Even in the Quiet Places

Christopher K. Doyle

APRIL GLOAMING

©2021 Christopher K. Doyle
Cover ©2021 Kari Hubbard

-First Edition

Publisher's Cataloguing-in-Publication Data

Doyle, Christopher K.
    Even in the quiet places / written by Christopher K. Doyle
ISBN: 978-1-953932-01-3

1. Fiction - General I. Title II. Author

Library of Congress Control Number: 2020950682

To my mother and father

It was his notion that the moment one of the people took one of the truths to himself, called it his truth, and tried to live his life by it, he became a grotesque and the truth he embraced became a falsehood.

— Sherwood Anderson, *Winesburg, Ohio*

Part One

Part One

1

HENRY SAW THE BOY WATCHING HIM from the woods. The boy was tucked behind a fern on the far side of the towpath and jangled a fishing rod above his head whenever Henry hauled up another piece of junk.

"Okay," Henry said, pausing on the grassy lip of the canal, "I can see you there, and I ain't done nothing wrong." *I ain't*, Henry thought, before hauling up a rusted bedspring and crumpled bicycle, an old leather suitcase and cracked furnace, before resting near a television he'd found with a gunshot in its side. Standing by the TV, he counted on his fingers all the things he'd found as the boy stepped out of his shady spot.

"I didn't think you were doing nothing wrong, mister. I just never seen nobody work so hard." The boy had caught a small-mouth bass with a brown line along its back and eased his sneakers onto the rickety slats of a footbridge spanning the canal. "Do you mind if I come across?"

Henry heard the boy's bright voice echo along the canal. Henry hadn't talked to anyone, not since buying biscuits seven days ago at a store, and he liked hearing the boy's voice. The boy's voice was light and made his belly tingle.

"I don't mind," Henry mumbled, and he brought his fingers to his lips, covering them in case the boy was only here to stare. Though as the boy hurried across, Henry saw he was only here for the TV, considering he went straight for it.

"What's it say there?" the boy said and pointed to an inscription on the side: "JOHNNY WUZ HERE: 1969. Shoot, that's only three years old."

"Well, it's mine now," Henry said. "I found it."

"Sure you did," the boy said, setting his fishing pole down. "Do you mind?" nodding at Henry. "I just wondered why anyone would throw out such a swell little set." The dull screen slanted unnaturally in the frame.

Henry watched the boy trace the reflection in the glass, outlining the abandoned lockhouse and mountain behind. "It's like a mirror," the boy said, and he held the set up to Henry's face. "Look."

Henry's face was different in the screen. That was one of the things Henry liked best about it. His neck didn't look so wide, and his hair didn't look so orange. His whole body was washed out in the black glass. It was like he was held beneath the river far off, where the reeds caught in the rapids and stuck out like antennas from underwater radios.

"You look like Charles in the screen," the boy said, putting the set down.

"Who?"

"In your arms. With how he swings them out wide coming home from the Elks'. He takes Momma there mostly. Says she drinks like a fish."

Henry wiped his forehead with his sleeve. His red cheeks puffed out when he spoke. "Hiram drank too," he said. "Hiram said this was our canal if we fixed it, if we did it right. Hiram said he played at this same lockhouse as a kid—before the Amtrak come and the cars." Henry pointed to the railroad before looking back at the boy. "But Hiram said no one else lived here, so no one else would see."

"See what?"

Henry rubbed his hands below his waist and along his leg. His thick work boots edged up and down in the mud. Orange rays were rising above the trees. The light framed the crumbling lockhouse behind the canal in a spreading cloud, and Henry turned to the black flies and gray mouths that would die soon because of the cold so he wouldn't have to look at the boy. He wanted to look at the boy, but not with him so close.

"Well, *we* sure live here," the boy said, nodding to the hill behind the lockhouse. "Can't you see all them houses?"

Henry glanced along the ridge and tried to count on his fingers the houses, but there were too many and his mind didn't work that quick, so he looked at the canal instead. He looked and thought of doing what Hiram always wanted them to do—to fix the canal, to make it right—even though Hiram died ten days ago in the hospital. Henry remembered counting the number on his fingers. He left Baltimore that same morning.

"So how much you want for it?" the boy said. The bass dangled from his belt. Henry had hauled the TV up only yesterday and liked watching his thick lips in the dark glass. He didn't talk so well and only wanted to see what other people stared at when he spoke.

"But it's broke."

The boy watched Henry's unmoving face. "Well we can clean it, can't we? You'd help, wouldn't you?" The boy patted the slick side, wiping the glassy ON/OFF knob with his shirt. "Then I could pretend all night with Momma always at the Elks' Club." The boy set the shiny bass on a boulder beside the lockhouse. "Because right there's about the best fish you'll ever eat. Go on. Check her out."

Henry sat next to the fish and touched the open belly. The flesh flaked in white strips beneath his fingernail and Henry's stomach grumbled.

"I catch them nearly every day. Cook 'em right there." The boy pointed to the highest house on the hill. "I'm Barnum," he said and stepped closer, sticking out his hand. "See, this is what people do when they meet. They stick out their hands and shake. I even seen Momma and the principal shake last month."

"I'm Henry." Henry's fingers were pale and swollen from the water that soaked them these last two days working in the canal. *They feel like worms*, he thought, as he watched his own fingers squirm against Barnum's.

"So how about that fish?" Barnum said, his fingers fluttering in Henry's fist.

"I like crabs more than fish," Henry said, letting go. "Hiram steamed crabs and we picked them."

"Well, they ain't no crabs in that river," Barnum said and laughed. Henry heard the rapids a quarter mile off. The sound jingled above the valley like a handful of coins. "And I don't know what you been eating down here all alone, but it can't be as tasty as that." Barnum pointed to the flaky white flesh.

"Smells clean." Leaning over, Henry bent stiffly at the waist. His right leg—an inch shorter than his left—quivered from his hips to his toes. Pushing his wide nose down, he smelled the river water like fern leaves in the meat. "It's white, like what the crab cakes were white before Hiram fried them and they smelled like linen."

"*Linen?*"

"In the fire," Henry said. "I picked up the linen and burned the linen so Marshall the manager could give me my pay." Henry saw Barnum watching him and brought his hand to his lips. "In the hospital," he said. "I worked in the hospital, punching the clock."

"Oh."

Behind them, the lockhouse door swayed open. Inside a thick canvas tarp was heaped in folds in the corner by an old radio. A mattress, pushed against the back wall, slumped behind a wood stove. "Well, you got a stove right there," Barnum said. "You could burn things all day. Eat whatever you want."

"They's only biscuits," Henry said, rubbing his belly. He kept the biscuits in a sack beneath the stove. In a cupboard, he'd found a tin cup that he filled with water from the cistern in the basement. But he didn't like going to the basement too often, not with the rats he heard that first night. They scuttled above the windows in the walls. "I bought the biscuits from a lady," Henry said. "She said if I were walking all the way to Harpers Ferry then I should take as many as I could haul."

"*Biscuits?* You been down here all alone just eating biscuits?" Barnum's bright voice giggled as he ticked off the words. "I don't know if I'd be eating biscuits all this time—but about that TV. I could give you something for it, something you could eat." He motioned to the fish.

As Barnum spoke, he worked his hands through the gunshot in the TV's side to where the vacuum tubes were mashed into a jumble of spaghetti-like shapes.

"I didn't even know it had stuff like this." Pulling out a black transistor, he wiped it on the grass until the black sludge stopped running down his finger. "I bet this makes the picture not fuzzy anymore. I bet it brings them in from up in the air, or wherever the picture starts out, in New York or Hollywood maybe. They got all them ranches out west too," he said. "That's what I like best—horses running along a cliff, and there's always a river to cross—and I never understood why they're so afraid about crossing a river. I do it nearly every day." He cupped his crotch with his free hand, giggling. "I just suck in my stomach whenever the water crawls around my jimmy."

Henry wanted to smile at Barnum's words, at how fast they came. *But my mouth don't move like that*, he knew. So he pressed his finger to the scar above his lip instead, until his dull teeth showed like a warm wedge of cheese in the middle of his face—until he smiled.

"And this suitcase, I could sure use a suitcase like this." Barnum wiped the dull clasp and spun the numbers on the lock. "Do you hear it? It clicks with the same kiss Momma gave Charles this morning. And I told Momma if I save all the money I make from selling fish to Rommel, the janitor in the church basement, then I might need my own suitcase to go to New York or Hollywood too." He stared at Henry. "That's where my real Daddy is, though Momma only says he works somewhere with pictures, somewhere out there." Barnum nodded at the TV and the suitcase spilled open with a soggy clump of leaves. "Well, here we are then," Barnum said and smiled at Henry. "That's what Charles says on the phone, whenever the cars he fixes don't run right. Here we are then," and as Barnum giggled, Henry leaned over to touch the broken suitcase and watched the leaves sag to the grass in a clump.

2

ENRY LIFTED THE TV because that was what Barnum asked him to do. "Besides," Barnum said, "you could sure use a break from all that work you done."

Henry agreed to trade the TV for the fish, though he had a condition: he wanted to know where Barnum was going to put it. "So I can look in it," he said.

"Well, sure, where'd you think we were going?" Barnum said, peering over his shoulder. "Anyway, it wouldn't be fair if we traded and I wouldn't let you look in it. I'll even give you an extra fish for as long as I can. That seems fair, don't it—*for a TV?*"

Henry liked how Barnum spoke to him as if they were the same size and Henry's right leg being shorter than his left didn't matter. Of all the words Barnum spoke he hadn't once mentioned it, teasing or nagging like Henry thought he might, even when Henry limped on the trail beside him. *And maybe that's why my stomach tingles*, he thought as they walked along the trail—*just to be near him.*

"See, this makes us partners," Barnum said, as the words hung between them. "Well, don't it?"

"*Part-ners.*" Henry felt his dry lips stumble on the sound.

"Well, that's what they say, ain't it?" Barnum watched Henry shift the TV in his arms. "We're aboveboard and shipshape and all that, though I don't think I've ever had a partner as big as you." Barnum inspected Henry's shoulders. "You're just like Charles, only bigger. And if he could see us now." Barnum snorted and had to stop a moment from laughing, leaning on his knee. When he did, the fishing rod jangled at his side and Henry watched the laughter rise like a wave from the boy's feet. Henry wanted to laugh like that too—laughing with his whole body—but could only wheeze with two loud bursts from his chest.

"Whoa..." Barnum said, as Henry's rasping echoed around them. "I bet you haven't laughed like that since the hospital. Because that'd be about the best job ever. Just building the fire up, throwing in more things to burn." As Barnum rubbed his hands together, Henry's arms ached from carrying the TV. He saw the railroad rise to a gravel slope, another hundred yards ahead.

"The linens made the ashy smell," Henry said.

"The what?"

"The ashy smell..." and as the tar from the railroad rose in a haze, he remembered the hospital. He remembered pushing the cart through the aisles and thinking the ashy smell was from the people who'd died and fallen into the flames—that the ashy smell was from their hair and teeth and bone. Hiram told him the hospital only wanted him to *collect* the linen after the people were redeemed. That they were up in heaven now and couldn't hurt him where they were, not with the Lord holding them, and he didn't have to worry. So he didn't. He even touched the linen before dumping each sheet into the furnace. He wanted to see if touching the linen was like touching the people, so that he might be closer to them and know who they were, now that they were gone.

"Well, I know all about the ashy smell too," Barnum said. "I know about the fire smell and the fish smell, and you should hear Momma yell when my fish bucket tips over—but I ain't never found a TV like this."

"Didn't you have one before?" Henry said, panting.

"A big one—but not since last spring. So we might have to put this one in my bedroom just in case. That way Momma won't see we dug it up from the water. She says I bring flies in when I fish." A few black flies circled when Barnum waved at the sticky sides of the bass. "Now just wait a minute," Barnum said. They'd reached the base of the gravel slope, and as they climbed, Barnum raised his hand and touched Henry's arm.

Henry felt all the hair on his arm rise up until his stomach spread into a tingling shower below his waist. No one had touched him since Hiram those days ago.

"We got to be careful. We got to watch before we cross."

As Barnum peered along the tracks, Henry looked to the mountains. The trees spread out shimmering in the sun, and when he looked from end to end, the orange and red colors of changing and living and dying spun until they blurred into a large quilt he hadn't expected. He'd only kept his eyes on the canal these last few days. But now the mountains seemed propped up like a broad teepee. The trees spun all the way up to where the faint clouds of cotton and linen drifted by.

There's linen in the sky, he thought. *I see people in the sky. They're redeemed.* That was what Hiram told him, and the nuns before Hiram in the rectory, when Henry shied away from the children so they might not laugh at his leg. The nuns said the sky was where you went when you die—no matter what your leg was like—and Henry believed them. And as Barnum pointed along the hill, Henry watched the clouds move in circles above them.

"You can see them now, can't you," Barnum said, "all them antennas from the houses. Up the hill?"

The town stood on the side of the hill facing the canal, and as Henry started counting the gray antennas, "One two three four five six seven eight nine..." he heard the cars make a sucking sound as they went into a pass behind the ridge.

"Mine's the one on top. Next to the white house with the hedge."

"*Fifteen*," Henry whispered. He hadn't realized it, but he'd said one of the numbers he had so much trouble with before, when the nuns had tried to teach him to count. Henry didn't like the numbers past ten. *One two three four five six seven eight nine ten zero*—those were the ones he could hold. Whenever he needed to know how many linens to burn or how many sandwiches to eat, he just counted on his hands and there they were: the numbers. But zero was his favorite. Zero had its own beginning and end, and all along the canal he'd drawn zeroes in the mud. He liked looking inside the zeroes, because looking inside was like looking at the TV. There was a picture inside the zero, something set apart from the rest, and didn't that make what was inside different, on its own? He thought so, and as he watched Barnum crouch above the railroad tracks, he felt the same way now. What was inside the metal lines was easier to see—it was different.

"Look here, Henry, can you see it—how the tracks are starting to buckle?" Barnum pointed to a small section of the line.

Leaning in, Henry set the TV along the slope. The railroad was long and barren, and he smelled peat moss and shredded rubber between the rungs, but he couldn't see it buckling. What he did see were worm-eaten wooden ties and weeds sprouting between the gravel. Reaching out of habit, he plucked the weeds one by one, scrunching them in his hands; he didn't want this line to be as messy as his canal.

Because it was *his* canal, wasn't it? Hadn't he walked seven days and nights to get here? Hadn't he looked out for it by hauling away stones and stumps and trash? Nobody else was. Not the funny dressed people on bicycles. Not the one ranger he'd seen in a green jeep. Not all the hikers and joggers racing past. Their orange and puke-yellow shorts made a swishy sound coming round the bend. And often, when they stopped to stare at him as he worked, it felt like he was back in Baltimore, on the bus, when the children stared at him on his way to the hospital and he had to shake their staring away. The staring brought the black smudges to his eyes so that he couldn't see them anymore—he couldn't see anything—just blackness where their faces were.

"Wait a second," Barnum said, cupping his ear. The tracks hummed, ticking against the bolts. "See, I told you! I told you!"

"*A train's coming,*" Henry whispered.

"*Oh, boy!* Here she comes, Henry! I said, '*HERE. SHE. COMES!*'"

Henry looked inside the lines—at the space between the humming lines. What was set apart was different, it was special, and now it was ticking.

"Bet you it's the Amtrak!" Barnum squealed. "Just put your ear down. I said, '*PUT IT ALL THE WAY DOWN!*'" Barnum screamed because the metal groaned as the birds fluttered louder in the trees. Henry even heard the water rushing in the rapids. The whole world grew louder as the train drew close.

Since he'd arrived, Henry had already found himself falling into the Amtrak's schedule. In the top of the sleek silver cars he watched people sleeping on their way to Baltimore and Washington, and then back again at night when the Amtrak went clear up to Martinsburg, West Virginia and maybe even Cumberland beyond that. All he knew was that Harpers Ferry was the next stop up, considering he'd heard those bright-green and puke-yellow joggers talk about it when they ran past. Though he'd never once thought about going beyond his lock.

"Well, it sure ain't no Amtrak," Barnum said as he tugged Henry down the slope. His high-pitched voice brought Henry back to the billowing smoke rising from the line. And for a moment—as the train rumbled past, as it took with it that clouded veil so that they could see again and the mountains rose up brown and orange and towering—he found himself counting the red painted cars rolling by: *One two three four five six seven eight nine ten zero. One two three four five six seven eight nine ten zero.*

They weren't like any boxcars he'd seen. These were older, slower. They were built with panels and wood trimming and didn't look at all like the Amtrak with its shiny aluminum tubing. Or like the cattle cars with their metal slats. Or the automobile haulers, with cars stacked on shelves behind a mesh of holes. This train had a fresh new paint smell and an engineer even leaned out and waved from a front window as he passed. Though before Henry could count all the way up on his fingers again, it was gone, and Henry whispered, "*Zero,*" as the red shiny caboose disappeared around the northern bend. Henry whispered, "*Zero,*" and drew a wide circle in the sand at Barnum's feet.

3

"**N**OW MIND YOURSELF," BARNUM SAID, "we've got to be quiet around this hedge." Barnum pulled back a willow branch along the outskirts of a neighbor's property. "Momma said the old man here was a policeman once. I even heard him shoot at poachers before—in broad daylight."

"*Poachers?*" Henry looked at the TV in his arms. Sweat dripped from his face.

"You're okay, just as long as you tell me you seen that train just now. Because I ain't never seen a train like that." Barnum's eyes were wide and he rubbed his brow. They'd climbed for what felt like a lot longer than a quarter-mile, though Henry couldn't tell what a quarter-mile was. He just remembered the mile markers ticking off those seven days and nights along the canal. Mile markers like bright orange stumps at his feet.

"That train looked more like a picture book if you ask me," Barnum said and held a rickety gate open for Henry as they crossed another yard. "Or like in those westerns, because the robbers are always chasing a caboose. But I never thought trains like that still ran, especially since we're not anywhere close to being out west. We're here."

Barnum stood by the cellar door. He touched the rusted handle and the door swung open, creaking on its hinges. The musty cellar spread around them full of clothes and cardboard boxes and old exercise equipment. "Momma and Charles work weekends mostly, so it's just me and the cat." Barnum leaned his fishing rod against a shelf of dusty tools. "But I don't let the cat down unless I hear the mice, and I ain't heard the mice in weeks." Barnum knelt by a wood stove, opened its small iron hatch, and a faint light reflected off the ceiling. "Put it by the wall."

Barnum nodded to the TV in Henry's hands and pointed at a table. When Henry set it down, Barnum turned to the stove and twisted a small hand shovel until the brighter coals glowed above the ash. He added a few splintered logs.

"Won't be long now," he said, raising his hands to the grate. "Then we can cook that fish and pretend to watch all the shows I used to watch."

"*Pre-tend?*" Henry's voice died against a brown mattress as Barnum grabbed a spoon hidden under his pillow. He'd already hung the fish from a hook on the wall. Beneath the fish sat a bucket where other fish tails were heaped. The bucket was covered by a blue plastic lid, and when Barnum accidentally nudged the bucket, the lid fell off so a sour briny cloud overtook the room. From the top of the stairs, cat paws scratched the door.

"Quit it, Josephine!" Barnum called, staring at the brown door. His voice echoed above the exposed frame leading up either side of the wooden steps. From the frame, fishing poles and nets hung down. An old green plastic tent and rusted tricycle were propped on a dusty dresser. Eight broken radios were piled on a shelf of cinderblocks and plywood. Henry moved next to them when Barnum started cleaning the fish, scraping scales into the bucket.

"I just use a spoon turned over." Barnum held up his hand. Iridescent scales speckled his flesh. "The light makes them look milky, don't you think?"

Henry looked at Barnum's glowing hand in the firelight.

"But Momma don't give two shakes. I tell her we could put the scales in the kitchen window. Wouldn't that be nice? Milky sunrise all over everything. Make things glow for a change."

Henry saw the glowing light Barnum described and touched his finger to each radio until he counted to eight. The radios reminded him of the junk he'd hauled out of the canal. He'd found an old wooden radio with three glass dials his first day. He put the radio in the lockhouse near the mattress, and each night he rubbed his hands along its sides as if it might start singing. He wanted to hear the voices. To hear the music drift across the room like when Hiram used to sing so he wouldn't have to hear the rats in the walls, or feel alone.

"I don't want to hear them rats," Henry said.

"*What rats?*" Barnum looked from his bucket and a milky scale dangled from his chin. "They ain't no rats down here, and if there is, I'll let Josephine down for sure."

Henry looked at the radios.

"*I want to hear the singing*," he whispered. He could still see the way Hiram touched him below the waist. Hiram's touch had the softening feel. Henry would stand before Hiram those nights after Hiram drank from his bottle, until Hiram's hand was a single cord moving against Henry's body. After, Hiram listened to the radio and Henry watched the fire escape in the moonlight. That was what Henry liked most: light falling on trees, on chimney tops and lampposts. Moonlight working like sleep across the street.

"They sang then," Henry said. He had his hand on the highest radio and spun the dial. "Them old singers with their trumpets and pianos."

"Who sang?" Barnum said. "You can touch them dials all you want, but they won't sing. I took them all apart."

Henry raised his hand to a twisted antenna until Barnum turned away— and Henry saw Hiram turn away instead, when the loving was done. On those nights, Henry helped Hiram to bed and then looked to make sure no one saw him limp down the stairs at the end of the hall just like Hiram told him to. In his one-room apartment he slept on a cot by the radiator. Heat came off the coils in waves, and long after the moonlight lifted into the air, he still heard those smoky trumpets and pianos in his mind.

"It's gonna be cold again tonight," Barnum said. "You can bet that. Momma's got an almanac and it's got just about everything you want to know, about trees and harvests and tides. Each morning it tells me when the sun rises."

"It tells you that?" Henry's bottom lip gaped open, dry and chapped.

"Sure, like this morning—it was hotter than most this late in fall—but the almanac told me about it. Said it's gonna be a lot colder tonight, and you can already feel it."

Barnum was right. Already on their walk up, the sun had gone behind some low clouds, and it was as if that train might not have been a train at all. That it might not have gone by them like Henry knew it had. It seemed more ghost or dream to him then, with the light clouding over and the wind moving in, a dream that brought a cold chilly air, until he shivered at Barnum's cellar door. That was why he was happy to see Barnum light the fire as quickly as he had. Gutting the fish, Barnum put two fillets on the stove. The sizzling sound hissed through the room and Henry's stomach groaned because he hadn't realized how hungry his work in the canal made him. Not until he had his first steaming forkful.

"I bet you been eating grubs and them crabapples I seen by the canal, even berries from the brush. And just biscuits all those nights?" They sat on a low bench near the stove. The heat had worked through the cellar until Henry turned his sleeves up to dab the sweat that pooled in the scar above his lip. "Ain't it a beaut?" Barnum said. They stared at their reflection in the TV. Years of moisture were steaming up from inside, and Henry moved the table the TV sat on near a few boxes with old Christmas decorations. Watching Henry maneuver the TV, Barnum grabbed a shirt from the foot of his bed and wiped the dull black screen.

"Just want to make sure we can see those cowboys when they come, when that cliff rises up like it does." Barnum pointed to the upper-left corner. He wiped a last runny smudge, and with the firelight bouncing off his body—and the TV held in a sort of wavy heat—Henry felt something below his waist and looked away from Barnum's glistening face.

"Told you it would get hot." Barnum was at the cellar door and opened it a bit, letting in some cold air. "It don't take long with this stove." Sitting back on the bench, he leaned against Henry's shoulder, settling himself. "But where was I? Oh yeah, the posse…because you know that posse always gets its man no matter how far he runs, or how many señoritas fall in love with him."

Barnum set his plate on the floor.

"You've seen them? All them señoritas? How they hide the outlaws in their hotel so they can watch the posse ride through. Or in the barroom, where they gamble on the spinning wheel." Barnum stood in front of the TV and only stopped long enough to stuff his face with another forkful. "Can't you just pretend…with all them girls?"

When Henry watched Barnum dance he saw the rectory stage, and Barnum was like the boy who played Jesus in the manger. That was when snow fell, when ice coated the streets. The docks were spread out with a light crunchy feel and the bay stretched beyond the window. The whole rectory was focused on the singing of one little boy, or on the three wise men who brought the gold-colored boxes that Henry liked best. Henry liked pretending that when he woke the next morning the gold boxes would be at the foot of his cot and all the kids would crowd around and he wouldn't have to move his lips at all with his hands to smile—to be with them. *"Pretend,"* Henry whispered, and when Barnum leaned down to hear what Henry said, Barnum's ear brushed Henry's lips.

Henry's stomach tightened when the boy stood back up, swaying in front of him. Henry remembered Hiram leaning in like that, when Hiram's belly rested on Henry's, heaving up and down as he breathed, when he held Henry like no one else had. Barnum had brought Hiram back for a moment so that Henry felt Hiram's pink breath circling the shelves, the radios, the mattress—even his own glazed skin.

"Pretend is all we got down here," and Barnum fell giggling against Henry's shoulder. "Cause there's always a shoot-out with the main posse too, when the warden calls out the outlaw. Because the warden always says: *'Rex...you know what you got coming, so just come outta that saloon and get what you deserve.'"* Barnum hitched up his pants and ambled toward the door. "And then Rex is always like: *'So, you found me, and I ain't never thought you'd make it past the Red River rapids. But you can bet your last shoe polish I ain't going in.'* And then BANG!" Barnum jumped by the stove screaming. "BANG! BANG!—the warden fires back..."

Barnum raced to the railing.

"BANG! BANG! BANG! The warden's got men on top of the building when Rex runs for his horse. And O!—Rex is hit. He's slumped behind a whiskey barrel, and we don't know if he's been hit and neither does the warden, so he says: *'HOLD YOUR FIRE!'* as he moves closer to see."

Barnum sprawled beside a Christmas box. Shifting to his side, a few tin bulbs rattled on the linoleum. The tiny bulbs sounded like Barnum's coughing voice because Henry heard a rattle in the boy's throat:

"Warden..." Barnum rattled. *"I ain't never meant no harm to no one. I was just trying to get by as best my Pappy taught me how."*

Henry couldn't look at anything but the pain in Barnum's face, with how he held his hand to the TV.

"Warden, just tell that sweet little señorita Maria Vargas I meant all them words I said last night, that I always wanted to be there for her. And BANG! BANG!—Rex has been foolin' the warden all along. The warden's hit now too, and his men fire back hitting Rex for good." Barnum grasped his heart and rolled across the floor. "Till they both lie side by side in the dusty street."

Barnum was motionless.

"Henry..." Barnum whispered. He didn't move, but spoke from the side of his mouth. *"Come and lie beside me and be the warden for a minute."*

Henry rubbed his belly to think he might pretend with someone else's mind.

"Just till the scene's over," Barnum whispered.

Henry stood and limped to where Barnum sprawled against a plastic angel. Kneeling at first to get into position, Henry slumped with his stiff legs against Barnum and felt another tightening in his stomach when he brushed his hand along Barnum's hip. When he turned to face Barnum, he saw a dark mole above the boy's left ear.

"Now you're the warden and you're gonna *die*, but before you do, you need to tell Rex that he's going to the real bad place of fire and spikes, while you—the warden—you're going to the real good place, of clouds and air." Barnum pulled Henry close with a delicate tug. His narrow fingers fluttered against Henry's ribs. "Just say the words, '*At last, Rex...I caught you*,' and that's how you can begin."

Henry counted in his head: *One two three four five six seven eight nine ten zero.* He remembered doing this when Hiram tugged below his waist. *Because counting made it better. I didn't have to think about the kids in the rectory and what they might say. I only heard the numbers, and the numbers were right.* When Henry saw the clear circle of Barnum's face, he reached out with his finger to draw along the boy's flushed skin. *Zero.* What was on the inside was set apart, and he wanted to touch what was inside. So he held his hand to Barnum's belly and squeezed the soft skin between his fingers.

"Um…Henry?"

Henry pushed his fingers into the boy's flesh until the hot tightening in his stomach spread to his groin.

"All you have to say are the words…"

But Henry was moving. Pulling himself up, a tin bulb shattered against his boot.

"To end the scene, Henry! To end the scene!"

Out in the early chill, Henry heard Hiram's voice for a moment in Barnum's complaint. Hiram's reedy voice worked through the wind rising above the ridge, and Henry watched a pink breath stir the weeds at his feet as he limped down along the trail.

4

HAT NIGHT IT GOT MUCH COLDER than any of the other nights since Henry had arrived and he built a fire in the lockhouse. Passing his hands along the radio, he thought about the singing again, always about the singing. Stretching the antenna with his hands, he moved the metal prongs because he'd seen Hiram do that often enough, when only a static fuzz reached their ears, when Hiram said, "Shit, shit, shit," because he couldn't get the sound to come in right.

Hiram always drank another drink then and asked Henry for one of the gold-colored bottles he kept in the cabinet. Hiram sang then too, when only the static came. He would peer from his chair at Henry and Henry couldn't look away then, not with Hiram's gray eyes on him, not when Hiram started talking:

"Why don't you sing with me?" he'd say. "I can show you. Then you wouldn't have to sit by that window and look out on God-knows-what all night long." Hiram had a glass of gold-colored water. He took a swig and blew out a breath of hot pink air saying, *Oooooohhh*, like he was full of ocean water.

"Come and sing with me," Hiram said. He wrapped a gentle arm around Henry's waist, and his pink breath fell against Henry's cheek. "This is how we're redeemed. You know that. This is how we're redeemed for hiding up in this goddamn apartment."

Hiram had a purple mole above his left ear. Henry watched the purple mole move in circles when Hiram spoke.

"You know it wasn't always like this, not during the war. Not when people did what they wanted and nobody watched."

Henry wanted to reach out to it then, to touch the purple mole, to see if it came off on his finger, but he held back. Hiram was singing:

Amazing grace, how sweet the sound,
that saved a wretch like me

"Come, Henry. You can sing, can't you?"

Henry brought his hands to his lips.

"*Don't touch your lips! Don't touch your goddamn lips!*" Hiram raised his hand, grasping Henry's neck. "Your lips are perfect. Your skin is perfect. Your eyes perfect." Hiram dropped his hands to Henry's wrist. "It's all right, Henry, it's all right. I'm here."

Hiram's eyes were bloodshot in the light.

Henry had one hand on the window and the other on Hiram's chest. When Hiram leaned in closer, Henry felt the cold glass of the world. Moonlight fell on him. He watched the moonlight work across the tips of his fingers, his arm, and felt sleepy. His body swayed as Hiram moved his hands along his chin, his mouth, until he raised the ends of his lips with his fingers—making him smile.

"Just sing with me. Would you do that? Would you just forget about your leg and lips for once—and those goddamn kids?"

Henry looked at his fingers against the glass. He counted five fingers—and then counted to ten when he looked at his other hand. "I tried to count," he said, wriggling his fingers. "I always tried when I scrubbed."

"I know you did. In the rectory. When you scrubbed the walls."

"I dipped the rag in the soap. The soap had the roses."

"Shhh, Henry. It smelled like roses, I know."

Hiram stood at the window with Henry. "And you held your hand in the water with the black bits of hair and paper and breadcrumbs. You counted on your fingers the pews and walls you scrubbed. You did this until everything was done, but it wasn't enough—still you got teased for counting wrong—and it hurt to think you couldn't do it. I know. But all I want you to do is sing now; can you sing with me?"

Henry looked at the radio in the lockhouse. He saw Hiram's purple mole move in circles in his mind and thought of the mole above Barnum's ear. He hoped Barnum wasn't sad about how he'd left him lying there on the floor. *I just felt the numbers calling me, and heard that warm place, where me and Hiram were, where I saw fire escapes and moonlight, and I wanted to get to that place, with Hiram. So I stopped touching Barnum's belly. I stopped touching the boy because I didn't know what Hiram would say if I touched someone else.*

"Come here, Henry, come here." Henry turned to the lockhouse door and saw Hiram motioning him back to his chair, away from the window. They were back in the apartment. "We can't stand by the window; you know that. We can't show anyone."

Down in the street, Henry watched moonlight work along the passing buses. Each night he saw the pretty lady with the black curls smile back. She rode the #31 and looked up at Henry standing in the window. He'd stare back at her powdery face because it was creamy and electric, like electric lines came off her in waves.

"Come along, Henry," Hiram said and slumped back to his chair, fiddling with the radio. "This is how we're redeemed. You know that."

Nothing. Static.

"Shit, shit, shit," and Hiram rocked in his chair, balancing the gold-colored glass in his hand. "Well, then. We'll sing."

> *I once was lost,*
> *but now am found,*
> *was blind, but now*
> *I see...*

As Henry looked at the canal, he knew he would have listened to Hiram's raspy voice forever. He would have sung anything if only to stand there each night with the buses rushing below, with the streets outlined in moonlight, if only to see that lady's eyes stare back at him, to see her smile. A lady had never smiled at him before, and so he'd never thought of ladies like that—that they could love him—not like how Hiram did. Though as he stepped into the night now, he thought of that lady when he remembered Barnum.

"Look at me now," he mumbled, watching starlight reflect in the puddles he'd cleared of junk. "Lady?" he said. "Are you there?" Far off on the river, Henry heard the rapids. Closer to the mountain, the faint sound of cars sped past: *suck suck*. "Can you make me tingle? Because if you can, I might not think of him anymore. I might not think of touching someone who's not Hiram, and I'll set myself apart because of it, because of your smile. I'll think of it and I'll be different. I won't touch anyone and I'll be in a zero all by myself."

He stared into a puddle for the lady. The puddles winked with stars turning on and off in the night. Bringing his hand to the lockhouse, a dusty stone crumbled at his side.

"Are you there," he said, "watching?" Easing his body into the canal, mud squished beneath his boots. Leaning down, he saw the stars. The stars were eyes watching him. The eyes were far away and silver, but they weren't hers, he knew—she wasn't there. Holding his right leg, he didn't see her, the girl who might distract him, who might make him think of someone else. So all he could think of was Barnum's glistening body, of Barnum raising his hand in front of the TV as he pretended and danced and died.

"But I can think of work instead. I can think of work instead of the boy." Henry looked along the length of the canal, at the logs and weeds and stones, and knew it wasn't enough to just get here. Even Hiram would have said that.

"It's not enough to just live here either. To light the lantern and burn the fire that's now my life. I have to clear away the junk. To clear away everything until it's old again, until it's straight. Like when the lockmen raised the barges fifty years ago. Like what Hiram said, before these houses shot up with the train."

Henry turned to the towpath and trailed his hand in the air. "I can see it, how the water will be blue between the rocks. Then the lock will move barges and boats with mules on the towpath." He imagined where mules walked. "That's what Hiram said, that mules pulled the barges. They pulled them up and down, and when they pull them up and down again this place will be old, like before—and the boy won't matter to me. The boy won't matter because I'll be right, like the numbers. They'll be straight and even in my mind and Hiram can't say I ever touched anyone else, that I strayed. He can't say I ever strayed."

5

"**Y**OU SHOULD MOVE THAT BOULDER over there." Barnum shook his fishing rod, pointing. "Then maybe you could thresh them weeds so the canal empties out like you want." Barnum stood on the lip of the canal and watched Henry's progress in the mud. It was Monday and Barnum hadn't been able to fish before school like usual, since his mother wanted him to chop wood instead. But now, "Here I am," he said, flashing a smile of crooked teeth. His straight brown hair was greasy from the baseball cap he took off—and then put on—never quite getting the right fit with the too-big hat on his too-small head. "I was at church Sunday and then Momma and Charles took me to the diner because of all the psalms I read out loud for the *con-gre-ga-tion.*" He repeated the word, sounding out each syllable. "The priest called on me because he said my voice was, '*Quite affecting,*' whatever that means. Do you know what affecting means?"

Henry looked up from the canal.

"Well, I read all them psalms out anyway and got a hot fudge sundae with whip cream and a cherry on top to boot."

As Barnum spoke, Henry smelled the hot fudge dripping in the cold cream and stopped threshing with a hickory stick to think of the sweet fudge on his lips. Every Friday after work he bought a hot fudge sundae with banana slices and nuts. He'd sit behind a tinted window in the cafeteria and watch families come in the front door. They couldn't see him from where he sat, and it was nice to sit high up in a dark corner, the hot sugar dripping off his spoon. The children couldn't follow him with their eyes there. They couldn't count his limping steps either, like they did in the hospital, and it made his leg tingle after finishing each gooey scoop to think he was above them—watching.

"And if I were you, I'd start on that trickling creek." Barnum pointed to the mountain and to the houses among the trees. "It's stopped up in that pipe closer to the tracks. It pools in the bottom of Ms. Hansen's yard."

"Pipe?"

"Sure. The stream goes in there like a drain or something before heading to the river." With their eyes, they followed the path the pipe made down the mountain. "If you make it come this way, you'd have all the water you'd want. We could even find some old boat, ride it as far as the water goes."

Henry saw a bright image of the finished canal. The lockhouse had two coats of whitewash. Weeds were pulled and the water was blue and drawn all the way to the bottom of the lock. *After I fix the lock, after I replace the stones, I can get a boat too,* he thought, *just like what Barnum said. Maybe I'll even get a skiff or rowboat, so I can push myself with a pole. Then I can dip my fingers over the sides and feel the cool water, and I won't have to think about Hiram being gone—I won't have to think about Hiram at all.*

"Maybe the people would stop then too," Henry said, not realizing he was speaking until he heard the words.

"You mean them goofs jogging by all day?"

"Maybe the swishy-clothed people might watch me with smiles on their faces instead of staring." Henry touched his lips and coughed.

"Sure they would. They'd ask to ride in the boat too." Barnum held up his hand and Henry watched the boy keep it flat and steady before moving it in the air along the canal. "And they'd ask why you done it, but none of it would matter because they'd say it was beautiful what you've done, just beautiful. Because I can see how you're gonna clear it out and make it work. And they'll all call you Henry and me Barnum because we'll get bright new shirts with nametags on them, like what I bet you had in the hospital. Did you have nametags on your shirt in the hospital?"

As Henry nodded, he remembered the crisp blue shirts Marshall the manager handed out each morning. He remembered touching the letters printed on his chest—his name raised above everything else.

"Maybe we'll even wear straw hats to block the sun?" Barnum took off his red baseball cap and dropped it to the ground. "I'd sure like to pole one of them boats too, if you'd let me—would you let me?"

"Sure. You and me—poling."

"And they'll all call you Henry and me Barnum and it'll go on like that forever, until the whole canal works. Then we could ride it all the way to the end."

Henry breathed in with two long sipping breaths thinking about *forever*, and what it would mean to live here peaceful, poling atop the water.

"So why don't you come fishing with me then?" Barnum said. "And take a break from all the work you done." Barnum trailed his fingers along three rusted barrels, an overturned barbeque, and the torn hull of an old water heater.

"You even got two American flags," he said, pointing to the cloth draped across the water heater. "Feel them holes. They go all the way through." Barnum fingered the holes in the flag before running his shoe along the worn tread of a knobby tire. "Hey," he said, when he saw the upper torso of a store-window mannequin. He stopped inspecting everything else.

Henry had propped her on an old sawhorse, so that the torso surveyed all the other objects scattered around.

"Would you look at that?" Barnum whispered, caressing the shape. "She's even got bumps on her chest where Momma's got bumps." He turned to Henry. "You know all the other fellows at school call them, '*Breasts*,'" and Henry heard the word tumble from Barnum's lips. "But I wonder..." Barnum said, setting his fishing rod down, raising his shirt. "I wonder about them bumps...if they're the same." He rubbed the smaller bumps on his own chest till his lips drew tight lines across his face. "You should feel my nipples after I been swimming, they pinch-up something awful. But this mannequin don't have nipples or a face. It's all just worn canvas and dark."

Henry watched Barnum from the canal. He watched the boy pass his hands across the mannequin's chest. That made Henry's eyes stare hard. It made Henry's eyes see black smudges in the corners, until the boy's face passed into blackness.

"But about fishing," Barnum said, and his high voice snapped back Henry's attention. Henry focused on the river then, now that he imagined Barnum casting the bright line from his reel, pulling up a strong bass, and he wanted to be with Barnum, to walk beside him to the water.

"Let me put my things away first," Henry said, and the words came out so steady and clean from his lips that Henry said it again: "Let me put my things away first."

"Sure. I can help," and pulling the mannequin from the sawhorse, Barnum held the damp torso between his fingers.

Inside, he wouldn't let go, even when Henry said he could put the mannequin on the mattress beside the radio. Henry hauled all the other things to the basement, piling them near the cistern and all the other junk he'd brought in, though when he came back upstairs he had to count to zero in his mind to see the boy still holding the mannequin. Henry stood back and let the boy know he was ready by focusing his shell-blue eyes on the boy's thin neck. "Let's go." Henry said, and the boy finally let go and led Henry down along the trail.

6

THE TRAIL WAS NARROW AND OVERGROWN, and a thick minty closeness swallowed Henry as he followed Barnum. Sprinkled with moss and loose rocks, Henry had to hunt and peck with his right boot to find the safe spots so that it looked like he crossed a bed of crushed shells.

"Can you hear it," Barnum said, "all them rapids?" He looked at Henry before racing off. A thick-walled forest swayed around Henry, and as he limped along, he could see the leaves change the closer he got to the river. The leaves turned orange to yellow to green, growing younger it seemed as he went.

"Barnum!" he called, but only the rushing water hummed close by, and he stopped to smell a fern at his side. Trailing his hands along a leaf, he bent to touch a mossy rock where a butterfly alighted, its thin rice-paper wings folding into a single sheet. The wings hid a pearly color that reminded him of the clams he bought after walking ten blocks to the fish market. Those were the days Hiram steamed clams, when Hiram liked showing Henry their deliberate opening shells.

Hiram said, "It's nice breaking something open like this," and he pointed to the boiling pot. "Can't you see how much prettier everything is inside?" Henry had never pried anything open like that before, but he liked watching the shells in the deep mottled kettle. They opened as if on cue, once the steam worked inside their knotted muscles.

One night Hiram even hung a picture on the wall beside the window Henry looked out of. "It's a rice-paper drawing, from when I was in Korea." On nights after the tugging was done, when the fire escape was dark, with the moon hidden, Henry stared at the picture instead. He stared at the blue wavy mountain and green river until he thought he *was* the picture— that his mind had merged with each point of light rising like a butterfly from the middle. He always hoped he might rise like that too, rising without limping. And as he watched the butterfly now, he wondered how the air could let such rice-paper wings rise like that. How can you rise up while being so fragile?

"*Henry!*" Barnum showed his head from behind a yellow bush. "We ain't got *too* long to fish. Momma wants me back by six-thirty. The Elks' got Bingo at seven. But I was wondering," Barnum pressed his hand to Henry's side. "You could come up after Momma goes. Then we could watch another western."

"I could look at the TV again?"

"Sure. Because I think there's gonna be a story about a river on to-night and some settlers moving west, to the Frontier." When Barnum start-ed talking, Henry let go of his hand. He thought he might fall because his right leg lagged behind, and he wondered if Barnum would ask about lying on the floor before, when their bellies had touched. "Look," Barnum said. They'd reached the river's edge. The bank was marbled with pebbles and overturned trees, and beneath his boots Henry remembered the rich brown sand.

"I come down here the other evening," he mumbled.

"You weren't scared then, with just the moon out?"

"I just waded to them rocks and sat down. I didn't go too far cause I can't swim."

"Oh, I know," Barnum said. "Down in Carter's Coffin, in the rapids. Almost like a chair carved out."

"Yeah," Henry said, and he remembered how the water rushed over his shoulders, holding him close. "But I kept my head up. I breathed."

"Well, sure you did. Especially if you can't swim."

"I never learned how." There wasn't any fear when Henry said it. He didn't feel any fear in the water and hadn't since he first started walking beside it those days ago. *Because it feels right, and I even like the sound of it. The sound don't bother me when I sleep, or when I stand in the canal listening. The water sort of talks to me then, chattering through the trees, and I know it couldn't hurt me chattering like that—the water can't ever hurt me.*

"Well, there ain't nothing to swimming," Barnum said. Slipping out of his shoes, he stepped into the shallows. "I could show you in a minute." As Barnum fiddled with his fishing lure, Henry was already wading in behind him, his boots back on shore. "But it's high now, Henry, it's high."

Henry heard some joggers say it was high the other day and believed them, even though he'd never seen it otherwise.

"Anyway, we're fishing now. We can swim later." Barnum gave Henry a net and pointed to a white glowing beech leaning above a line of stones twenty yards into the river. "We're just going a little ways out. You'll be fine." The log had carved its own ledge in the water. Barnum said there might be large bass there. He'd struck a few on Saturday but lost them when the leaders broke. He lost a few flies too that Rommel the janitor in the church had tied for him. "Just ease yourself around the side, Henry. That's it. So you can stand real still with the net."

Barnum sat on the beech trunk. He slithered along the slimy surface that glowed with the late sunlight cresting over the ridge. Not another person was on the river. Henry stood still once he reached the other side of the log, not too far from Barnum. Only the river rushed past Henry's legs. The water was cold above his belly. His legs felt like they were expanding beneath him, that the river was spreading through every inch of his thighs and knees and toes, until he felt like he would never fall in. That the water was holding him up.

Leaning over to test his new sturdiness, he saw his face in the fast-moving current. His orange hair raced away from his eyes, and his lips didn't look so thick. They looked like river water—and seemed held out in a thin line as he swayed to stand up again. His right foot was on a rock that must have been an inch above the rock his left foot stood on, because he'd never stood so level before. *Even in my special right boot*, he thought. Then way out on the river, a bass arched high up and made a zero on the water.

Henry trailed his hand in the current, making his own zero. His other hand held the net, and as it rested on his shoulder, he watched where the zero the bass made dissolved in the shadows. He saw zeroes appearing and disappearing all over the surface. Even at the end of the log, small swirling zeroes spun off from Barnum's dangling feet. Henry tried to count the zeroes but didn't want the numbers in his mind to wash away the silence of the river. It was quiet and he liked it. He liked only hearing the water and the zeroes the fish made when they arched up in the shadows before falling.

"OK," Barnum said. "I'll bet they just waiting to bite what I brought 'em."

Barnum cast with a great looping throw until the fly landed twenty yards in front of the beech. Henry liked the sound of the whirling reel because the line sounded like ticking all over, like the wings of birds ticking in the trees. But then a bass arched high up with the line in its mouth, and Henry heard the line tick off as Barnum dipped the pole to let the line run. Barnum whooped real loud as his arms pulled in great strands of line. "It ain't as little as I think, and he's got some real fight to him."

Barnum snapped the pole and the bass surfaced. Henry saw the brown mottled mouth when he dipped the net into the water. The bass was tired. His mouth was closed where the hook bit in. Henry raised the net around him, and the brown shimmering sides caught in the mesh. When Henry brought him out of the river, the bass let out a loud gasp, and Henry heard the faint sucking sound of water run off his slimy lips.

"You got him. You did it!" Barnum pulled the bass out and held him by the bottom lip until he dug out the hook. Then he put the bass in a long sock slung across his back. The sock sat deep in the water and billowed out with the bass shaking his head beneath the surface.

"It's like we been working side by side all these days." Barnum was tightening his leader and Henry wondered how long, 'all these days,' really were, because he'd lost track. He tried counting the trains that ran by, but he'd counted to zero twice already and then thought he wasn't even counting the trains he might miss being in the river like this. So he stopped counting. He didn't think of the days like that. *Not when there's only the bird's ticking wings now, or the trains clacking by.* He heard their sound and it was movement and he liked it. *Because I can look in the canal and see what I've done, with the stuff I've cleared.* Though he knew his progress would be slower with it getting colder each morning, with winter coming soon.

"Let's try again; there's light for one more cast."

Henry looked across the surface; the light had gotten purple without him noticing. The water ran purple across his skin, and when he looked, there were orange flares on the sides of his reflection. Though when Barnum cast again and the ticking reel echoed across the valley, Henry thought a great bird must have swooped above him because the line spun out next to his ear.

Striking the line, a bass arched high up near Henry's end of the log. With the fish so close, he saw a thin line of scales underneath its body in a tight weave, and Henry thought he saw all the blood and bones and air stripped down and perfect inside the fish. *Just like a perfect ticking clock*— but he shivered when the fish went down next to his leg. He shivered to see the zero the fish made around his waist.

"Did you get him?" Barnum slid in from the log, the river up to his chest. Henry pulled up the net and the bass hung low, his wide mouth gaping in the prickly mesh. "You got him," Barnum said and let out another loud whoop.

7

BARNUM'S THIN LIPS HAD TURNED BLUE when they made it back to the lockhouse. Henry put two logs in the wood stove and blew on the coals left over from the morning. "Stand over here," Henry said, pointing to the stove, and as Barnum moved closer, he started taking off his shirt.

"It's what Momma and Charles always told me to do whenever I shiver, to just take off my clothes and get near the fire." Barnum rubbed his hands along his nipples and then slid his hands down to his cut-off jeans before unzipping his soggy shorts.

Henry stood behind him and could see the lowest notch in the boy's back, where his buttocks pushed out from his soaked underwear. That was what Hiram had called them, "the buttocks." Henry always thought it was an odd name; it sounded like an animal. And often, after the tugging was over, after Hiram rubbed and sometimes clawed Henry's skin, Henry felt his own round fleshy bumps and wondered if everyone liked the wavy feel of their own round skin, because Barnum sure did. Henry watched Barnum slide his fingers up and down along his buttocks before grasping the top of his underwear and pulling them to the floor.

"I'm just gonna hang these up."

Barnum bent over to pick up his sopping underwear and Henry saw the thin ribs stick out from the boy's side. Peering closer, Henry saw the line between the boy's buttocks. *It looks just like he's joined together with two halves. Like the bass was when it jumped near my eye.* And for a moment, Henry wanted to trace his hands along that smooth line. He wanted to hold the boy close to find out how he was sewn together and made—though he hoped Hiram didn't know how he felt.

So I won't touch him, he thought. Though shuffling closer, he looked along the boy's back and felt a pink breath like Hiram's surge through him, so he tried to think of the mannequin next to the radio instead. He watched the firelight flicker on the mannequin's breasts. But when Barnum leaned up to a shelf, Henry watched how the boy's water-slick body held the orange stove light. Henry even thought he saw all the bones and blood glowing inside Barnum's body.

"As soon as we get that fire up, I won't chatter no more." Barnum's jaw shook as he hung his underwear and shorts near his shirt. "Cause they ain't chattered like this since last winter, when I fell through the ice."

Barnum's legs were perfect. They came out straight and even at the bottom—each as long as the other—and Henry rubbed his dry lips when he saw Barnum's bare waist. *Because it's hanging right there, the boy's dangling thing,* and he knew Hiram would have held the dangling thing if it'd been Henry who was naked. Hiram would have brought him closer to touch.

"Why don't you take your shirt off? You've got to be as cold as me."

Henry hadn't felt his own shivering skin for so long standing there, that the words brought him back to the tense shell of his body. His skin was blue at the edges. Feeling along his dripping shirt, he shook the sleeves from his arms. Heat was moving through the room. An orange glare strung wide shadows across the walls.

"You sure got a swell radio," Barnum said, edging closer to the mattress. "I bet we could hear all kinds of westerns on it. Like in the days Charles and Momma talk about, when the radio played shows."

Barnum was moist. Henry saw all the sweaty beads on the boy's arms and legs. And when Barnum turned to pass his hands along the radio's glass dials, Henry slid his trousers to the floor.

"I bet Sonny and Cisco are on there right now. And if we eat our fish quiet like, we could listen to all the cattle rustlers and card dealers in the saloon."

Henry leaned on his right foot and brought his hands to cover his dangling thing. He was careful not to touch it, so it might not grow like when Hiram touched it, when Hiram held it and made the sound with his lips. *I don't want it to grow around the boy.* But he felt a rising hardness below his waist and tried to count against it in his mind, to see Hiram instead: *One two three four five six seven eight nine ten zero. One two three four five six seven eight nine ten zero.*

The slow tightening was rising even as he looked at Barnum bent near the radio. Shadows from the firelight crossed the thin line of the boy's two halves, so that his buttocks looked moist near the stove.

"Aw, shoot. We already missed Momma. I forgot she leaves by six on Bingo nights." Barnum spun his hands across the dials and saw the mannequin. "Well, well, *there* she is." Reaching over to the mattress, he brought the smudged shape to his chest.

"No," Henry mumbled when he saw the mannequin's breasts in the boy's hands. He stepped closer, raising his hand. Henry had never said no to anyone before, not even to the children when they teased him in the rectory.

"I just want to see her is all." Barnum looked at Henry, his eyes blank and searching, and it reminded Henry of when they first shook hands those days ago.

"That's mine," Henry said.

"You mean, it's *ours*, don't you? Ain't we partners?"

Henry moistened his lips with his tongue, spitting at the stove. A few drops hissed in the heat, and he grabbed the sides of the mannequin, pulling the body from the boy.

"*Henry!*" Barnum cried. "I'm just trying to share."

Henry felt his right leg quiver as he leaned harder on his heel. The quivering came all the way through his stomach and arms, and in the corners of his eyes he saw the black smudges. The smudges blotted out the boy.

Pulling back on the torso, all he saw was darkness then, and he heard Barnum cry as he slid against the wooden sides of the radio. Trying to catch himself, his moist arms sounded like skidding tires on the highway. When Henry shook the darkness away, he saw a glassy knob had come off in Barnum's hand.

Stepping above him, he held the mannequin to his waist and could see beneath Barnum's dangling thing to where the line of his two halves joined. Henry sucked in with a rush of sipping air. "You okay?"

Barnum didn't answer.

When Henry bent closer, the mannequin rubbed against his groin, and he felt his dangling thing grow when he looked beneath the boy's rounded flesh. The boy's dangling thing rested against a creamy thigh, and Henry held the mannequin closer—he couldn't press close enough to stop the rising, so he started rubbing instead. He rubbed the mannequin up and down because it made the tightening feel better, like the tightening was meant for something. Like it was meant for the boy. But he kept the mannequin close and wouldn't let go.

"*Henry?*" Barnum's voice wavered in the shadows. "What happened?"

"You had yourself a fall." Pulling on his boots and damp trousers, Henry covered his feet and waist. His thick lips gaped open, and when he looked at Barnum, the tightening faded from his waist. Barnum was covered in dust, and his marble skin was sick to look at in the light. Bits of leaves and twigs were smeared against his side. Blood drew a thin line along the side of the boy's face. When Henry saw the blood, he remembered seeing his own face in the mirror after Hiram slapped him each night and said they were, "Redeemed now for doing it. Redeemed now for loving. Redeemed now forever. So slap me, Henry. Slap me so I know what I've done."

Henry had never slapped Hiram. Those nights he only touched his lips to see the red drops in his hand. Then he would touch his lips and look at Hiram, at the tears in Hiram's eyes. And in looking at Barnum's bloody head, he wondered if they were redeemed now too—him and Barnum—after coming so close to the loving?

8

THEY ATE THE FISH AFTER THAT, after Henry unfolded the old canvas tarp he'd found in the lockhouse. It covered Barnum so Henry wouldn't have to see the boy's creamy thighs in the red firelight. Henry had found a few wild berries in the morning, and they ate the berries so that a wild berry flavor coated their tongues after the smoky meat was through.

"Best dinner you ever ate," Barnum bragged. The words came slower from his mouth. He stood to take his clothes from the shelf and giggled when his shorts came away like a stiff board in his hands. "Looks like they've been cut from an oak."

Barnum beat the shorts with his hands until they were softer. As he beat the shorts, the canvas tarp fell around his ankles and the boy's buttocks tightened. When he leaned up for his underwear—which looked like it still held his two skinny legs—Henry watched the twitching muscles in the boy's thighs. All the downy hair on Barnum's skin was aglow. Henry hadn't noticed that before, the downy gloss, and he traced the outline of Barnum's legs with his hand in the air.

"I forgot the fire did this to things full of water." Barnum crouched and slid on his underwear. "Feels like I'm putting on something right out the dryer, like at the Laun-Dro-Mat."

He jiggled left and right to get his underwear situated and laughed as he watched Henry watch him move back and forth. As he did the same with his shorts, Henry felt along his waist. His groin wasn't growing like he thought it might. *I'm all right*. Though when he stood, he wobbled a bit on his right leg and he almost had to reach out to the stove for support, but Barnum was there. So Henry put his hand on the boy's shoulder to steady himself.

"It's all right," Barnum said. Henry wobbled for another second before reaching up for his shirt. The sleeves were still damp but he slid them on anyway after Barnum put his small fingers to Henry's chest so Henry wouldn't teeter.

"Thanks."

"We're partners now, and that's what partners do. Don't you know that?"

"Partners," Henry said, "yeah."

"So we gonna listen to that radio or what?" Barnum spun the dials slower in his hands. Letting go, he rubbed his eyes. Henry saw the faint blood crusted from where Barnum hit his head, and as Barnum fiddled with the radio again, Henry placed the mannequin in the small kitchen by the window. The window had plywood nailed over it in rotting sections. Henry hid the torso behind a splintered rectangle.

"We gonna listen to Tex and Dale and the Red River Gang when the sheriff's in town..." Barnum yawned and rubbed his head where the cut had clotted. His hand brought away a mushy blood-smear like a chewed up jellybean. "We gonna pretend?" Barnum slumped to the edge of the mattress, yawned again, and was quiet.

Henry listened to the crackling log. *The heat made him sleepy; it makes everyone sleepy*. Henry breathed in twice, listening to the boy's soft exhales.

"The rats should be back soon," Henry said. The boy's eyes were closed, and he yawned at Henry's voice. "We'll hear them in the walls for sure." Henry nudged Barnum, but Barnum didn't wake. "That's when we can pretend all we want with the radio. Then we can listen for the train to come through."

"*Well, just call down Josephine for the rats...*" Barnum muttered. He was slumped against Henry's shoulder, asleep.

Holding the boy up by his arm, Henry put the canvas tarp over the old mattress. The mattress was usually covered in leaves and flattened cardboard boxes, but Henry brushed the leaves and boxes away.

"See, the music from the radio is smoky and comes from up in the air like your pictures," Henry said. Setting Barnum on the mattress, he spoke over him. "Moving you is just like hauling a stump. The ones pulled up after all the roots have rotted through. They come up easy from the mud. Like hands letting go."

Barnum rolled over to one side and Henry wrapped the tarp over him and stared at the rafters.

"Now, I count the stars," Henry said. "I count them on my hands." Between some of the shingles, fuzzy points of light glittered. "Usually when I get to zero once and then to zero again I'm asleep. But then the train rumbles past and all the dust drifts down. But I'm getting used to all the things you don't know about. Like even the rats in the walls. I don't hear them no more. I even take a bucket down to the cistern now. I set aside that tin cup I found a while ago." Henry looked at Barnum's head, at the red smear above his ear. "It's good sometimes when you don't talk."

Henry turned to the mannequin on the shelf. The dark smudgy breasts edged out from behind the plywood. These last nights, after hauling her up from the canal, he'd slept with her pressed against him. *It's because I smell the canal on her. She's got bumps on her chest where I don't have bumps or where Barnum don't have bumps, and I like passing my hands where I'm supposed to put my hands on a girl—on her bumps.*

"At least, that's what Marshall the manager said in the locker room, when he showed me the pictures in his pocket. And you're right, Barnum, she's a girl, and maybe she can make me tingle just like you."

Barnum rolled over and Henry felt the boy's warm breath. Barnum's lips were dry. His hand stretched out to Henry, touching his side, and Henry watched him breathe until after he counted to zero once, and then to zero again. He watched Barnum until the stars fell away, after the midnight train rumbled past. He watched Barnum until he forgot all about the mannequin and the bumps, until he forgot about holding her close and rubbing her against his hardening waist, until he was asleep.

HENRY WAS UP AND WALKED STRAIGHT AND EASY. His legs were the same length, and his feet touched the trail one after the other. He was on the towpath hauling a thick muddy line. Looking over his shoulder, he saw a low boat in the canal. *He* was on the same boat he hauled the line of.

There were ladies in white dresses too. Smoky music sounded all around. Sunlight and leaves reflected off the water, and the Henry that was on the boat—the Henry he was watching as he hauled the line—was smiling. That Henry had a brown hat, and thin fingers, and he didn't have to raise his lips with his hands to smile. Though when he *did* smile, when he let out a broad laugh, Henry heard the screaming voice near the railroad ask for Barnum:

"Barnum Jacob McClain, what is on the side of your face!"

Then Henry sat bolt upright and heard Barnum mumble back, "I don't know if it's blood or not, but my head hurts."

Henry rolled over and felt the warm place where Barnum slept. The sandy river smell of the boy was still there. Through a hole in the window, he saw Barnum beside a woman in a white wrinkled shirt. The woman was much taller and thinner than the boy. It looked like she was standing to the side with her body turned, even when she was right in front of him. She leaned down until her straight brown hair merged with Barnum's hair, and Henry thought two heads had merged into one.

"I didn't know you were looking, Momma—honest." A low moan came from the boy as his mother cried overtop him, and Henry watched until the low moaning came across the dry weeds separating the railroad from the lockhouse.

"I'm just glad you're here."

Henry watched Barnum point to the lockhouse. When he did, Henry shrunk close to the floor with just his nose edging over the windowsill, and long after Barnum went up the trail, Henry thought about Barnum's pointing finger the rest of the day. "Maybe he was mad I didn't let him hold the girl? It looked like he wanted to rub her like the way I rub her these nights."

It was much colder. Henry had to stamp his feet in the canal to loosen the weeds. He heard birds in the trees ticking above him and wondered why they hadn't flown to where it was getting warmer instead of colder each morning. *Isn't that what the birds did in Baltimore?* They flew to *Flor-i-da*. Hiram told him that, and Henry liked the sound of *Flor-i-da*, with how the starting and stopping sounds melted on Hiram's lips. *Flor-i-da* sounded like a melting place.

"But Barnum might have been mad I pulled the girl away, and he hit his head because of it." Henry watched the birds settle into groups above him. The trees had lost their leaves these last days. It happened all at once. One moment the trees were green and he'd walked the trail those seven days and nights. Then the trees turned blood-orange and gold-green, towering up the mountainside, and the trees were bare. Now packs of birds twittered here and there. They wove nests like thick knots of yarn high up.

"He probably wants the girl," Henry said. "And I could have given him the girl just like the TV, but I wanted the girl for *myshelf.*" Henry hissed this last word and felt his lips; his lisp had started again. Spittle gathered in the pit of his mouth. "I could give him the TV and radio for sure. That would be easy. And maybe even the bicycle in the basement, and almost everything else I find—but not the girl. The girl makes me right. She makes me right by how she feels. By the bumps I press with my waist. She's not the boy." He said this last part low, so his lisp wouldn't come back, so the spit he hated and had to wipe from his lips wouldn't return. "She's not the boy. She's not the boy," and he started in harder, threshing the weeds.

9

ᴴENRY DIDN'T SEE BARNUM FOR MANY DAYS after that. When Henry rested each afternoon from his work, he expected to hear the boy's high ringing voice, but there was only more work in the canal and less swishy-clothed people jogging by. Once, during those days, Henry saw a horse with a woman on it in a red riding jacket. She sat in a red saddle and stopped with the towering horse on the edge of the canal. Henry was wading in the frosty grass, his boots slick with mud, when the horse snorted at Henry's face. Backing away to the other edge, Henry feared the horse might charge, but the woman clucked her tongue and the horse shuffled off. Two dark clumps of dung crumbled from its rear as it turned on the towpath. Those days were hard for Henry. Barnum had once brought him food. Now it was colder, and the berries didn't grow. Henry went to the river to fish, but he didn't know how to work the rod that Barnum left, so he used the net instead. There were many hours when Henry stood alone in the water, the net dragging through the shallows, minnows and perch slipping through the mesh.

Wading by the banks once, he found a turtle when he lifted a rock. The large gray head looked up at him with its snapping mouth, and Henry was so startled that he dropped the rock back on the turtle, killing it by mistake. When he held the broken turtle in his hands, its purple-green shell passed like bits of a broken bowl in his fingers, and he cried to know the turtle wouldn't snap anymore or sleep his winter sleep in the thick mud.

"But I'm gonna need you," he said. "I'm gonna need you and make you like me, so it wasn't a waste what I done." Henry brought the broken turtle into the lockhouse. He placed him on the stove, and the turtle bubbled out of his shell. Henry ate him standing there, leaning on his right leg, the steaming turtle meat sweet with the taste of river water.

Henry even had a visitor once who wasn't Barnum. Henry watched from the other side of the towpath after he came up one morning from wading with the net. His stomach groaned as he hid behind an oak. The man wore a green and gray uniform. His white and orange-checkered truck was parked in front of the lockhouse. The truck took up the whole towpath and Henry heard the man's radio stutter and fizz: "Ron…Ron?"

"I'm at lock 31," Ron said. "The reports of activity were correct. The canal has been cleared out somewhat, and it looks like someone might have been squatting in the lockhouse. But I've put the chain on; it should be fine."

"Over and out," the crackly voice said.

Ron got in his truck and drove away.

It was true what Ron said. Henry stood at the lockhouse and passed his hands across a loose chain that ran around the door handle and through an iron loop on each side of the frame. Henry wheezed in with two deep breaths. His stomach tightened when he thought of the mannequin. He stood for a long while and felt his right leg tingle when he wobbled a bit from standing without moving. Shifting to his left leg, he pulled and the door gave half an inch, but that was all. He pulled again and it gave another half inch, but that was all he could pull. His hands were chaffed from the effort, and as he sat on the large stone in front of the lockhouse, he peered into the canal.

"I still have work to do," and he glanced at the stubborn door. "She's in there alone, and I said I would hold her forever; I told her." Then to distract himself from thinking about the mannequin and the bumps he might never hold again, he thought about the canal instead. He thought about finishing it. "Because I can pretend." It was something he had started doing by accident, after Barnum had showed him how to pass into someone else's mind. So Henry pretended what the canal would look like.

"I have the pictures in my head. Like what Barnum sees. The pictures help me forget about my stomach and the cold—about everything."

Leaning back on the stone, he closed his eyes.

"Because I can feel the pictures getting bigger when I want them to. Then smaller, when I'm almost asleep, so that all the colors come out. The color of the water and of the red saddle the lady sat in. I hear the birds ticking in the trees, even when I know they're mostly gone to *Flor-i-da* now. And I wonder if Barnum would believe me if I told him this ain't never happened before—to see so many pictures and hear so many sounds inside me. Even in the rectory by the docks. Even when the other children were led off and I stood there alone, the bucket and soapy water sloshing against my waist. When all I saw was the wall, and my hands moving across the wall."

Henry raised his hands and scrubbed against an imaginary wall.

"But now I have pictures. Now I can see how the canal will be blue and full of water. Leaves will shine all orange and red on the surface; then green and gold during spring." He leaned up on his toes to see the towpath. "And there'll be mules too. Mules with red saddles like the lady's red saddle. I can see them red saddles right in front of me, just like that horse above the canal. Hiram said mules were used back then, when the canal was working, and maybe that's all I need to bring it back—so it's new."

Henry heard Hiram's voice in his mind then. A whispering moved across the puddle below him to make it ripple.

The mules did the work, Hiram rasped. *And you can bet they were happy doing it. They walked all day and got fed carrots and drank water when they wanted. The trail is so flat you don't even notice it rising up. Even with your leg. Barges rode up and down and brought flour to the lockhouses and news about wars and Washington DC. They even brought stories. The lockmen got all the stories and told everybody everything.*

In the apartment, when Hiram talked about the lockmen, he told Henry the story of the half-moon scar on his belly. Hiram talked about the war too, about Korea, and how the half-moon scar showed God had a plan for him, since he survived. "And since God has a plan for me. God has a plan for you too."

Looking from the towpath to the wet grass, Henry remembered how Hiram drew close to him those nights. How he said what they did each night was redeemed because of the half-moon scar, of what it meant. *But I never knew what that half-moon scar meant*. He only remembered when the tugging was done that Hiram pressed his fingers to his scar saying,

"That pink scar above your lip is a sign of God too." In his mind, Henry saw Hiram pointing to his lip. "He puts one on everyone. So when He recalls them to heaven He knows which is which."

In the canal, Henry pressed his finger along his pink scar, along the raised curve. He couldn't remember if he got it in the rectory, when the children slapped him at night, or if Hiram raised the scar with his own slapping hand, with the gold ring he touched beneath his handkerchief to make it shine.

"Or maybe the scar's from before?" He picked up his hickory stick and started threshing the weeds. "Maybe I got it before the slapping and tugging begun—and it really is a sign from God, from before the beginning?"

He didn't know what *before the beginning* could mean, but thought it might have something to do with the colored pictures of glass he remembered from the church. "With the pictures of men holding up other men and the light passing over their bodies." Henry passed his hand along his right leg.

"All their legs were the same length in the pictures," and he felt his hip tingle from the moisture in his joints. "And I wonder if before the beginning my legs had the same length?" Pressing his hand to his hip, he felt his leg ache. "If only there were nuns," he said and looked to the towpath. Beech trees swayed on the other side. Their long branches reached out like fingers to him. "If only there were nuns I could ask. I never asked. My mind wasn't like it is now, with the pictures and the pretending."

Leaning over a puddle, his mind made the pictures larger in the water. He saw the picture of the rectory. He watched his hands rub across the high walls and windows with the rag—and he remembered seeing his face for the first time with the scar—in its pink and curving wonder, etched above his lips. A sudden thunderstorm had risen across the bay, darkening the shimmering glass he was cleaning, and he trailed his fingers along the shape, rubbing over the scar's crease.

"The church," Henry said and focused on how wild his orange hair looked in the late afternoon light. Tight curls spilled over his forehead. Spitting on his fingers, he rubbed his hands along the scar's curve and remembered the rectory yard. He saw children making him stand in the middle of the seesaw, right at the point where he could neither rise nor fall. As the children took their turns, he always traced their legs with his hands in the air, watching.

"But maybe I could go to the church and ask?" He didn't know when he'd started mumbling like this, but he liked hearing his voice; he liked hearing the words. "I'm getting better with my lisp. My words don't sound anymore like the swishy joggers going by. I sound like Barnum instead, with his voice echoing in the canal." Henry looked to the trees. The limbs were bare, and a breeze started the limbs ticking against each other. "But Barnum ain't around no more. They ain't even any birds." He wheezed in with two deep breaths and heard the canal echo with his breathing. "But he talked about the man. Rommel. That's what Barnum said, the man in the church basement. So I'll just walk the way Barnum took, but instead of going up—I'll head down—into town." Henry said all this to the puddle. He spoke and watched his pink scar and drew a circle in the mud with the stick around his face.

10

THE RAILROAD'S TARRY SMELL stayed with Henry when he made it to the road. The highway was farther up, on the other side of the hill. It went into a pass beyond where the houses were, and Henry paused to look both ways along this smaller road before limping to the other side.

"That was the way Barnum went," he said, pointing along the pipe that came down the hill. "I remember the TV and the wide hedge, when I went up huffing and sweating. But I don't go up there now; I stay down here and walk into town."

Henry looked along the edge of the road leading into town. Bare oak limbs hovered above him on both sides like a twittering cage. As he watched the branches, the wind shook the mountain, and Henry didn't realize how cold it was. With the chain on the lockhouse, he hadn't been able to get in and light the coals from last night. His trousers were dripping from wading in the river; his boots were filled with pebbles and sand.

"*Orange jackass!*" Henry heard a voice yell from a pickup truck. As it sped by, a yellow-haired man leaned from the window. He pointed at Henry with his fingers like he was firing a pistol. Henry watched the red pickup drive into town. The road curved around a bend and went up along a hill. Henry limped to the bend where another road intersected before running off south following the railroad.

"But I *am* the jackass," he said, snorting. "If that yellow-haired man ever saw me hauling frigerators and stones to the towpath, arranging bicycles and bedsprings, he might know he was right."

Henry thought it was funny to picture himself like a mule on the towpath, hauling away junk. "I am the jackass," he said, and wheezed in with two deep breaths, slapping his hands.

Tracing the intersection with a raised finger, he saw a soda machine beside a gray building across from where he stood. A row of gray apartments ran along the road that followed the railroad south. A few antennas jutted up from cracked rooftops. A low green wall lined the other road, heading east, up another hill, away from town. The houses' metal doors opened above the low green wall, and dogs rummaged in the trash bins. The dogs stopped and looked at Henry standing there on his one short leg and whimpered before returning to their rummaging—it sounded like they were laughing at him, laughing at his leg.

They are, he thought, watching the dogs.

"But this ain't Baltimore," he said, and his stomach grumbled.

Off the road, Henry saw the church beside the bare limbs of a maple. He tried to count the steps from where he stood, but he had to lean into the road, and before he got to—*three*—a car honked and a man raised his fist in the window so that Henry limped back toward the gutter. Caught on some twigs in the drain, a blue and yellow plastic bag fluttered with a swishy noise, shaken by the wind. The swishy sound reminded him of the towpath and the people staring at him in their puke-green and orange clothing, so he limped up the—*one two three four*—steps to the church door.

It opened with a slight push, and then Henry was inside like in the rectory. The church had that cloistered smell—of waxy roses and rose-soap and iron kettles—and it took Henry a few moments before his eyes adjusted to the darkened glimmer. On the far wall, the altar was lit from beneath and a few women were in pews spread along each side. Henry tried to count the number of rows and stood until he got to zero but stopped because his right leg tingled, so he slid into one of the back pews.

"*Hmmmm*." Henry heard a woman moan from one of the front pews. Most of the women he saw were toward the front and rocked gently to some song they must have heard inside. So he tried to rock gently too. He tried to hear that smoky music from the radio Hiram used to play. He tried to make the sound louder in his mind until even the tingling in his leg was a song rising from his toes to his arms—but only a few words returned to him.

I once was lost,
but now am found,
was blind, but now I see

It was the song Hiram sang from the radio those nights, when Henry watched the buses in the moonlight. *And the song has a rising in it, a floating up.* Though he wasn't sure why he remembered it now. It felt like the song was a current that had brought him in from the wind, his shoes and trousers dripping. As he sat in a pew shifting his legs, his boots made a squelchy sound of grinding sand, and he thought the ladies in front might turn to look, but they never did.

"*Hmmmmm,*" one said, all the way up front.

Henry squelched his legs and right boot again.

"*Mmmmm,*" another said.

"*Mmmmm-hmmmm,*" another said. She was closer to Henry, only— *one two three*—pews in front.

Henry raised his finger to trace the outline of her head. She had white hair with blue streaks along the sides and the long white strands were brought to the back of her head in a bun. The tight braid was what Henry liked, and he trailed along the outside of its circle until all the ladies stopped saying, "*Mmmmm-hmmmm.*"

They filed out then one by one, their heads bowed and feet shuffling until Henry was alone.

"They didn't even look at me." Henry stood then because his stomach had a fluttering feeling and fell away from him, like when he was younger, when all the other children were led away from the rectory. He remembered standing in the morning, a bucket of soapy water against his thigh, and he wanted to make the fluttering feeling stop. It always did when he started scrubbing the walls, scrubbing up and down and left and right. The scrubbing was a quiet thing.

That was what the nuns said back then: "The quiet things are good for you." He heard their voices rise above him as he stood in the center aisle. The church was warm. Colored windows lined each side of the nave and he saw light falling on figures in the glass, on their perfect arms and legs. The light was purple and blood-orange and looked like the mountains before the leaves fell all those days ago. *It reminds me of the leaves in the canal, on those days the mountain was a wave of color, and I stood there for hours watching the colors drift to my feet.*

He limped next to a window with a man in a white robe. The robe fell along the man's skinny legs, and Henry trailed his fingers along the legs to see how both feet rested together: they were the same length. He reached down to touch his own leg. He loved how the white robe was creased and full of folds. As the light caught in the folds above him, it made his stomach flutter. But this was a jumpy fluttering—a flying feeling he knew was good and which he'd felt as recently as this morning, when he rubbed the mannequin against his waist before going fishing. *It isn't the falling away, like when I'm hungry, or when the nuns left me alone in the church. This is nicer.*

The window frame had black iron lines on the edges, and the edges looked like the railroad tracks Barnum made him lean over when that strange train went by before he drew the zero in the sand. He remembered watching the conductor lean out from the brass trimming and red-painted panels. He hadn't seen a train like that since though, and he knew he might never see pictures like this again—not with the perfect glassy legs—so he stared even harder at the light.

"That's the third Station of the Cross, when Jesus first fell." A scratchy voice rose from near the altar. Henry saw a gray-haired man in a blue shirt lean on a mop by the candles on the front wall. "The weight is unbearable and Jesus falls under," he said. "He feels the weight and is not sure if He can continue, but He is pulled up and *made* to continue." The man started mopping after he spoke.

Henry watched him mop for a while.

The man had a limp about him too. *But the limp ain't in his legs*, Henry thought, *because I can see his legs. They're the same size and move across the floor from the same height. The limp is higher up, and comes from his waist or hips.* Henry watched until the man noticed Henry watching him, until he stopped to ring the brown water from the mop.

"Jesus emptied himself out too." The man pointed to the glass Henry stood beneath. "You can see how emptied out He made himself. Emptied of all the light of heaven. All so He could walk the way He did and fall the way He did—for us—like us." The man drew himself closer to the altar. He squeezed the mop again and straightened up, saying, "He emptied Himself out and humbled Himself and hauled the cross up Calvary."

The man took another step toward the altar, but he didn't step over as much as limp over, or shuffle. He moved with a tense jerking motion that started first by throwing his waist out so that it looked like he might fall face forward. But right when he was on the point of teetering over, both his feet came from behind and caught up to him and were under him so that he was ready for the next loose thrusting-out of his waist.

"The burden is His can't you see? But it's not just His burden." The man's black eyes were pinched shut, and his small face had a pinched look about it, like it was pinched together with invisible fingers at the sides. "The burden was never the burden of Jesus alone. The burden is ours in each day and night, in each decision and word."

Henry's thick fingers hesitated on the white robes falling over the perfect legs. "And even the burden of legs?"

"Yes, son, even the burden of legs. And even the burden of lips and eyes, and the burden of sleep and hands. The burden of many things are found in that first burden—the burden of living."

The man thrust-out his waist and his legs caught up to him, and he thrust-out again and was closer to Henry. He rested his hand on a pew when he was only—*one two three*—rows away. His pinched face had become unpinched because he was smiling now, but his smiling face had lines in it. A spiderweb spun out from all sides, like the lines on Henry's hands.

"Do you worry about your leg?" The man smiled as he looked at Henry's special right boot. Henry turned to the light falling on the white robe and on the perfect legs of Jesus, all straight and the same size. He touched the ends of the legs with his hands, before feeling the glass.

"What is your life like?" the man said.

"My life is in the canal." Henry didn't lisp when he spoke; he didn't look back either. He kept his eyes on Jesus and the white robe.

"In the canal?"

Even in the Quiet Places

Henry heard the man thrust his waist out, and his legs came shuffling after him—once, then twice—and with each step Henry wanted to turn to help the man, to hold him up if he fell, but the white robe and perfect legs were what Henry wanted to hold. *I want to pass my hands over the white robes and legs, and maybe even rub my waist against them; I want them so much.* "In the beginning," Henry said, "were my legs the same?"

The man had thrust-out and shuffled-up till Henry could tell he was only a pew away, maybe only another thrusting-out and shuffling step. Henry smelled a mixture of charcoal and bleach on him but didn't move, even when the man put a warm hand on Henry's shoulder. Henry just stared at Jesus in the white robes. He stared until he felt his eyes tremble with water.

"Son, you needn't worry any longer about your life in the canal. You're here now. There are dry clothes in the basement and an extra cot." Henry remembered his squelchy clothes when the man nodded to the wet puddle beneath Henry's boots. Henry looked at the old man, and the room glowed in the white light. The water, trembling in Henry's eyes, ran down his cheeks and made the room refract blue and red and yellow like leaves falling from the mountain.

Part Two

11

THE WEEKS DID NOT HAVE NUMBERS after that, and the people were many. Henry stayed in the basement with Rommel, the man with the mop and blue shirt, and it was easy to find the church new. It was easy to find the rooms in the basement and the windowsills new, to lose himself in the storage shed where they kept the manger decorations. Or to let his mind wander during the mopping he helped with that first day, after Rommel let Henry look through the cardboard boxes for clothes in the basement. He picked a pair of gray overalls and hung his blue jeans on a line near the furnace. He also found some thermal underwear and a blue flannel shirt that Rommel said went well with his orange hair. The days found a new rhythm, a pattern that felt like his new clothes—worn a little at the ends, frayed and loose, but comfortable, and easy-going. There wasn't any kneeling in the mud, or eating berries from the weeds, and Henry enjoyed this newness, he thrived with it.

"After mopping each day, after the furnace is clean and the toilets wiped, then I get to scrub the pews." Henry breathed in with two wheezing breaths and rubbed his hands together. "That's because Rommel can't bend like he used to with his back the way it is. And I don't mind the pews at all. I don't."

Scrubbing the pews was the part Henry liked best. It was after the priest finished his afternoon service. After all the silver-haired ladies came and mumbled, "Mmmmm-hmmmm," for an hour or so, rocking to the songs inside themselves—and it was after Henry helped Rommel make the soup.

Rommel said, "Just open the cans. We stir the beans so they don't burn the sides." Rommel shuffled to the cupboard and grabbed the peanut butter for the sandwiches. "We'll make a cook out of you yet. You're stirring the Lord's pot now."

It was only after all this that Henry found himself alone with the pews. As the stained-glass windows hovered above him with a stillness he felt working through every inch of his limbs, he focused on his scrubbing hands and let the memory of the mannequin return to him. He thought about the mannequin's bumps. How he rubbed the mannequin against his waist those nights, and he watched his hands move across the worn grooves in the wood. It was only when he thought about the mannequin that he saw the lockhouse and the canal again like he pretended it those days ago.

"It will be blue," he said and rubbed the soapy rag along the pew. "It will be blue and glisten with the orange and gold leaves falling to the water." The colors brought back the canal's minty smell; he heard birds ticking above him and turtles gulping on the banks. Then he missed his life there and repeated his promise: "To make the canal new. Like when it was older. To make it new and let the river back." After he repeated his promise, he scrubbed harder to forget about the days he was spending here with the weather cold and the earth frozen. *Because the days here are different*, he knew. *The cold brought me in, and the cold will say how long I stay.*

He watched the canal in his mind grow smaller then. He wasn't sure why he'd come to the church, and there was no one to ask. Usually, when he scrubbed the pews, Rommel napped on his cot in the basement. The priest had already gone to his house. Henry watched the priest leave each day, down the—*one two three four* steps—across the road, then past the soda machines and garbage bins to his gray house. The silver-haired ladies were gone too. They'd already teetered down the aisle, wrapped in scarves and hats, but he wouldn't have asked them anyway. He wouldn't disturb their prayers. *I remember why I'm here, even if there's only the sound of my scrubbing hands to give me the answer.*

He watched his hands work the waxy soap in the late afternoon light. The light came through the window with Jesus and His perfect legs.

"I'm here about His perfect legs. His perfect legs keep me here to look at and to touch." Henry trailed his fingers in the air. "And 'before the beginning.' I wonder if my legs were once perfect, that they were the same before the beginning."

Though when he stopped scrubbing and felt along his short right leg, he thought there had never been a pair of perfect legs beneath him to begin with.

"Even before the beginning there might have been just this." Kneeling, he thought about all the priest's words from these last two Sundays. The priest said, "Everyone was the same. Everyone was free before the beginning, but he never spoke about legs." But then he remembered seeing Barnum that first Sunday, and how it frightened him. He hid from Barnum in the coatroom, avoiding the boy's eyes. Thinking of Barnum now made him rise from his knees and worry about his short leg. He worried what people would say if they noticed it.

"Because what if the cut on Barnum's head don't heal? And Barnum's Momma thought I done it? All she has to do is ask and that would be it, if she saw me." It made his stomach tighten thinking about Barnum's mother going to the lockhouse and finding the mannequin. Henry knew Barnum's mother would hold the mannequin up in church, saying, "See, I told you he done strange things to my boy. Just look what he keeps and rubs against him. Just look at his rotten body! And his short leg! It's a sign, with how it marks him. It's an unholy man you've let walk at your feet, scrub your pews, eat from your cupboard!"

Henry knew the church might rise against him then. Even Rommel might rise against him, saying, "I always suspected him, but never knew it until I seen the mannequin. Because I've heard him rubbing with his hands most nights in the cot. I thought it was just his feet then, that he rubbed his leg because of its shortness."

Henry shook his leg out when he pretended what Rommel might say. *But aren't Rommel and me in on something with how we limp like we do?* "He wouldn't rise against me if he found out about the mannequin. Not with us being the weakest like what the priest said." Henry looked to the third Station of the Cross. "Because I remember that first sermon, when the priest talked about 'Redeeming our fellow man.' The priest said it was our greatest charge. That 'Our fellow man does not know what he does to the littlest among us, nor to the weakest.' I remember how he brought his handkerchief to his face then. When all the people said, '*Yes, Sir,*' and, '*Yes, Lord,*' and, '*Yes, God.*' When they said that, I knew we were all together. I could feel it in my stomach."

Leaning over, he remembered the golden feeling from that sermon. "I saw the light dance from the window with Jesus high up, with how the light passed from stomach to stomach, and pew to pew, and I wondered if the other stomachs could feel that light too? Could they see when the priest wiped his forehead and cried out for redeeming?" Henry set his rag down and saw Rommel grow bigger in his mind when he thought of them together, in on something, with how they limped. "Rommel would never rise against me—he even give me my bucket."

Leaning on his right leg, he remembered how Rommel bent awkwardly above the rows that first day, showing him how to scrub the pews. "You see my back, don't you? It don't bend like it used to, but I still do the Lord's work like what Beauregard taught me. Beauregard came before and taught me and so now I'll teach you. You can sleep in Beauregard's cot, if you don't mind."

"I don't mind," Henry said, and ever since then, whenever Henry scrubbed the pews, he repeated those words. "Just by saying, 'I don't mind,' makes me silent," he knew. "It makes my body silent and ready to look when I have to look."

Henry turned to the lighted windows and to Jesus' white robes. The white robes were silent—but somehow singing. Somehow he knew the glass and white robes were singing to him by being so silent. So wetting the back of the pew, he watched the sudsy water drip along the grainy wood. It glistened after the water dripped down, raising a deep, crimson hue. The rich mahogany and rosy soap bubbles mixed with the wood until it smelled like the trees on the trail above the river, and he saw the wide current then. How it stretched like a black line across the valley. Since he'd come here, he hadn't seen the river in his mind. Not like this. Not so clear.

"That was many days ago. I need too many fingers to count the too many days," and so he focused on the pews instead. "When I scrub the pews I start on top like what Rommel said, then I put the rag to the side." He brought a stiff brush from where it was clipped to the bucket. "He told

me to scrub from the top down and squeeze the rag till all the suds run along
the slant to where the seat meets the back. Because I've seen how the water
pools there in the edge, and I'm just gonna scrub harder to move the suds."

He pushed down with the brush, whisking out in circles.

"See, I don't mind." Leaning closer, he saw his face shimmer in the
water until his skin looked like a smooth grainy stump, swirling and moving in a pattern that was much older than he could ever count. "Zero," he
said.

He pointed to the pew and traced a wavy zero along the grain.

"And zero zero." He pointed as the soap sloshed in circles along the
plank. *Saying 'Zero,' makes me feel quiet inside. It's like what the church
is now, with the velvet feeling falling down.* In the late afternoon light, he
saw violet waves falling through the white robes in his favorite Station of
the Cross. "He's all purple now. Like what He shouldn't be, not like what
Rommel told me."

"What did I tell you?" Henry saw Rommel by the basement stairs, a
matchbox in his hand.

"I thought you were napping?"

"Well I was, but then I heard you talking. And I decided if you had
something loud enough to say, I should probably hear it."

"I was just looking at the stations. Then I tried remembering what you
told me about them, but I couldn't think of it yet."

"Just look at the pictures. Then when I point to them, pretend like
you're inside them. Just pretend you're with Him."

"Pretend?" Henry said.

"Sure, because you can see Jesus is condemned to die in the first
station? How He wears a crown of thorns when they mocked Him, even
though He was King of Men."

"A king," Henry repeated and leaned on his right leg.

"In the second station, Jesus carries the same cross He dies on. See
how big it is? He carries a cross for you and me." Glancing back, Rommel pointed at Henry, and it was as if Henry felt a wooden cage hovering
above him, a cage Rommel had forced into being with his words. "But then
there's your favorite, the one you looked at when you first came: the third

Station of the Cross, when Jesus first falls." Rommel breathed heavier and set the matchbox on a pew. "The weight is unbearable. He falls under the weight of all our sins, and yet is made to continue."

Standing very still, Henry watched Rommel thrust his waist out before shuffling his legs up once, then twice, standing closer to the third station. Rommel stood near the glass, and as he raised his hand to the white robes, Henry let out a bright hissing sound before covering his lips with his hands.

"What is it, Henry? What's wrong?"

Henry turned from the third station and saw how the other stations held other pictures and scenes and he wanted to move Rommel away from the third station, away from the white robes and perfect legs. So scouring the other images, he saw how Jesus was stripped of His robes in one station, and how a woman wiped His face in another, so he pointed to the sixth station.

"She has His face on her veil," Rommel said. "Just by touching Him, she has His face. Veronica wipes his face for Him. He has just been beaten and rejected."

Wondering at the word—*rejected*—Henry saw Rommel inspecting his face and his pink curving scar.

"His face shows the signs of it," Rommel said. "Just like everyone who has suffered. Like everyone who has lost."

"*She touched him.*" Henry passed his hands across the scar above his lips. "But now she has His face and can touch it whenever she wants. She can touch Him. He made His image perfect for her."

"He made His image perfect for us too. So we can share His perfection."

As Henry looked across the stations—from the pictures at the beginning with the white robes, to the later ones, with the purple glass—he felt the stations shift across a darker line. *But the stations with the purple glass don't shine as much. The air beneath them is darker, and I wonder if Rommel knows that too, if he sees it?*

"You know," Henry said. "I hurried beneath the darker ones before, scrubbing on the first days I was here, I hurried and was scared."

"I didn't know that." Rommel looked at Henry's bowed head.

Henry hadn't spoken like this since he arrived.

"I thought they were heavier, with the darker light. I didn't think they floated as much as the white robes. But now I need to stay in front of them, I think. I need to stay in front of them longer now that I been here some weeks and have watched them."

"Watched them do what?"

Henry dipped his rag into the bucket before squeezing the sudsy water on the pew. "Rise."

Rommel watched Henry scrub the pew beneath the fourteenth station, where Jesus was placed in His tomb.

"They rise with the light. The white robes rise because they have the floating feeling—whenever I trace my hands along it—whenever I touch it."

"Jesus floats above us everywhere. Don't you know that? Even in the darker pictures, in the darkness."

Henry held his hand to his lips; they were dry and chapped. As Rommel's pinched face stared at the gray tomb, a hint of late afternoon light pierced the purple glass, and Henry felt the tomb was floating now—like the white robes—that it floated within the falling light to the floor.

"See, it floats with the light high up. And I can stand here longer beneath the purple glass because of it. Because I know I haven't cared for the pews beneath the purple light like I should. I've only shied away from them like what a sinner would do, so they don't shine as much."

"It's okay, Henry. It's okay."

Henry breathed heavy. "But my face don't shine like in the other pews. Even when I squeeze the rag—even when all the zeroes spin out on their own. It don't shine."

"Zeroes?" Rommel leaned across the watery pew.

"I don't mind the zeroes because they're mine now." Henry squeezed the rag and the suds spun out on the wooden plank. "But my face—my face is darker in the wood."

"The darkness isn't bad, Henry. Not if you make it your own, like even you said—if you listen to the Lord."

Henry reached into the slanted edge where the water pooled warm and sudsy. His hands were covered in the rosy smell. The smell came all the way up his arms, and he knew Rommel couldn't smell it like he could. *I'm closer to the pews now than he is, because it's becoming mine now—all of it.* Scrubbing slower, he felt his arms tighten into cords so that he might push so hard to come out the other side, pushing through the zeroes of the wood to stand in the light of the tomb in the fourteenth station.

"They take the body of Jesus to his resting place," Rommel said and thrust his waist out so that he stood closer to the window. "The stone over the tomb is the final sign of death. But they didn't know He would rise and overcome the death they'd made for Him, overcoming even stone."

Henry reached down and touched the outline of the tomb on the floor. "But I hauled up stones all day from the canal and even sat on one at the door and never seen death in any of them. They was only something I hauled. Though when you say it, I can see a picture of death in them, when I pretend like this."

"Sure. Just pretend. See yourself with Jesus, and you'll always be with Him. Then the stones won't bother you anymore. The stones will be a wonderful thing. They'll be a sign of an everlasting life to you."

"I've taken away my stones," Henry said, and stretched his arms into the falling light. Henry heard Rommel coughing as he traced the tomb again, tracing the final stone. *But he does not know I took the stones away from the canal, that I didn't know they were death when I hauled them. But now I see. The stones were death and I put the death in the woods, but still I must work with the lock. I must make the lock rich with the death of the stones, and I hope You will help me, Jesus.* "I hope You will help me haul the death away and mold it into life?" he whispered.

"Henry?" Rommel squinted as he shuffled closer to the altar.

Henry realized he was talking to Jesus and not just saying, "I don't mind," so he bent over the pew scrubbing harder to be silent like the church.

"Mind yourself, Henry—this is the candle hour."

Without noticing, the velvet feeling had fallen across the church. Henry saw the sun setting beyond the glass and knew this was when Rommel usually woke from his nap to light the candles, and Henry always hurried to finish his scrubbing. *But now I don't have to hurry. Not since I know about the life and death of the stone. Because the candle hour is when the girl comes to pray for her mother, and I must dry the pews for her so that her mother feels better, and her prayers are heard.*

"Can you light the candles tonight?" Rommel's face was pinched shut when he spoke, and Henry hadn't seen his face creased with lines like that since he spoke about the third Station of the Cross.

"Me?"

Rommel had never let Henry light the candles before, though he'd shown Henry how to light the long match so that it didn't burn up faster to hurt your fingers near the end. "You can get the girl her candle too," and Rommel winked with his pinched-up eyes before shuffling down the stairs.

12

THE GIRL CAME EVERY NIGHT after Henry finished scrubbing the pews. Henry liked watching from the basement door. He liked the whispering prayers she spoke with and the still way she kept her body. She sounded like a stream when she prayed. The words came from her as the river water—shimmering and unceasing—though she did not say a word when she entered. She went to the same middle pew on the left side. After she sat, she did not look up. She only pulled the brown hair from her eyes. Then with her shoulders bent and her hands clasped, she whispered. Henry watched her each night until he blinked after counting to zero once and then to zero again, though he was not sure if she was breathing with how still she sat, and he did not want to disturb her.

"*She's here again,*" Henry whispered. Rommel was in the basement cooking. Henry could smell the burgers, so he limped down to the kitchen to chop the tomatoes before remembering the girl did not have her candle. He had not replaced the candles to have the low light like she might want. Henry also had to bring in the ladder to change the bulb above the altar, but he would wait to do that till after the girl was done. So instead he went to the cupboard and picked from the box twelve wide candles. He piled them high in his arms, and when he limped back to the bottom step, he felt the smooth round edge of one jostle his cheek. The candle against his cheek made him say, "Tallow." *Like the tallow Hiram would light in the apartment, after the tugging was done.*

He took in two wheezing breaths and saw how after the tugging was done Hiram's face looked milky in the light. Like egg-whites, his eyes. "I looked to the fire escape then, when his eyes glazed over. I looked because the streetlights glowed like candles. Then Hiram would ask for the, 'Tallow,' and I had to give him a new candle from the drawer."

His right hip tingled to his toes when he remembered touching Hiram's hand, and he felt a pink breath circling the stairway.

'Tallow,' is the old word for candle, Henry, and I bet they didn't teach you that in the rectory. Henry heard Hiram's voice and breathed quicker to feel how close he was. *Because the old words are better than the new ones. Because the tallow was made from the boiled fat of sheep and cattle.*

Henry coughed and looked at the flickering light. *The girl was in the flickering light,* he knew, *upstairs. But Hiram is down here with me.* And shifting the candles in his arm, he heard Hiram's pink breath moving along his cheek.

"I know you're here because you know all the things I said, and what I've done."

What you've done?

"With the boy," Henry said, "in the lockhouse."

But you didn't do anything with him. You had him all to yourself and you didn't touch him like I wanted you to. So now I'm here, and you can't get away from what I want, with the older ways before.

"Like when I brought you candles?"

Yes, like when I said, 'Tallow,' to you each night. Because now I'm sure you'll say, 'Tallow,' to the girl. You'll talk to her.

Henry blinked at the wall. "But I mustn't disturb her. Or pass across her streaming prayers. No matter what you want."

It's not what I want. It's what you want—like with the mannequin.

Sweat beaded Henry's lip. The stairway was hot and he limped up faster to be away from the circling voice that knew about the mannequin. From the doorway, he watched the girl in her pew. Words floated in a constant stream in the room, drawing a white current above her stillness. "*Tallow,*" he whispered, biting his bottom lip. "Tallow is what I can say to her, to know her."

Setting several candles by the altar, he lit them with a long matchstick. When he blew the matchstick out, shaking it with his hand, he listened to the word on his lips: "*Tal-low.*" Leaning closer, he saw his face reflected in the polished altar. His yellow teeth jutted out from his lips when he said the first part of the other word, "Can." When he said the second part, "dle," the stump of his pink tongue stuck between his teeth, and he didn't like the feeling of the other word on his lips. "That makes my lips dry. Then they crack and I have to lick the cracking away." *Tallow, sounds smoother*, he thought. *Tallow would be a much better way to speak to her. Because I've always wanted to light the candle for her, as soon as I first saw her.*

A noise stirred behind him and he looked, but the girl hadn't moved. He could only see her from the waist up. Her head was bowed and the words whispered from her in the same shining stream. Turning to the metal stands along the wall, he lit another matchstick, holding his hand steady before his eyes. "She makes me steady," he said. "Just with the stream she prays with she makes me steady, even though I've never lit the candles before. Even though Rommel didn't know if I could. But I'm steady around her. And if I was to talk to her now maybe 'Tal-low' would be better to say than 'Can-dle,' so I can know her, so we're close."

That's right, Henry. Hiram whispered, and Henry shook his head when he placed the candles in a line. He didn't want to hear Hiram's voice with the girl so close—yet Hiram's low grumble surfaced in his mind: *What's older is better. It was made first and right and not cheap like what that girl is. Just look at her. Just look at those shabby clothes and dirty arms. You can tell she was on the street because she's cheap and you and I have a much cleaner way of loving, don't we, boy? Why would you want her anyway? Why would you want her like the mannequin?*

"Stop." Henry shook his head because he didn't want Hiram to know her or see her or say the things he knew Hiram would say. But there he was again—as soon as Henry thought of holding her torso and maybe rubbing her against his waist.

She would be different than the mannequin, but the same.

"You're wrong. She would be different than the mannequin. She would be real."

She would be a sickness and not a redeeming. She would not give you the redeeming like I gave you—or like what the boy would give you.

"Not the boy," Henry said. "She's not like the boy at all," and he shook his head to stop the words he thought might disrupt her prayers. But she didn't move.

The girl was the only one in the church beside Henry and he watched her torso now that he limped behind her to the front door. She was much smaller than he thought and reminded him of Barnum, with how thin her neck was and how she pulled her brown hair back from her eyes. Standing behind her, he thought her skin was like some of the clay patches in the canal. The patches that were delightful to stand in because the sun warmed the shallows and the grass beneath the puddles was soft and wavy, and it was like he stood within a warm falling waviness. Often, when he rested from his work, he stood in the warm waviness for as long as he could.

"She'll be different because she's warmer and she won't slap me." He looked to the rafters because he wanted to stop Hiram's voice, to stop his speaking. Though even when he spoke louder he still heard Hiram's slurping lips; he heard Hiram tugging at his waist, so he shook his head and closed his eyes to stop the noise. "Her sounds will be much nicer than yours, much nicer than the 'Mmmmms and Ahhhhs' you made when you sucked down below. When I rub her against my waist, it will be like she's singing then. She'll be singing in the lockhouse, and she'll sound much clearer than the radio ever could."

Henry said this last word too loudly and opened his eyes. He thought he saw the girl move, that her prayers were over. Limping closer, the matchsticks rattled in his pocket, but she didn't stir. He was in the center aisle, only—*one two three*—pews behind her, and watched her breathe but couldn't make out her words.

She said something like, "Ever…and with me…by the grace of…" and his right leg tingled once he stood there for much longer than he should. He counted to zero once and then to zero again, but still her torso did not move like what he thought it would when he spoke too loudly.

"*Because she'd sing without static,*" he whispered. "*She'd sing if we were closer, and I held her.*"

In his head, he saw the lockhouse where he held her in his arms. "I can see her near the wall, and I will bring the canvas tarp to cover us. Because she has bumps like the mannequin. The small bumps like Barnum's, red and soft in the air. Red coals shine from the stove—so that her cheeks look cinnamon in the light—like a red leaf has fallen across her face."

Henry reached with his hand to his dangling thing. It was hard and stood up against his waist. *"My lips kiss her cheeks as she sings with the radio... and down below, I can feel her heat. I'm only pretending though,"* he whispered, to stop the heat. *"I'm only pretending she would hold my dangling thing."* But the heat continued through his hand, and as Henry coughed, he thought she would move at the noise—but she didn't. So he watched her breathe and traced the outline of her torso with the candle in his other hand.

Zero.

He drew a circle around her in the air.

"She would hold it like Hiram held it," he whispered. *"Her hands would move back and forth like Hiram used to move."* And he watched her cinnamon hands move up and down in his mind. "This is like the floating before, in my stomach, with her small fingers grasping and holding me. I feel lighter now, like I can pretend." His dangling thing was stiff against his trousers. He had to nudge it to the right so that it did not hurt him as he watched the small image of the girl move her hands back and forth in his mind. Then she made the good noises, the sucking and kissing noises as she moved her head back and forth—until the hardening was about to burst all over her hands and mouth and face.

"Sir?"

Henry heard her voice but did not know it because he still saw her kneeling in front of him, so he had to shake her lips away.

"Do you have the candle?" She had turned from her prayers now that they were over. Her face was smooth and reflected the light so that a cinnamon glow radiated through her thin ear lobes.

"The tallow?" Henry said and held out the candle. The word did not raise his lips to show the girl his yellow teeth. His hand did not shake either because he said, 'the tallow,' so smoothly and low that the flying feeling came back to his stomach.

"Thank you." Holding the thick candle between her hands, she cradled it like a cup. He watched her fingers resettle on the wide candle and counted to zero as she held her head down looking at the unlit wick.

"Milk," he whispered. He smelled milk now that he was standing so close to her.

She looked up and blinked both eyes shut before opening them again.

Leaning over, he wheezed with two deep breaths, and his nose was full with her warmth. "And cinnamon," he said, "even though it's cold now, with ice in patches on the steps."

"*Ice?*" Leaning over the candle, she smelled it.

"No, on the steps. When I break the ice with the shovel. But you're not like the ice at all. You're like cinnamon and milk."

She looked up at him and when he breathed again, he smelled the river water of her hair. He smelled the lockhouse too and saw them lying on the mattress; she was singing as she moved her head down along his legs. Coughing then to shake the smell away, he tucked his stiff dangling thing against his waistband as he shuffled to release the stiffness. As he did, the matchsticks rattled in his pocket, and he remembered what he must do. "The tallow," he said, "and the matchsticks..."

He motioned to the girl, and when he looked along her fleshy brown lips, he thought he saw a thin scar nestled below her nose. It looked like a thin zero.

"The match?" she said.

Henry looked along her narrow seated waist as she shifted her legs.

"For my prayer," she said, holding the candle.

Henry took out a long matchstick and struck it cleanly against the box. The flame leapt orange and blue before settling into a cool wavering yellow. He brought the yellow flame with a steady hand (just as Rommel had instructed) to the wick the girl held up.

"Thank you," she said and looked at Henry before moving off on slow conscious steps. As Henry watched the girl bend at the altar, he thought of Barnum. *The girl reminds me of Barnum bent near the stove shaking the water from his legs. I seen under the boy then. I seen all the way to the line between his buttocks.* As he watched the girl bend and place the candle before the altar, he felt he wanted to hold her up and see that connecting place in her too. *Because she'd be as light as Barnum. She'd be as easy to lift, like I lifted Barnum to the mattress after he fell.*

Reaching out in the air with his two strong hands, he pretended he was holding her close. He pretended her underwear came off with an easy tug, and then he made a sipping sound with his lips. In his mind she smiled and reached out with her hands to touch his waist; she wanted to pull his trousers off too.

"She would say, '*Henry*,' with her soft brown voice. Because she would smell like honeysuckle in her warm dark place. Like honeysuckle and fern."

"Amen."

Henry heard her gentle voice near the altar and looked up from the bigger picture he had pretended. She had placed her candle on the altar and wrapped herself in her yellow knit scarf for the cold outside. She also had on a bright yellow slicker over a gray wool sweater, and looked plump in all the warm layers of cloth and glistening color.

"Thank you for the tallow," she said beside him, and he watched the faintest smile trace the plump edge of her lips.

"It's nothing." He saw again the scar above her lip; it was flushed. Little beads of sweat like dewdrops had formed. With her wool sweater and slicker on, she needed to be out in the cold where she could be comfortable.

"Excuse me," she said and he leaned aside as she started past.

Henry was in the middle of the aisle and brought his hand to his lips to make sure they weren't cracked and dry in front of her. "Certainly," he said, and a falling away slipped in his stomach as he watched her fasten the belt that swung around her slicker. She had stopped to look back at him, and as she opened the door, the winter wind rushed in and all the candle flames fluttered so that the church became darker for a moment, and all the Stations of the Cross seemed to lean in beneath the shadows of the flames to watch. Grasping the metal railing with her thin yellow mittens— she seemed a bright golden zero held against a snow-white field—and he sipped in with two wheezing breaths as the cold rushing air swallowed her completely.

13

ĦENRY SAW THE GIRL nearly every night after that. With Rommel slipping into a tiredness he couldn't explain, a tiredness that kept him in the basement, Henry stayed upstairs and did the things Rommel had done before. Henry changed the bulbs in the lanterns. He replaced the candles near the altar and along the walls. He put the old candles in a metal bowl on the furnace so that the stubs melted into a soupy mixture that Rommel poured into the molds he kept under his cot. Rommel made all kinds of wax figures with the leftover candles. Shepherds and angels, doves and trees, steeples and stars, and was intent on showing Henry how to make the wax figures too.

"So you'll know how to do it for the Christmas pageant. This could be another task for you, another part of the Lord's work."

"Do I still get to scrub the pews?"

"Of course."

Henry still scrubbed the pews. He also swept the snow from the church steps and along the stone path to the parking lot. He even helped the priest and laundry woman with the tablecloth for the altar. Henry shook out the tablecloth, grasping it with both hands before tucking it back into place; and often, in its folds, he remembered the linens from the hospital. *I bunched the linens like this too, before taking them to the fire. The linens held the souls of the people who'd passed before. But this tablecloth holds a different soul.*

The priest was in his study; the laundry woman had left with the priest's black vestments in a bag. "This tablecloth is God's soul maybe," Henry said. "Because it lies under the golden chalice and plate, with the body and blood." Henry passed his hands across the cloth. He saw green and black threads blend with blue and white threads along the etched lines. He looked inside the etched lines to the smooth surface. Holding his hands beside the body and blood, he wondered if God had a soul too, or if God was the soul of everyone else, of even him?

"Because if God has my soul, then maybe God has a shorter leg too? Maybe I could ask the priest when he's not writing or taking confessions or speaking with the silver-haired ladies in the pews. I'll just wait like what Rommel said I should—to wait and ask him all the things I want to know."

Henry didn't mind waiting to ask the priest. He had other tasks to keep him busy and could think of what he wanted to know when he took the coats and hats and scarves from the parishioners on Sunday. He put the coats and hats and scarves in the coatroom and brought them out when the service was over. Rommel said that was his second duty. "Second only to your first duty—the duty of saying the Lord's Prayer."

Henry had started praying out loud around Rommel so that Rommel knew he was paying attention to his first duty—to saying the Lord's Prayer. But even when he said the Lord's Prayer, he couldn't concentrate. Instead, he thought of all the things he wanted to know when he did his other tasks. Like spreading salt along the icy steps. Or taking donations at the basement door. He put the donations in the boxes marked: Food Stuff, Toiletries, and Clothing. Rommel pointed out the boxes because Henry didn't have his letters as well as his numbers, but Rommel said that was okay. "Just as long as you work on that too—and that could be your third duty."

Henry held up three fingers so Rommel could see he was thinking of his three duties. But as soon as he watched the girl pray with her streaming words those nights, after the church was empty, Henry forgot all about the things he wanted to ask the priest—and from anyone else. *Then it's only me and her, and we have a habit. As soon as she's finished praying, she nods, and then I walk to her saying, 'The tallow?'*

She always smiled when he said it and responded, "Thank you, Henry," bowing her soft brown eyes. She'd asked his name a few days ago, and he'd told her with a slight slur. He wasn't as smooth anymore when he spoke to her with the things he hadn't rehearsed. So when she did ask, it caught him unawares, and he hoped she hadn't seen his yellow teeth. But she said, "Thank you. I'm Mabel, and my mother thanks you."

Henry didn't say anything after that. But he watched Mabel bend at the altar before wrapping the yellow slicker around her body. Then at the front door, as she pulled the yellow galoshes slurping up over her shoes, he wondered how old she was, because he'd seen her on Sundays when the children were led to the classroom for their studies. She seemed older than the rest, more sure of herself. After everyone sat together listening to the priest a while, she stood and led the children to the basement, and he always watched her walk with Barnum to the steps. And he watched her now.

It was the Sunday after Mabel had told Henry her name. Church was over, and folks crowded the aisle. Henry limped back and forth to the coatroom to get the coats in big heaping armfuls so people could search the piles on the table by the front door. When he looked down after rushing back with another armful, he saw Barnum and Mabel. They came up from the basement together. When Barnum saw Henry, he smiled and pointed to his head. Henry slunk down then because he knew the boy was pointing to the cut he got that night in the lockhouse, and Henry knew he couldn't hide anymore.

"It sure has been a while since I seen you. I didn't know you worked here."

Mabel lingered with a group of children in the aisle. Henry watched her listen to something Miss Abigail, the Sunday school lady, said.

"Momma and Charles sure wondered about you."

"They did?" Henry looked for Barnum's mother but hadn't seen her or the man named Charles in weeks. He'd only seen Barnum at their normal spot in the pew: Barnum smiling and dressed in a wrinkled shirt. Now here he was.

"I said this fella was down in the lockhouse hauling out rocks and stumps. But when they went with me a few days after my head got cut, the door was chained."

"Is it still chained?" Henry looked into the boy's eyes to know for sure if what he said was true.

"Sure is. When Momma seen the chain she said, '*Good riddance*,' even though she never met you and I thought it was strange how she sneered."

The children around Mabel dispersed, and Henry watched her stand in the aisle.

"Where's Rommel?" Barnum's high-pitched voice brought Henry back to a pile of scarves. Grabbing Mrs. Simpson's gray muffler, Henry limped to the door. "I ain't brought Rommel a fish since winter started. Make sure you tell him I still watch the river though. I know where all the fish are, even when it freezes along the banks."

"*It freezes?*" Henry had never thought of the river freezing. He couldn't picture the zeroes freezing in his mind, because the zeroes were always moving, weren't they? The zeroes were always spinning off the ends of logs and stones in the middle rapids, releasing their lines and edges. He hadn't seen the river in so long that he stopped to think about how it might freeze along the banks.

Barnum pushed his body against Henry's right leg. "Don't worry—it never freezes over all the way, not like what you'd think."

"Never?" Henry paused and looked at Barnum.

"I thought you of all the people would a knowed that…but I can't believe it's over already—the service—and the people sure are crowding around like the rapids now."

With the boy clinging to his leg, Henry felt the rush of people like what Barnum said and wondered if they saw how the boy clung to him. He looked at Mabel: she stood with her arms folded, leaning against a pew. *And it looks like her face is a clay-brown shallow, with how her brown eyes catch the light. Maybe I could go to her*, he thought. *Just to stand beside her, to be close.* Though as he stepped toward the aisle, all he heard were the river sounds of the people: arms and fingers clambered across the table by the front door, clambering for their coats and scarves and mittens, pulling him back.

"But the river ain't like this," Henry said to Barnum, "not all the way. When I'm scrubbing the pews, I see the water shine all over the wood and it's like the rapids in the middle, rushing over the rocks—but it's different—it's smoother."

"You scrub all these pews every day?"

They both watched Mabel drift to the last row.

"But the scrubbing is closer," Henry said. "You'd know, you been there. You seen how the river was smooth far away and hollow when it sounded, even when I stood in it over my waist."

"I been in it my whole life," Barnum said.

"So you know how the river sounds far away even when you're in it, even when I saw the fish make the zero." Henry drew the arc of the fish jumping in air.

"I know what you mean, how the sound fills up the whole valley."

"But when you're alone, the river is always a lot farther away than what my hands and feet could feel. It's farther away." Henry stepped back from Barnum and remembered standing in the river with him. With no one else on the river, with the rocks gray-white and cresting and the water rushing around him loose and solid, and even the mountains falling beneath the purple sunlight, the river felt more like it was flowing up in the mountains than down at the base of the hills. *The river always seemed higher up, like a higher floating wing, and I still wonder about that river gliding sound, which even when I stood in it was much higher than I was allowed to be.* "No, it don't sound like this place," Henry said, "not all the way." He limped back to the coatroom. "The sound here is *here*," and he raised his strong flat hand and held it level with his shoulders. "It ain't higher or lower or nowhere—it's just here—on my hand when I scrub."

"I ain't talked about the river in weeks with no one." Barnum struggled against the rush of arms and legs as the crowd converged on the coatroom. It seemed someone was missing a scarf, and they wondered if Henry knew where it was. The voices and people came at Henry from all sides.

"If you could just look, Henry, it would be ever so kind."

"You're doing a fine job, Henry, a fine job. Make sure you say hello to Rommel. Tell him I hope he feels better."

"It's this color, Henry. It's brown. It's a scarf."

The reaching of the people and the speaking of their words was like another current above Henry's waist, a current up to his eyes and ears.

'*See...*' Henry turned to Barnum, mouthing the word. Henry's eyes were darkening. He saw the blackness of the crowd pushing everything aside. *And I told him they were like the river sound, but different. I told him they were up to my thighs and even over my thighs, but they ain't any higher than that; they're here.* He held his hand to his mouth and breathed—counting to zero with each rise and fall of his chest. Turning to the piled clothes, he saw the scar above his lip. It was reflected in a glass cabinet. It glistened with sweat, and he brought his hand to touch it. "These are my duties," and he held up two fingers. "This is my second duty, second only to the Lord's Prayer." Behind him, the crowd hovered in the doorway, and he knew that he had just been among them for a moment. "I was just with them, when they reached for their coats and hats. I saw it."

He watched his lips move in the glass as he spoke.

"Then I limped back with an armful of coats and the sound of the asking and grabbing, with their arms putting-on jackets and zipping-up zippers was much louder than I thought. It was much more than a duty...And yet." He turned to look at the crowd waiting at the door, at all the darkened faces. "I'm standing on the edge of that sound even by being in it. I'm standing inside their lines, but I feel away from them—separate."

"Henry?" Barnum had pushed back through the crowd with Mabel trailing from his hand. "This is Mabel; she says she knows you cause you give her a candle each night when she prays for her Momma." Barnum pressed against Henry's leg again, and Henry felt a tingling in his groin when he felt the boy's waist. The tingling spread to his hip when he saw Mabel pressed against his other leg. The rush of people fell away then as Henry heard the front door opening more often. Every once and a while when someone was bundled up—plump and wooly—the cold air swept in with a great sudden burst, and it felt like icicles rushing up his nose. Then the lingering people shuddered all at once and a few snowflakes drifted in. The snowflakes shimmered on the floorboards, and Barnum would say, "*Snow! Snow!*" and shake like a dog against Henry's waist.

Barnum wanted to get out into the snow and find the sled he kept in his cellar. "I keep it right next to the TV you brung me. I've got a sled and saucer and an inner tube that I use in the river, but which is just as good going down Clarke's Hill any day. That's on the other side of the ridge, near the highway. Though Momma don't like it when Dwight's home and he takes me to Clarke's Hill. Says we'll sled into traffic."

"Dwight?" Henry looked at Mabel who was listening to everything

Barnum said because Barnum sort of sang when he spoke.

"Dwight's my step-brother who worked the quarry, but you never seen him. Dwight's taller and more yellow in the face. His hair is yellow too and everyone says he's taller but he was older, so of course, I told them—of course he's taller—and they all laughed when I said it, but I told them it was true."

"Where's Dwight now?" Mabel said.

"He's been gone a while, after his girlfriend turned him loose. He's in the army: stationed down in Flor-i-da somewhere."

"Flor-i-da?" Henry said, touching his lips. He remembered Hiram saying, *Flor-i-da* months ago. *Flor-i-da* had a lingering feel, a feeling in his stomach like when he was eating, when he could eat some more even though he knew he shouldn't: That was *Flor-i-da.*

When Henry said it, a few parishioners heard him and chanted along until "Flor-i-da, Flor-i-da," rang all around them. Then someone said, "Henry said it! Henry said it!" and a pocket of laughter broke out as all the shuffling feet edged closer and a strong hand patted his shoulder saying, "Lord, Lord, Henry, don't make it harder for me to go out there. It's bad enough with the snow. But now all I can think of is *Flor-i-da, Flor-i-da.*"

The man with the smell of Hiram's colored drinks laughed in Henry's face. He wrapped a flannel scarf around his neck before opening the door. Another blast of cold air rushed in and more snowflakes sprinkled across the floor. Henry knew he'd have to get the soap when they all left. *I'll have to get the mop and bucket too, to keep the floor shiny like what Rommel said was best and what the priest likes best.* Though keeping the floor shiny was also what Henry liked best, especially when Mabel came, and he could look at the shiny floor from any part of the church. That way he could see her reflection wherever he was—so she was always there—beside him.

"Why don't you come too?" Barnum's squeal carried over the people. The door had opened again, and another group shuffled out until the rushing feeling from before had fallen away. Even the priest had shuffled out. He'd given Henry a pat on the shoulder and smiled before leaving. The priest hadn't said anything about Henry's leg, and Henry wanted to ask him about before the beginning, but not with so many people around.

"*Yes!*" Mabel squealed, clapping her hands. "You can come, Henry. We're going sledding in the hills!"

Henry saw the hills in the city when she said it. He saw the children from the rectory when school was closed, when he didn't have to scrub the walls with the rosy soap bubbles. Those were the days bundled up in layers, when they put Henry in the toboggan and held onto his leg for luck, saying, "*Hold onto Henry's leg!*" He remembered rolling in the snow when they fell at the bottom, ice shivering his neck. Some of the children even laughed when he tried to make a snow angel, considering his angel's right leg was shorter than the rest, and after the children started up the long hill to where the nuns stood waving for them to return, he stayed behind. Crawling on his knees, he sat at the edge of his angel and erased its shorter right leg. With his cold mittens he redrew a leg that matched the others as best he could. Looking up the hill, he wanted to show the other children, but saw Barnum instead, tugging his hand.

"We can go to my house," Barnum said. "When we get the sled maybe we can watch TV before we go?"

"You have your own TV?" Mabel said.

"Henry brought it for me. And I think there's a Christmas show on tonight about Rudolph and Santa, because Mabel and me are gonna be in the manger scene, Henry. Did you know that?"

"Manger scene?"

"I knew he didn't know." Barnum had a big grin on his face. "I bet her you didn't know and I was right. She's gonna be Mary and I'm gonna be Joseph."

Henry watched Mabel as Barnum spoke. Her neck was bowed, and he thought she was praying standing there.

"Josh and Mabry from gym class are gonna be two of the wise men—which I don't think is the best casting personally. I told Miss Abigail that after we voted, but she said something about being fair, and I said, 'Fair-schmair, they'll ruin the play and end up throwing rocks at Baby Jesus.'"

The church was empty. The rush of people had gone and Henry watched Mabel pull her yellow slicker on. She stood beside Barnum as he buttoned his denim jacket.

"Well," Mabel said, looking at Henry, "are you coming?"

"Let me get my coat."

But Mabel didn't hear. She'd already walked out the front door. Henry watched her through the window as she stood on the front porch—a brilliant golden zero, leaning on the railing. She watched Barnum jump down the steps. Though as Henry limped off for his coat, he stopped to listen to how quiet the church had become in everyone's absence. Standing by himself, he had it in his mind to stay under the white robes of the third Station of the Cross. Just to be there. To listen to the rhythm of the falling snow on the roof. *Because it seems like it might be quiet like this forever. To just hear the lonesomeness of things. So that no one is asking for jackets, or calling out prayers, or asking for the floor to be mopped or for their mittens and scarves to be brought to them.* And he remembered what it was like by the river, without so much noise in his mind. *Maybe I could be silent like this too? Maybe I could stay beneath Jesus' white robes forever, or just as long as it took until the silence of His perfect legs became my silence.*

Though when he saw Mabel giggling beside Barnum, their arms held up to the twirling flakes, and the town quiet except for Barnum's talking, he hurried to be with her, to be together. Racing down with Barnum laughing and talking as fast as he always did, with the speed of the sled holding them on its bright falling wing.

14

"JUST LOOK AT THAT TV. See how pretty it is with the hole along the side." Barnum pointed to the gunshot. "You can see all the way into the tubes and gears."

Mabel stood near the woodstove. Thick waves of heat worked through the room. "But it's broken."

"Oh, no it ain't. I can make it work whenever I want. Ain't that right, Henry?"

Henry stood behind Mabel as Barnum talked. He looked at the girl's soft neck in the light. He had helped her up the snowy slope, after Barnum went running on ahead to get the fire warmed and the milk from upstairs with the cups. Barnum had three tin cups set on a table by the fire. He poured milk into a kettle on the stove and was spooning in cocoa powder when Henry and Mabel made it in.

"He's right," Henry said. "I seen it."

"Because that show about Frosty the Snowman is coming on soon. You know the one, with the kids who ride their sleds with lanterns and Frosty melts since it's so warm his hat falls off." As he spoke, Barnum began to move around the cellar. He rummaged through boxes and shelves looking for his hat and gloves, because he'd need another layer to run the sled down the hills in the snow. The furnace in his body couldn't hold off the cold forever, especially after he rolled in the snow like he said he wanted to. "But it won't matter. We'll be out there moving around so much anyway; it'll keep us warm." He pulled a loose basket from behind a bucket and let it fall to the floor. "And we can catch that show later too, after we come in from sledding Clarke's Hill—and maybe even Jimson's Hill after that."

"Jimson's Hill?" Mabel said.

"*Barnum!*" A voice called upstairs. Henry knew at once it was Barnum's mother.

"Yeah?" Barnum stopped beside the bottom step, his hand on an inner tube.

"Don't stay out all night. You still might have school tomorrow. And put some more logs on before you go."

Henry slumped against the wall when he heard the voice. He watched the small square at the top of the stairs open a bit when she called down and felt a low falling in his stomach to think she might see his lips and the thick hands he held to cover his face. *So I'll watch Mabel instead. I'll watch Mabel and how the snowflakes drip from her yellow slicker.* Henry watched the snowflakes turn from white to gray to blue as they melted in a puddle on the linoleum floor. He watched the folds in her slicker and tried to count the way the yellow folds crinkled under her arms. He got to the end of seven crinkles before he saw there weren't any more. So he thought he knew more about Mabel then, with seven being the end of all the other numbers beneath her arms. Though when he held his finger up to rub the seven crinkles, Barnum's mother called down for more logs again, so he took his hand away from knowing Mabel deeper.

In a second, Barnum had the inner tube in his hand and brought it near the stove where he pulled out a pump. He gave the pump to Henry. "Make sure we can bounce all night on her down the hills, because she'll be our fastest sled—the one out front—pulling the others." Barnum stretched his hand in the air. "We'll fly along, just like floating down the rapids." Barnum said he wanted to tie three sleds together—the tube, saucer, and runner sled—all with the rope he found inside a milk crate near the water heater. He bundled the rope at Mabel's feet. "Can you untangle that? I still have to find the saucer and runner sled, and then the cocoa should be ready, but I need to put on some logs." Once he threw the logs on, it got hotter and Mabel sat down to untangle the rope while Barnum skittered off under the stairs.

"I hope he's okay," Mabel said. She took off her slicker because of the heat. "We've got all kinds of things in our basement too, and I'd hate to think what I'd find if I ever had to look." Taking off her hat and mittens, she unbuttoned a white wooly sweater. As Henry watched her undress, he loosened his own canvas jacket. He took off his gloves and the wide knit hat he found in the church basement. They bundled all their clothes on Barnum's bed, but still it wasn't enough. Mabel stood and started to shake off her long-sleeve shirt, smiling at Henry, and he saw how her lips glistened with sweat. She had a tank-top on underneath. "Too many layers," she said.

As her white tank-top inched above her waist, Henry looked across her brown belly, and a slight stirring rose along his thigh to his hip before he watched her sit back down above the tangled rope.

"Found it!" Barnum threw a silver saucer out from below the steps. Its dented shell clattered on the floor and Mabel shivered, putting her hand on Henry's leg. As she held his knee, Henry's dangling thing moved against his waist to feel her warm brown fingers.

"It scared me," she said. "Sounded like a gunshot." She moved her hand back to the tangled line. "Sounded like how they hunt in the hills." When Barnum returned with the runner sled, Mabel held up the rope for him as far as she could reach.

"That's fine, but look at this." Barnum held up the runner sled, drawing his hand along the wooden slats. "Found this beneath a beanbag. Didn't even know we had a beanbag." Barnum was sweating and took off his denim jacket and wrinkled Sunday shirt. He only had a white T-shirt on now. "Saw all these old tennis rackets back there too. If it snows any more, we could strap them to our feet. I seen that on TV. They strapped all these tennis rackets on their feet and walked up a mountain." He put the runner sled down and stirred the cocoa. "*Oooohh*—it's all steaming now." Leaning over the kettle, he breathed in the hot chocolate vapor. "And I'm about as warm as I ever been," he said, shaking out of the T-shirt so his pale chest was rubbed red by the firelight.

Henry saw the boy's red-blossom nipples. *But they ain't hard like before*, he thought, *they're soft and blossoming. Like smeared rose petals*.

"Here." Barnum held out a tin cup of cocoa for Mabel and then for Henry. "Won't be long now." Barnum drained his tin cup before pouring it full again. He took another sip and wiped his forehead with his hand. "Won't be long now at all."

THEY WERE OUT IN THE SNOW AFTER THAT. Henry had watched Barnum and Mabel dress side by side, with Mabel sliding on her yellow slicker, and he remembered her skin.

"*She was all brown*," he whispered, and as they trudged in the snow behind Barnum's house, he remembered Mabel's belly too. "Her belly was skinny and held in, and I seen the top of her trousers where her legs started." He paused and sipped with two breaths the cold falling air. "Then I counted to two. There were—*one two*—legs on either side, two legs diving down below her waist, to where she's held together by her seam. Just like Barnum is below the buttocks."

Henry held out his hand then, like he was grabbing her shoulders.

"And I wonder what her seam looks like—if it's like the boy's—and if I could hold her down and look, like I pretended in the church that night. Then I'd know for sure." He looked down at the antennas of town. He saw the church spire through a veil of snow. "But now she's all yellow again." He turned to watch her walk in front of him. "She's changed from all brown to all yellow just like that."

Mabel walked a few steps behind Barnum. Barnum was all blue in his denim jacket. He had on a blue wool hat and blue plastic gloves and led them from the cellar to the higher pines that ran along the ridge.

Reaching up with his hand, Henry trailed in the air along the tops of the houses far below the ridge, drawing an arc. "Them houses look smaller and far away, not like houses at all. They look more like pictures of houses, like the houses in the snow globes on Hiram's mantle above the fire." And he saw the snow globes in Hiram's apartment. But he knew he couldn't touch the snow globes unless he was told to. Henry brought Hiram the colored-water in glasses and the tallow and the long-stemmed matches. Then he brought Hiram the snow globes from the mantle.

"This one's from Kor-e-a," Hiram said back then, draining the gold-colored water. Henry remembered Hiram saying *Kor-e-a* because it sounded like when Barnum said *Flor-i-da* in the church. Both words had a lingering sound that made Henry rub his belly. And with Barnum way out in front, just entering the first pine, and Mabel in-between, with her quiet galoshes and yellow slicker glistening with flakes, the world was fading into a row of snow-whitened zeroes along the edge of his eyes.

"All those trees are pictures now," he said and shook his head from side to side, as a hazy dimness fell over the edge of what he saw. Only the bigger snow globe of the world was revealed to him. It held the whole hillside in its glassy dome.

This one's from Ok-i-na-wa. Hiram had come back and circled in the wind. *Where the little brown girl like the one out in front of you tried to touch me, but I wouldn't let her. Not with the sin she carried. I wouldn't let her touch me at all.*

Henry stopped walking to shake Hiram away. He set the inner tube down because the line he dragged from the tube was twisted in his gloves. When they'd started from the cellar door, he'd felt strong. Barnum and Mabel had watched him pile the sleds up and even offered to help haul them, but he said, "I'll haul them. I'm like the mule now." And he watched Mabel's shimmering eyes follow his strong arms to his shoulders, and he knew he'd done right by saying it, that he was stronger than both of them and that this was his task. But now, he didn't feel so strong anymore hearing Hiram's voice. Instead, he felt hollowed-out, as all his insides clenched together.

And that small brown slut at Inchon wasn't a redeeming either, Henry, I can assure you that.

Henry spun to look at the tops of the trees where he heard the voice.

She wasn't a redeeming. Because I sure didn't see across her brown belly like you just did. I didn't see her brown bumps either, like you want to, holding her down to see the seam beneath. I bet it's all you can think about to see the seam beneath.

"She's not like that at all. She's not."

The hell you say...because I'm not just talking about the girl.

Mabel and Barnum had disappeared. Henry looked along the ridge and knew he was alone with Hiram and that Hiram knew everything he'd ever done. Hiram knew how he'd looked under Barnum's dangling thing. Hiram knew what the boy's dangling thing had done to him, how it had raised the hot feeling below his waist, the same hot tightening he felt now, rising in his groin.

"This ain't about the boy."

Of course it's about the boy, because the boy wouldn't be a sin, Henry—not like the girl. You know that. He wouldn't be a sin. The boy would be a redeeming like me. Because he's white and perfect—but you don't want it. You say you don't, but I know you do. I can feel it rising inside you.

Henry reached down and felt his dangling thing rising against his waist. It was rising and the hot tightening ran from his thigh across his hip to his groin when he thought of holding the boy. Looking at the fresh-strewn path the boy and girl had left, he knew what he must do. So bending over and grabbing a handful of snow, he shoved it down his waist. *"There!"* he screamed, and searched the tops of the trees with his eyes. *"You see that! You see what I done!"*

The cold clumps moved in a burning wave down his waist, and right away he knew he shouldn't have done it, so jumping up and down, he shook from side to side and grabbed handfuls of snow out of his pants. "But at least the hot tightening's gone," he said, after jumping so much. "At least it's gone and so is the tugging with Hiram forever, because he's dead now, he is. You're dead now, and I don't have to talk to you because it ain't about the boy anymore. *It ain't!"* Henry scoured the woods, but Barnum and Mabel were gone. The tall pines were covered in coats of snow. *But I have the sleds. They'll need me if they want the sleds, so they won't go off together too far—not without me.*

He sipped in another bright rush of air and looked at the inner tube with the saucer on top and the runner sled covering the saucer. Barnum had some more rope with him and would tie them together when they got to Clarke's Hill, which wasn't too far away he'd said, once they started out.

"It's right up the hill. But Clarke's Hill only runs down part way. It rises up at the end though, so we won't go flying over to the highway, because that's Jimson's Hill then. That's Jimson's Hill, for sure."

Mabel had shivered when Barnum said that last part about flying over to the highway. And when Barnum opened the cellar door, Mabel had put her hands on Henry's side, whispering, *"Don't let me fall over the hill, Henry."*

Henry swore to her then, with Barnum trudging off, that he wouldn't let her fall over, and that brought a smile to her lips. He would have smiled too if he could have, but instead he just stared as she buttoned her yellow slicker and pulled her boots over her socks. And now with the woods spread out before him and the flakes falling, he would have given anything to see her yellow galoshes. Or to hear her whispering prayers. But he couldn't see either of them. There was only Hiram's cruel voice rising from deep inside.

You left the lockhouse for this? For the church? Where they make you scrub the pews and haul their coats and stir their soup?

Henry didn't speak.

Oh, you'll talk to me. You'll talk to me or I'll make you do things, by God...things you can't imagine.

"But they put the chain on the door." Henry didn't want to talk, even though he knew Hiram would make him do things if he kept quiet, and he didn't want to know what those things were.

I thought you were going to clean it, Hiram continued. *That you were going to make the lockhouse old like what we said. That you'd have the canal cleared by now.*

"The cold stopped everything." Henry shivered with the last snow dripping from his pants. "And inside the church it's warm and there's the white robes with Jesus and His perfect legs."

Oh, those goddamn legs—but what about the canal? What about what you promised?

The pines fell behind Henry as he turned to the river. The river was a gray line, sludgy and stiff. He knew the river must be moving; a blackbird flew along the surface. He watched its glossy wings cross the canal and railroad and heard a faint washing sound—a faint falling away. Off to the south, following the bird's arc, he heard that sharpening blade again. He hadn't heard it for so long, he'd forgotten how it felt.

I forgot how it rumbles, because I was so used to it, and I probably didn't hear it even when it rolled past the church. That's because it's part of me now. It's another part I can't feel no more, but that I know is there—always.

"Being up here changes things," he said and raised his hand along his lips to feel if they were cracked, but they weren't. "With how the mountains on the other side race up white and brown in patches, and I could just keep climbing them if I wanted." Raising his hands, he trailed along the outline of the other mountain. "You wouldn't be able to follow me then!" he cried to Hiram in the air. "I'd just keep climbing. I'd find another house far away. Far from where the people want me to bring them their hats and scarves and mittens."

But then you wouldn't see Mabel. Henry heard Hiram chuckle in his mind. *Or Barnum. No, you wouldn't go away from the boy. You wouldn't get to see them ride down the hills then, and you wouldn't be able to ride down with them, and feel all that speed.*

"Speed?"

Sure, like the sharpening sound, Hiram said. *Can't you hear it? Don't you remember how the speed felt? That's where you should be, down in the canal, to stop that damn speed, to make it slow again. To bring back the canal when everything was slower. So nobody has to rush off to another war again, so we can stay here—at home.*

Henry remembered standing close to the tracks. He remembered feeling the tracks buckle and tick with the sharpening sound approaching, and looking down, he saw the smokestack of a red engine curve below town. It was the engine he'd watched before with Barnum: the red train with the wood panels and smokestack. *The red train that didn't look like any other, except like maybe in the picture books in the rectory those years ago. Because I forgot all about it. But there it is*—and he pinched his eyes shut and opened them to believe it was really here.

"Well, do you see it? Don't you remember?" Barnum was beside Henry before he knew it. The boy's light footsteps had returned under the cover of the sharpening sound. "Ain't it just like before?"

Barnum and Mabel stood beside him. They watched the red engine curve below town, before moving closer to the lockhouse.

"That's the train that almost ran us over, when we had to jump off the tracks."

"For real?" Mabel watched Barnum point to the engine.

"Just ask Henry."

"It wasn't like anything I ever seen." Henry was surprised at how steady his lips were. "I remember the red wood and the engineer waving.

With how Barnum pointed to the tracks, and I remember the lockhouse and stones I hauled too—even the radio at night—when I thought it would sing."

Barnum and Mabel looked at Henry. He was sniffling to watch the train move along a sharpening line.

"What is it, Henry?" Mabel put her hand on Henry's side.

He couldn't say that maybe it was this sound that he wanted to keep, the sound of this train that was unlike any other. With how the engine shook through every part of him, and the clacking wheels moved in waves through his stomach, tingling along his right leg to his special boot. And that maybe it was this moment he held above any other. That it was this moment in a whiteness of silence and churning, with his stomach falling away and the hollow wind and ice held inside him. That it was this older sound that moved him more than anything he'd ever seen in the church or falling flakes. It was this sound and nothing else that he wanted to keep, with Mabel and Barnum close by, with the river washing away—and the zeroes spilling out and out—washing everything out.

"Henry? *Henry?*"

The sharpening sound was all around. As the engine churned, as his right leg trailed off into vibrations, he felt Mabel's small fingers dissolve into his side and he imagined holding her belly close to him, to help ward off the sound. *But I don't want to ward off the sound,* he knew, *not yet.* He wanted the sound to continue until it overtook everything in the world. Until he was left with the sound and the tingling of Mabel inside him. *Then Hiram would be gone forever,* he knew. *Then Hiram would be gone.*

"Henry?" Mabel said.

But he couldn't move. Everything was inside the sharpening sound and in the red paneled wood of the engine trudging up to Harpers Ferry. He even searched for Hiram's voice inside the sound. But even Hiram had been taken over by everything merging like the currents of the river. So he stood like that with the children around him without moving. He wiped the moisture from his eyes and felt his stomach rising back up once the sharpening sound drifted off, and he held as hard as he could to that moment and to Mabel's hand dissolving in his side.

15

BARNUM WAS QUIET ON THE WAY BACK to his cellar door. He was quiet when Henry and Mabel warmed themselves by the wood stove. When Barnum put more logs in and the embers flared higher, Henry thought he heard Barnum hum to himself once, but that was it. Barnum didn't once mention the TV. Or point to the screen. Barnum just sat there watching as the stove grew warmer and threw fat bolts of heat through everything—until Henry and Mabel were dry and ready to go because the sleep had them now. It was deep inside from sledding down and trudging back up the hills, again and again.

"I can feel it in my leg," Henry said. He stepped out into the gray night with Mabel. "I feel all the hills we rode up and down in my right leg. I feel all them jumps too, with how they come from all the way up in my shoulders down to my hands."

"I feel it too. I feel the sled and hills and jumps, and he didn't even say goodbye after all that. He didn't say goodbye." She slipped on the edge of Barnum's yard and Henry held her up with his right hand. "Thank you." She brushed her slicker with her mittens, shaking off a misty veil. "We were standing there so he could talk like he always does, but he didn't say anything."

Mabel walked behind Henry as the path narrowed. Pine trees swayed above them and Henry reached out to the branches, holding them back as they passed. *The thin branches are like arms*, he thought. *Like thin young arms whisking back and forth above the land*. He watched the wind kick up as snow spun in circles around them.

"In zeroes." He raised his hands to his lips before realizing he'd spoken. They were standing in a swirling zero so that he had to talk out loud about the floating feeling of the zero. "You're in the zero too," he said and nodded back to her.

"The what?"

"You're in the zero with me, and you probably feel like me now too, with how everything inside the zero is set apart. With how it's different from everything else."

"Different?"

But he didn't hear. The wind kicked up some powdery snow, and Henry kept walking through the lower yards. He led her to the road and then across the road. It was a path he remembered well, a path he hadn't followed in weeks. *I haven't come this way once*, he thought, *but now*. He looked at the spinning zero in front of him. *No matter where I limp to—to the right or left—that zero keeps me and Mabel hidden from everything on the other side. It's like we're held apart from the rest of the world.* He watched the zero as it led them toward the railroad tracks. *The rest of the world is gone. The rest of the world is on the other side of the zero.*

"Are we going to the river?" Snow danced around Mabel's face as she stepped to Henry's side. "I remember how Barnum talked about it up there sledding. It was one of the nicest things he said. How he talked about the snow falling on the river when he would fish in it. How the snow falls around you and the water rolls past and makes all these swirling pictures in the rapids." She paused and stopped Henry short, holding him with her hand. "I liked the sound of that. How he made a picture with his words. The picture reminded me of my mother, in her bed at home before they moved her to the hospital. You talked about the hospital too, about the long white hallways. Where you said you burned things."

"The linens," Henry said.

"Yes." She watched Henry's wide back as they started again. "I saw the picture of my mother in her bed sheets when you talked like that. I saw the sheets bunched up around her body that last night. That was when the fever set in, when I held her hand. She couldn't open her eyes anymore. But I talked to her anyway, and she kicked her legs and threw her arms out, and the bed sheets were like a current then. Like the rapids whenever I see them. So when I look at all the snow now, it looks like bed sheets to me. With how they're folded over and cold, cause my mother feels so cold to me now. Can't you see them? Can't you see all the bed sheets?"

"I see the linens everywhere. I always do."

As she pointed along the tracks, they watched the snow drift in folds on the sides.

"But the sheets ain't up in the sky no more."

"No, they're not in the sky anymore." She searched the sky before focusing on the woods. "They've fallen down to where we are, and they go on across the river like what Barnum said. Are we going to the river?"

Taking her hand in his, Henry stepped over the tracks.

"Henry?"

Henry heard her voice, but then another zero appeared like a lasso on the other side of the railroad. Through the icy weeds he saw his lockhouse; its white stones looked even whiter with the snow heaped on the sides. When he stood near the front door and looked to where he thought the chain would be, he let out a big steaming breath: *It was gone*—and Henry lifted his hands to the door before bringing them back down. He thought he would never enter his home again. That he would never see the radio and dip the bucket in the cistern. Or feel the mattress beneath him. That he would never listen to the trains go by in the night. Or see the stars twinkling through the rafters when he sprawled on his back, his eyes open to the falling dust.

"I thought Barnum said it was locked? Why didn't he tell me?" He pulled and the door creaked open. The wooden boards swayed stiff and frozen in the cold.

"Is this where you stayed before the church?"

Stepping inside, he felt Mabel close, felt her warmth. Standing by the stove, he patted the top lightly, and a white snowy cloud rose into being. "And there's the creaky chair I found in the canal. I put it beside the mattress so I could sit after working, after my body felt like it feels now, with the falling and sledding all through it. The hauling and pulling was like that; it was inside me then too, in my arms and legs and hips."

He leaned on his short right leg. It felt like all the muscles in his body remembered the house. Arching his back out, he saw the radio and remembered hauling it up, his arms clenched and moist. He remembered standing at the sink, how he looked through the holes in the blackened window as the swishy-colored people jogged by. *But that was when it was warmer and the frogs made the croaking sound, when the crickets fluttered in the breeze. Their wings ticked like clocks near my ear.*

He watched her yellow slicker. She was shivering. White sipping breaths came from her in short bursts. "Here." He pulled the stiff tarp from the mattress and a layer of snowflakes quivered in the room. The flakes captured some of the shine from the half-hidden moon and made the darkness silver for moments and moments. And suddenly, her skin looked silver to him. In an instant, he put logs in with wood chips and newspaper bunched like linens. He found the matchsticks under the stove—the same matchsticks he found that first night—after walking all the way here. "It won't be long now."

And it wasn't. The wood caught and the fire's yellow light fell across the room and the shadows seemed deeper. Mabel breathed easier with the cold subsiding but flinched as the crackling wood couldn't cover up some of the scuttling in the walls.

"That's just the mice and squirrels. They need a home too." He watched Mabel edge closer to the stove. "Don't be afraid. I'll take care of you." He felt along his lips and they were moist so he said it again, smooth and easy. "I'll take care of you."

"You're so good to me, Henry, you know that?" She touched him on the shoulder, and he looked away. "You make me think of my mother when you treat me like this. You make me think of her, but different. You're stronger. Because I saw your shoulders when you stood above Barnum. My mother was strong once too, before the fever made her thrash and sweat in her sleep at home. Before the hospital took her. She's still there, you know. I stay with my aunt now, but she hasn't said anything about when my mother might come home." Mabel raised her hands to the open stove. The warmth of the room was spreading out until the tarp was too much for her, and she unwrapped it from her shoulders. "I didn't know the corners were so deep here." The light had brightened the clutter somewhat. "Where do those steps go?" She pointed to the basement steps.

"To the cistern. Where the water is. But it's probably froze now; it ain't been stirred in weeks."

"So the rain drips down there, and it all collects for you?" She looked at the cracks in the rafters, now that she saw the snow. Glittering flakes fell across the sky. "That's how I still see my mother."

She kept her eyes on the rafters, and Henry watched the rafters with her.

"It's the quiet falling that takes over everything," she said, "like when I pray. You've seen me. That's when I think of her, when I hear you sometimes. I hear your footsteps on the edge of things, on the edge of my prayers and feelings, and I like knowing someone else is with me. You don't know it, but I make you part of my prayers then." She smiled at him and stepped closer to the stove. "I say, 'If Henry's here, righting the pews and placing the candles, then there must be someone with my mother, inside with her—always inside—righting her mind and soul.' There's always someone for everyone, don't you think? Even in the quiet places."

He watched her eyes, how they held the fire, and how the fire made her skin glow cinnamon again, like in the church.

"My mother used to say that to me. Whenever she woke from the fever, she'd say, 'There's always someone for everyone,' and I believe her. She told me to pray for her, to be with her in the quiet place as much as I can. But that was all before they took her to the hospital. She hasn't stirred once since she's been there. So now the falling snow sounds like the quiet of my mind in the church. You know how quiet it is there, with the colored glass in the windows and the sounds of your footsteps along the walls, with nothing but the sound of the words on my lips."

"The streaming sound—with how you whisper." Henry turned his head; his lips were dry. He felt the cracked edges and licked with his tongue.

"You listen to me? I didn't even know I said anything loud enough to hear. That's just how I've always prayed."

"It's pretty like the river is pretty."

"You think? I could say it for you if you want? So next time, you'll know all the words and can say them with me. Maybe you could be with my mother then, when I'm there, because it's quiet like this place is quiet."

The fire crackled, humming with heat.

"I'd like that," Henry said.

"So I'll show you." Mabel stood very still then and bowed her head.

"Forgive her, my Lord," she said. "See, that's how I always start. I always say, 'Forgive her, my Lord.' That's so the Lord will know it's me, even though I don't think the Lord would need reminding. But I say, 'Forgive her, my Lord,' and then I start, even though I don't think I have the right words for it yet, not like what the priest might or the silver-haired ladies. But I start right in with whatever's on my mind. Because I don't think the Lord would really mind *how* I say it, just as long as I feel it—that it's true. Look."

A haze of snowflakes had leaked through the ceiling. Henry stood beneath the misty light for a moment and then hunched over again at the stove. He gathered more twigs and logs to put in as the glittering flakes came all the way down from the ceiling.

"This house is like the church now," she said, watching the glittering air. "Look at how the heat's pushing the glittering flakes up until the glittering might disappear altogether. And then what? Then the church feel would be gone—just like that—just because of the heat. Look at it, Henry. Listen."

She reached out and took Henry's hand. She breathed in deep until Henry watched her back arch out once, then twice, looking up.

"Just look at the glittering and the stillness. It's like magic now, don't you think?" She squeezed Henry's hand and fell to her knees then, before the glittering rose all the way to the sky. Bowing her head, she brought both hands to her chin, "Forgive her, Lord. It's Mabel, and it's about my mother again. I know I'm not in Your church but You can hear me anywhere— if everywhere and anywhere are already Yours to begin with—so since I found the glittering feeling of the air just now, I thought You must be here too, so I thought I'd say a word about mother. That way You'll keep her in Your thoughts. You'll think of her sweating and thrashing and maybe take away the sleep from her. Just take away the sleep and the darkness so she can see Your white glittering sky again. Or the snow? Or the white glittering robes of the glass in the church, because she liked to sit beneath the glass in the church and feel the light of Jesus and Mary taking her to another place. That's what I remember most when she talked about the church. She'd say, *'It's like I've been taken somewhere, May, and I don't want to come back because it's so white and airy. But when I think of you and John,* *and Aunt Rosie and Uncle Edward, and I want to come back to tell every-* *one about the faraway feeling of the Lord.'* Isn't that nice? Isn't that nice to think about and never let go? So I'm just asking is all, while the glittering hovers in the room, while Henry stands quiet above me—and You'd really like Henry—considering how nice he is. But I'm just asking: take the sleep away from her. Then everything will be the same, like before..."

As Mabel continued to pray, Henry stepped back from the stove. He put his boots nearby so they'd toast up in the heat, so when he went back into the snow he'd be ready. But he wasn't sure if he wanted to go back out tonight. Not with Mabel praying beside him like she prayed in the church those nights. Not with everything like it was now. He was standing behind her before he knew it. He looked down on her head, along the part in her black hair that ran to her neck. She had taken her hat off after putting the tarp on the mattress, and with the heat rising, he knew she'd want to get out of her yellow slicker too.

But the prayer has her now. And she might whisper for the rest of the *night. Or at least until the prayer lets her go, after the prayer lets go of* *everything inside of what she wants it to touch. That was what the priest* *said. And Rommel said the same thing, whenever Rommel asked me what I* *prayed about before I slept.*

"You've got to let the prayer see every part of you," Rommel had told him. "You've got to let every part of the prayer touch you and hold you so that you can feel every part of yourself light up like the sunlight full of love."

Henry didn't want to tell Rommel he didn't have the words like what the priest used. Or what Rommel used. Or what the silver-haired ladies said when they rocked and mumbled in the pews. So he started to pretend for Rommel. With Rommel watching each night, Henry would struggle to his left knee. It was easier to bend and rest his weight on his left knee. Leaning forward, he'd close his eyes and whisper until his left knee tingled and he could hardly feel it anymore. Then he'd get up and limp to the sink and brush his teeth. When he brushed his teeth, he heard Rommel already snoring and turning to his side, so he knew it worked—his pretending—and it had worked like that for weeks.

But now she's praying right beside me. Now she's so close that I can feel the heat from the stove and the heat from her prayers. Henry wiped his brow. *Because the heat from her prayers has spread out to hold me, and this is not like the pretending before. The pretending always worked before with Rommel, and it made me feel light—until tonight. But now she's here and praying so close that the pretending isn't right, and I feel heavy thinking about my pretending standing beside her.* He felt his stomach fall away when he thought of his pretending. He imagined his lips whispering without really saying anything, when he used to close his eyes so Rommel thought he was sincere and true.

My prayers are not like hers. My prayers are nothing like the stillness of her arms and lips and eyes—nothing like her lightness. Henry saw the lightness of her, as he stepped back from her whispering stream. The lightness sparkled from the sky and set her apart from his prayers, apart from his older pretending. "She's different," and he stepped back to the sink because he felt he was missing something that she had. Something inside wasn't the same. Maybe the walls weren't as wide, or the floors as smooth. Maybe it was only Mabel's presence and close praying body that kept him from feeling the center of things. That they were off in this place. Touched differently from what he remembered. "*The mannequin,*" he whispered. The mannequin was gone from where he'd left it. He saw his thick lips reflected in the black glass above the sink. Running his hands over the wooden counter before raising them to his face, he watched his hands touch his thick lips in the glass, and the room was reflected and changed in the black glass.

The room is changed without the mannequin. The bumps are gone and I can't hold the mannequin close. I can't rub the mannequin against my waist when the hardening starts, when it grows hotter and I feel I might burst for the rubbing away.

He looked at Mabel in the black glass. She didn't stir. Even when he felt the center of the lockhouse turning beneath him, she didn't stir. And he wondered where the mannequin was, where that perfect torso had drifted to with the snow and sky falling all around. The glow from the stove increased until the room held a red humming light that softened around Mabel, but which kept the glass in front of his face dark and shadowed.

"Though the rest is softer," and he saw the softer floorboards and stones on the ends of the walls. The softer room returned to him when he closed his eyes and counted to zero. He had closed his eyes so the mannequin might reappear, so the center of things might hold. *But I can't hold it up*, he knew. *I can't hold the feeling up without the mannequin, and I wondered how I could have ever lost her?* "Though I have Mabel," he said. "And Mabel has her own bumps and her own torso and her own lighter feeling that I might rub below my waist." He looked at Mabel's reflection in the glass and licked his dry lips. "Because I can feel the hardening rising."

When he watched Mabel's reflection, the hardening started out with a slight stir as he stared at the red softening of the room, because Mabel wasn't Mabel when he looked at her in the glass. She was different in the glass.

"She's not herself," he mumbled. The whole of her seemed hidden under her yellow slicker until she became another person altogether: a yellow-slicker girl with down-turned eyes and folded arms. *She is a prayer now for me.* And he could hear Hiram's voice rising in him from the hardening center of his waist. Hiram was calling again about the redeeming of the body:

We use the heat of others—like you, Henry—like you and me and the heat we passed to each other when I held you. And then with my lips. I like the lips the most and I know you will too… even if it's just the girl and not the boy.

Henry didn't shake Hiram's voice away because Hiram wasn't talking against the girl like he did before. Hiram's voice was what Henry wanted it to say, and he let him continue until he thought the whole house might shake with Hiram's voice rising louder about the body of her redeeming:

The heat is what we like best, Henry. It melts us down inside, melting all the coldness and grayness, and so we bring the heat again and again, closer and hotter and harder. It's a harder thing to be close, to hold each other and to let the lips and hands go down to where you might not know the hardening starts and ends and holds everything up. Do you like this, Henry? Do you like when I hold you here?

Henry felt the stirring in his dangling thing growing against his waist. He felt it growing and rising, until he turned from the glass and looked at

Mabel. "But she isn't Mabel now. She's the yellow-slicker girl from the window. She has down-turned eyes and hair, and she's different—she's set apart."

He saw the moist drops lining her neck when he limped behind her. Bending down, he put his fingers to her neck. But the yellow slicker girl didn't move. He only heard her whispering when he put his hand on her neck. And when he reached around and put his other hand on one of her bumps, the light glittered where the heat met the night in the rafters, and the girl in the yellow slicker didn't move. She kept praying with her head down, as she swayed now too. And he knew that this was the redeeming. This was the redeeming because she was swaying. The girl in the yellow slicker. The girl who was un-bodied and different in the glass. The girl he had never touched like this before.

"Are you hot?" he said and wiped with his one hand along her neck while his other hand moved up and down on the bump on her chest.

But she didn't move.

So Henry took his hand away from her neck and reached around to the front of the jacket and peeled away the yellow slicker, so that she had to bring her hands down for a moment. He peeled the yellow slicker until it hung from her waist along the small of her back. When it hung in yellow folds, crinkled and glistening, she brought her hands back up to pray and a great rise of air and human smell like vanilla rose from underneath. Henry breathed in all he could and brought his arms around to her white wool sweater. He rubbed his hands along both bumps and she did not stir. She did not stir as he worked his hands beneath her wool shirt, under her white tank top, until he felt her brown skin. He could see the brown skin on her neck and remembered seeing the brown skin around her waist with her legs diving down to the seam beneath, in Barnum's basement, when she struggled taking off her shirt. But he wasn't sure if it was this girl or not?

"Was this the girl," he asked by her ear, "or was there another?"

He felt his dangling thing harden against the small of her back. He felt it harden as he leaned over to find the bumps on her chest. Her stiff nipples blossomed against his fingertips, and he heard her lips part wider, with the streaming words rushing out. *The stiff nipples like erasers*, he thought. *Like* *the erasers in the rectory when the other children went to school and wrote the letters. That was when I stayed behind. When I scrubbed the walls and got to write the numbers…*and when he held the erasers between his fingers that made the hot hardening swell even more against his pants. He felt the swelling like the great anxiousness and exploding he'd felt so often with Hiram. Or with the mannequin. Or when rubbing his waist on the cot in the church. He felt his whole body giving way to the body underneath, to the anxiousness and release.

"*Is it okay?*" he asked.

She whispered louder with the stream of her voice. Her neck moist. Her eyes closed. Her head lolled back against Henry's shoulder.

"*Is it okay?*" as he rubbed her erasers and smelled the vanilla skin rise beneath him until she let out a soft, "Oh."

She said, "Oh," as he rubbed harder against her erasers and back. The softening light in the room grew brighter as the hot center in him spiraled out from his right leg. It tingled up to his groin and dangling thing, expanding from the center of her back where he pressed his waist again and again.

She said, "Oh," and the great anxiousness swelled out of Henry in a bright burst, and then another, until he was sticky down below and the red softening welled-up over his eyes and mind and lips, until he saw the glittering up in the air. Higher up, the light was falling away, turning to gray and clouded pieces, and he thought he saw Hiram smiling upon him there. He thought he saw Hiram laughing as he slumped back toward the mattress. He had released her erasers; his hands falling along her stomach. As he rested against the mattress, the stream of her words dissolved, and he knew the prayer was over. She was quiet. And he was redeemed.

16

HENRY FOUND HIS TASKS IN THE CHURCH had a much slower feeling after that night with Mabel. He imagined the church moved around him like a wider zero. Like one of the zeroes on the river after the fish jumped beside him.

"It reminds me of those days when I first arrived. When the current dragged on the river, when it had that glassy feel." He wiped a rag across a pew and saw lines in the grainy wood. "Then the wind blew the surface so that the rapids didn't rush as much anymore, because the mountains looked wider too." Looking through the front window, he saw the mountains gray and white across the valley. "The heat made my legs drag in the mud then, so I felt brushed-out on all sides. And so it makes scrubbing the pews easier when I think about it. It makes scrubbing easy and slow."

Henry moved the rag across the pew in a broad arc. The puddles ran along the wood and drew glossy streaks over the planks.

"See how much easier it is to work slow, like on those nights in the canal. It's easier to work like this so I can watch Jesus' perfect legs high up. So I can see how I'm moving inside the zero." Standing, he drew a wide zero across the inside of the nave. "The zero spreads out on all sides, and it didn't do that before I was with Mabel. It didn't do that at all. Now it comes all the way around my arms and hands—and even my legs when I limp down the aisles. It even shows when I sit beneath the white robes of Jesus." Across the walls candles glimmered, and he looked to the third Station of the Cross.

Setting his rag aside, he turned a matchstick over in his hand. Scrapping the match along the box, the tip flared and he held the long matchstick for—*one two three* seconds—until the flame was down to his finger. When he felt the oily heat almost touching his skin, he blew the flame out, and the smoke wafted up in chalky white rings. The white rings looked like snowy circles to him, like the circles he stepped in with Mabel when the snow drew a zero around their lives.

"Now don't you think there's danger in that?" Rommel saw Henry holding the matchstick and called from the doorway, hitching his pants up. "Don't get careless now, son. Fire is one thing. Lighting a candle is another. But letting the flame burn down to your fingers is quite another. It's a notion I thought you might not have like some *children*."

Rommel said *children* with such a hard rasping, Henry felt the sound slap across his cheeks like how Hiram's knuckles did after the redeeming was over. Henry had spilled a bottle once on the carpet, and Hiram had slapped him like how Rommel had just slapped him by saying the word *children* with such shame.

"But I'm not a child." Henry felt the words come calm and steady from his mouth. He brought his fingers to his lips to feel how they arched up when he spoke. He was sitting beneath the third Station of the Cross, once drying the pews and lighting the candles was over. He had lit and let three long matchsticks burn down, and as far as he could tell, Rommel had only seen this last long, steady burn.

"You're not a child anymore, and I wonder, Henry. I wonder what you think you're doing here in the church. Living on the cot beside me. Scrubbing the pews and lighting the candles. Using the ladder when we need to bang down another shingle or when we need to change the bulbs. I wonder if you know what you're doing here?"

Rommel thrust his waist out, and his legs lagged behind. Henry didn't think Rommel's legs were going to catch up with this last thrusting-out, because he'd never seen Rommel's face as pinched-up as it was now. All the gray and brown creases on Rommel's forehead held a web of lines the world had spun, crossing and re-crossing like a nest of living and dying days. *I've never seen so close into Rommel's forehead before, or so slow— because his movements come to me now in pieces—like pictures.*

"What I'm doing here?" Henry wondered at the web of living and dying days as Rommel thrust-out his waist again before grabbing hold of the altar. Rommel held on and his knees buckled before locking beneath him. As Henry watched, the slowing down of the church started again so that the ripple of Rommel's swaying body spun out slower until all Henry could hear was the breathing in his own chest.

I'm breathing now too, and he looked up to the white robes of Jesus. He felt the white robes going in as he breathed. The air went down his throat to his lungs and legs, going in...in...before the white steady robes came out...out...and he felt lighter with each breath. He felt the words move in an arc across his tongue, and then they were spilling from his lips and filling the white space beneath Jesus with the white robes: "*What I'm doing?* I'm watching the fire and breathing the robes."

"No." Rommel's short bursting voice broke the wider zero surrounding Henry. "You're not here to watch the fire or breathe the robes. You're here to pray. You're here to be redeemed for the sin you carry and for the sin I carry, for the sin that even Father Whitney carries. You're here to testify to His life—and to testify is not to feel the robes in the light or to let the fire burn down to your fingers. There's covetousness in you, son; I've seen it, just as I've seen it in myself. There's sloth and envy. There's lust too. And the lust may be the hardest of all." Rommel rubbed his white whiskers as he spoke. "Do you still lust, Henry? Do you still lust at night in your cot?"

As Rommel stared at Henry's unmoving lips, Mabel swung the door open. Her eyes fluttered like brown wings when she saw Henry under the third Station of the Cross. Moving to her favorite pew, her hands rested in the middle of her chest, and both men watched how she moved on soft steps to her seat. As she sat, she looked up at Henry and smiled before bowing her head.

Henry saw her face flushed with scarlet streaks.

"*Lord*," she said and her whispering stream surged across the room. She sounded louder and slower than Henry remembered. "Lord, it's me, Mabel, and I know I've been quiet these last three days, but it was because I've felt things inside me that I haven't felt before, and I'm ashamed of saying I haven't even thought about mother as best I should. I haven't thought about her sleeping. I haven't thought about her arms thrashing in the white sheets of snow or in the white sheets of air, and I feel I've become something else since then…since Henry touched me."

Rommel's eyes flashed with smoldering sparks. His forehead reflected a glaze of sweat he wiped with his hands. *"What did she say?"*

As Henry edged closer to her streaming sound, he heard the furnace rumble in the basement. Heat poured through the vents as Henry brought his hand to his tingling thigh.

"Lord, I let him touch me while I prayed because I thought the feeling was good. I thought his fingers rising all over was like what You would feel like if You touched me. Because Henry is good, I know it. He was soft and tender—but with a jolt—with how he rubbed against me like how Your love might rub against me. That's what Aunt Rosie always says when we sit in the hospital watching mother. She says, 'It'll be just like a shock, Mabel, just like a jolt when it happens. She'll be up again and talking about the Sunday roast with sweet potatoes and rolls and she won't even know she's been away for weeks and weeks. And it'll be like that. She won't even know.'"

"Is this true what she said?"

Henry looked at the altar but didn't move. He wasn't sure if he should, if it might disturb the stream of Mabel's prayers.

"Come here, Henry," Rommel said, his voice louder.

"But I don't want to leave. Not the backward view of Mabel, with how she's leaning forward. Besides, it sounds like you'll only preach to me like what the priest would do. Preach about betterness and betterment, and already you've slapped me across the cheeks like what Hiram would do. Like what Hiram always did."

"Hiram? I don't know why you think you can talk to me like this, because I've done no such thing."

"You slapped just like Hiram would do with the way you said, '*children*,' like it was shameful me being a child. Just because I lit the matches and let them burn down to my fingers."

"Those damn matches!"

"See, I could never tell you what I'm thinking because of your preaching. I could never tell you I'm not a child anymore, that I was just watching the life of the flame. That the life was slow, and that I just wanted to get close to the slow life, to be around the slow life and the slow things—like Mabel with her prayers."

"And Lord," Mabel continued. "I can feel him behind me—my Henry. It's like how I think of You behind me, watching over my bowed head, watching my hands. I can feel his eyes like what Your eyes must feel like, large and piercing, yet soft and tender. His eyes seem to bring in all the sounds and smells of the air, because I can feel him there hovering behind me, and I know You must have sent him to be Your rising hands all over me with the warmth and rubbing jolts. You must have sent him to be Your limping leg too. Because even You have a limp in Your soul—a limp You would never want to hide."

Henry leaned on his right leg as she spoke, and the tingling went away when he watched her lips.

"So when I look at his lips now, and the way they never close, I focus on the scar above them. I think of my own scar, the one not many notice and which might only be another sign You wanted me to see—since both our scars mark us with Your touch. Then I think of how our lips might touch. Since that's what I wanted to do with Barnum before, but he wanted to keep going down the hill and it was too steep and I watched Henry follow me up the hill instead. And I knew I would kiss whoever followed me up the hill, because I wanted to feel my lips fall into another person then. I wanted to touch something bigger. Like what You are. And I knew You must have meant for all of it to happen. You've heard my prayers for bringing my mother up from her slumber, and I felt You brought my body up from its slumber too, when Henry passed his fingers along my skin. Because my whole life and body were asleep for so long before he touched me near the fire. And is that it, Lord? Is that what You wanted me to learn?"

Rommel looked at Henry as Mabel paused. "I knew there was lust inside you. I've seen it in your cot, and now I've heard it from the girl."

Henry limped a step closer to Rommel. He came down the center aisle so that he could walk past Mabel, if he decided to go all the way to the altar, though he wasn't sure.

"I see the eye you're giving me," Henry said. "It's the red eye with your head all scrunched into lines, and with me scrubbing all afternoon too, and carrying the candles to your cot. I did all that so you could make the wax molds for the manger Barnum talks about, and that Mabel will sit in. I would see her in anything, because we're close like that, after touching in the lockhouse. Even though it was another girl who was her for that moment. Even though it was another girl who I touched with my hands."

"*There was another girl?*" Rommel said.

"It was another girl who was inside Mabel. It was another girl who sat there quiet and still while Mabel was up in the air, un-bodied."

"*Un-bodied?*"

Henry glanced to the rafters. "She had to be un-bodied to sit there so steady, to feel my fingers go up and up and my waist grow hotter, until the tingling passed through me and my pants. Then Mabel came back to me. She came back."

Rommel swayed against the altar, closing his eyes. "My God, Henry, what have you done?"

"Then it was her again. When she come back to her body she put her slicker on and walked out the door, and I haven't seen her since. But now you want to take her from me. I can tell by your scrunched-up face. And you don't even know I love her like I could never love Hiram...like I never could." Henry felt the words on his lips. They were calm and steady on his tongue. "I love her because she's soft and Hiram was never soft. His lips were not like Mabel's, with the pink scar like mine."

"*Stop it! Just stop talking about it like it's natural!*"

"But it is natural. Everything's natural about her lips. Everything's natural about the stream that keeps coming out and out..."

"...because mother always said there'd be boys, but then she went off into the slumber and I only hear her in my dreams now, Lord. She says, '*The wide halls of heaven are love, Mabel. The wide halls of heaven and Earth are love, and only love will bring you through them. Only love will bring you through.*' That's what I hear her say when I listen for her words in my mind. I hear her when I open my eyes in the morning and when I close my eyes at night, and I hear her when I think of Henry's fingers rising along my chest. Because when his fingers rose up then I knew mother was speaking to me through him—and I'm afraid to admit it, but I thought about another thing then too. I didn't think about his fingers going up anymore, but about them…going down." Mabel shifted in the pew.

"For God's sake, make her stop." Rommel pointed to the Stations of the Cross. The late evening light was dark in the purple glass. "Look where she is. *Just look where we are.*"

"She's not finished. She's in the quiet place, and I would never stop her there." Henry stepped closer to her and felt the tingling in his leg. It shivered in his thigh and through his groin as the sound of her whispering surrounded him.

"Because, Lord, I think about Henry's hands falling instead of rising, falling beneath my waist—where the warmth tingled when his hands rose up. I felt warm in the spot below, and I almost reached out to You then, and to mother and Henry too. I almost reached out to all Your hands joined as one to bring them down below, where I heard mother's words the most, calling me. That's where she says the love begins and ends—down inside—and I believe her, Lord, I do."

With another step, Henry was beside her. He smelled the rich vanilla odor rising from her arms and took in two sipping breaths to quiet his heart. Looking up, he saw Rommel's black eyes fixed on his slow progress, but Rommel only swayed at the end of the church. *Yes, the end of the church seems to stretch out much farther,* Henry thought, *much farther than I ever thought. The church is stretched out into pictures.*

Henry saw the picture of the aisle, of the pews and windows. They were all far away from him. But he knew he would have to step through each picture, through each frame to get to Rommel, if he was to stop Rommel's fierce and staring eyes.

Henry looked down at Mabel. Her whispering un-bodied form was beneath him. *And she's like before, like in the lockhouse. She's un-bodied and away. With each word her streaming prayers go out and out until she's above me. She's higher up with her thoughts, with her mother and the stillness. And I want to be with her—un-bodied and floating—so I can feel those thoughts of hers and feel along her bumps and raise my hands up to see if her prayers are my prayers too.*

"How else do we see other prayers?" he said. The words came smoothly from his lips. "How else do we step inside without touching?" Though as he spoke, he thought he saw her move. He thought his words had re-bodied her, and he was ashamed to startle her if he did. So he limped in front of her so that he could not look down to her again, so he could not steal the grace of her prayers. "Grace," he said. As he limped in front of her. "That's the word I liked best from the rectory, when I was young."

"Do you think any of this has any grace to it?"

Henry saw Rommel's piercing eyes.

"The nuns said, 'Grace,' with the priest in the rectory whenever I sat beneath them," Henry said. "And I thought they were talking about me then, because when they said, 'Grace,' the nuns patted my shoulders when I drew the numbers."

Henry took another step toward Rommel and saw a zero drawn across the center of the aisle. It was the only number before him, and its curved line had such grace that he thought he would never lose the grace of that number again, that he would never lose that balance.

"I can feel it now," he said, and he looked at the zero in the aisle. The zero surrounded him; it covered the floorboards, the pews, his boots. "This moment of passing her is a moment of grace too; it's set apart from the rest; it's different. Because you're so far away from me now, Rommel, and you'd never know the slowness of the grace overtaking me and the aisle in the robes' floating light."

"What are you talking about?"

Henry took another step down the aisle. "You can't stop me from passing her with the grace this zero makes around us: only around Mabel and me." Henry drew with his arm in the air a zero, stretching above her as she continued.

"And, Lord, he is beside me now, and I can feel You beside me. It feels like You're passing me, that You're inside him and I feel the grace of Your soft passing and limping leg. Because he's watching me too, with his fierce eyes, and I know he's watching me because I can feel him through my eyes. My eyes are closed but they feel the room and heat and that older man on the other end. But he is so far off from Henry and me and You. That older man does not know what it is to be touched by You in the warmth of the lockhouse, with my skin rising up. It was like heaven was shining inside the lockhouse. A small part of heaven You were letting me see. And I thank You, though I know I haven't said one word about mother. I haven't spoken about her sleeping and the fever and the thrashing in the messy sheets, and I'm sorry to talk only of my skin rising up and Your hands rising up. But I know it's okay to talk of that first, to know that it was right. Though if You've shown her the same part of heaven, the same rising up and glittering, then I don't know if she should wake up. And I wonder if it's a sin to say that, to wish she's happy in her own part of heaven? Is it a sin to *not* ask for her back?"

Henry nodded at Rommel. "Now I'm past her. I'm past her and she knows I'm past her because I thought she moved her head to the side when I passed, and you didn't see that, did you? You didn't see her grace because you are too far off. You're at the other end of the church, and you can't see the steady grace of her praying, or the slight grace I stole from her by looking with a quick glace from the corner of my eye. So that I feel different now and set apart. Even my limp feels different." Shaking his right leg, he wiggled his hip. "Because it's easier to bring it up with my other leg now when I step. Can't you see?" Henry looked at Rommel. "Can't you see how my other leg came forward almost at once, when I stood straight? And I'm much taller now than you. I'm much taller and have you always known this—that I was taller if not for my limp?"

Rommel swayed against the altar when Henry spoke. "I've always known there was lustfulness in you, a lustfulness I could not shake loose." Rommel bent forward, releasing his hands from the red cloth and clasped them together. From a long way off, Rommel muttered a prayer. It sounded faint at first, but it came to Henry much the same as when Rommel talked from his cot when he would tell Henry about all the chores of the next day so that Henry could sleep on all the, "goodness of the chores they would do." And often, after Rommel said such things, Henry's mind would wander over ladders and lanterns and candles when he slept, until he was tired of seeing ladders and lanterns and candles when he woke. He got tired of Rommel's listing of goodness and chores, and he got tired of hearing Rommel's listing of lustfulness now—a listing he thought much too loud from a world so far away. Especially with the girl quiet and praying right here in this world of the zero: a zero that held only Mabel and him and could not be disturbed by such words.

"It's a lustfulness I know in you toward the girl," Rommel said. "It's your lustfulness and your betrayal that I pray for now. You have betrayed everything I gave you and that Father Whitney gave you and that the women and children of this church gave you by bringing you in."

"But they didn't give me this grace," Henry said. "Do you see the grace she's given me—only her." At once, Henry felt he was not limping any more, that the grace of Mabel—the small grace she'd given him—made his limp ease away. His body eased into a straighter line. His back felt held by strings from the rafters, and he thought that Mabel's higher un-bodied arms were holding him from her higher wandering place. "In the quiet place above," he said, pointing above Rommel's head. "She's helping me with the grace of her higher wandering."

"It is your lust that I cannot allow. I cannot allow it to stain everything I love. I cannot allow it with her being so young, and you...as young as a *child* when you think."

"You cannot hurt me with that word and your voice like shame anymore. Do you see?" Henry bent over then to remove his boots and kicked them off to stand in his socks even and straight. "Mabel is true. She's in the air holding me up. Look at how straight I walk—without any tingling in my leg—just look!"

Rommel had turned from Henry to the basement door. And Henry didn't expect to move so swiftly following him without limping. He was behind Rommel in a moment.

"And I bet you didn't think I could move like that, that a *child* could move so swift?" Henry stepped lightly and watched Rommel thrust his waist out and pull his legs underneath him toward the stairs. "Why won't you look? You won't even watch me move straight and swift across the floor."

"It's only the priest who may help you now. I have let it come to pass. I have let the light of Jesus from the robes you liked fall to nothing."

"You do not know me then." Henry stood to the left of Rommel's shoulder. "You do not know Mabel, and you do not know me to say it's only lust."

Henry felt his hands ball into fists. He towered over Rommel, who swayed as he stepped to the stairs, muttering: "I brought you too close to too many too early—especially to the ones you'd be tempted by most, by being a *child* like them, and I must change this life," he said, stepping to the doorway. "I must change this life so you may not change the lives of those around you, so that you don't ruin each child you touch."

Henry was behind Rommel, and each word echoed like in the rectory. He heard the children shuffling away when he had to stay and scrub the walls. They chanted at night, saying, *"Lonely Henry...Lonely Henry."* But he knew they couldn't hurt him anymore. Hiram couldn't hurt him either, not with the grace he had now. Though he knew Hiram was right about that older life, about the slower life being better. *I think the older ways are better now too. The ways of grace and of being slow and of letting the slower life hold you. Because Hiram and Rommel and the nuns can't hold me now—not with the grace of Mabel holding me up from the rafters. And Rommel can't talk to me like this either, not from a whole world away, not from the picture he's in.*

Henry saw how the picture of Rommel's life reached through the long narrow nave. He saw ripples in the shimmering air as he stood behind him. The picture of Rommel edged all the way over to dissolve into Henry and Mabel's zero, and so he put his hands out to push him away—to push his picture away.

"Forever." Henry felt his hands push Rommel away. "Forever," he said again, as Rommel's hips swayed out in a frozen picture. His arms flailed and his face pinched into lines as he landed in a broken mass at the bottom.

17

BY THE BEGINNING OF JANUARY, Henry was used to the cot beside him being empty. He was used to the churchgoers asking about Rommel's unfinished wax collection, about each angel and steeple, and he was used to telling them how he'd found Rommel at the bottom of the basement steps. Even though the churchgoers said if he didn't want to talk about that night they understood. Though with the way they acted, Henry knew they wanted to hear his words. They seemed particularly interested in *how* he said the words, as if his voice held some deeper meaning. They gathered around him when he spoke, crowding the pews. Some even took out rosaries and nodded along as he retold the tale. Others said, "Mmmmm," and "Ohhh-hh," and swayed to a rhythm.

With each retelling, Henry heard himself grow calmer, more balanced in his body. As he repeated the words, he didn't slur when he explained the accident. He didn't lisp or stutter when he described how Rommel's legs gave out, or how Rommel's arms flailed in the air. He didn't flinch either, when he saw Rommel's bruised and shapeless face in his mind. He reached up as he talked and the words came even and steady when he spoke about the last moments of the man they'd known for so many years but had never gotten close to, they all said. It was never enough to work beside him in the soup line or collecting canned food or hiding the Easter eggs for the children and not to know his favorite color? Or where his children lived? Or that he drank warm cocoa each night and that Henry placed the cocoa on a small tray with three biscuits dipped in honey. They all said Henry was a lucky man to have such knowledge of the life now absent from their world—a lucky man indeed.

For days after that, the priest would come to Henry and say, "Could you change the bulb in the lantern for me?" Or, "Could you scrape the icicles from the front door?" And standing there with Henry, the priest would tear up when he thought of Rommel changing the bulbs and scraping the icicles before. He'd put his hand on Henry's shoulder, remembering, just like how he'd touched Rommel, standing with his old friend. And as the priest touched Henry's shoulder now, on the second Saturday after it happened, Henry felt him tearing up again. They were the only people in the church, and with the priest wiping his eyes on his billowy sleeve, Henry's stomach bunched into a fist standing so close to him. Henry had wanted to ask the priest something for so long but never had the chance. *So this is my chance*, he thought. *Though I know the priest can only think of Rommel now; he only sees Rommel.*

All during Christmas and New Years it was the same—the priest's thoughts and sermons were all about Rommel—and every word only pushed what Henry wanted to ask further away. Henry couldn't remember the words, even though he'd held them in his mind for so long. *Even though they were the same words that made me come here in the first place. But I can't remember anything I wanted to say after Rommel fell away, after that touch of Mabel's grace.*

So Henry said, "Yes, sir," to the priest whenever he was asked to do a chore. He said, "Yes, sir," and walked off straighter because of the grace he'd gotten from Mabel—after Rommel fell. That was what he told himself during those weeks. "Rommel bumped into our zero. Rommel crossed over to where he shouldn't, and Rommel's falling away has changed everything. Even the manger scene was called off, and I haven't seen Mabel since."

He stood at the top of the steps counting to zero once and then to zero again.

"This is where I felt his picture moving into our zero." He looked to the light in the stained-glass windows. Moving his hands in the air where Rommel had stood, he drew a zero. "He was here," and Henry pushed out with his hands. "I can still feel his ribs. Then I watched him fall through slower and slower pictures. I saw the picture of his arms fly out. Then the picture of his legs. Until his face rested in a picture at the bottom."

When Henry remembered Rommel's face, his stomach un-tightened from its fist. He remembered walking down the steps to stand over Rommel and how Rommel's raspy breathing died away. Henry had counted each of Rommel's breaths: counting to zero once, and then from zero to six, before he didn't have to count anymore. Whenever he stood at the top of the stairs, he saw Rommel's body. But the picture didn't frighten him like when he first saw it. Instead, seeing the body only comforted him. It made his stomach stay where it was supposed to—flat and even in the center of his belly. As he looked at the un-bodied picture of Rommel, he counted his own breathing: *one two three* breaths moving in: *one two three* breaths moving out.

"Six," he said and held up six fingers to look at the number. "Rommel is in his own zero now," and he drew another zero in the air. "He was wrong to push into our zero with only me and Mabel, and now he's right. He's right at the bottom of the steps, in his own zero. Set apart from everything else."

Henry turned to the empty church and remembered Mabel from that night.

"She didn't even move or hear when Rommel fell. She was in the stream of her prayers when I walked back to her." Henry pulled a thick candle from his pocket and passed it from hand to hand. It was warm from being in his pocket. "She smiled at me then to see the tallow. And I thought of my hands rising up her belly, to pass across the bumps on her chest. But I knew she had to meet her Aunt Rosie to go to the hospital. She had to rush to catch the car that would drive her down the road. But I got to stand with her anyway, for a whole minute at the front door."

Henry started toward the front door. He moved smoothly on his feet and remembered how the wind had died down when they stood there together.

"When I said bye to her, the red color that I liked raced through her cheeks, and her face was all cinnamon above the snowy porch. Then I watched her cinnamon face move out beneath the night." Henry watched a gray car edge off along the street. Not another sound crept in as he opened the door to listen.

"It was quiet that night. It was quieter than I'd ever known." Spinning to the aisle, he touched his hip and wriggled his right foot. "Not even the wind rushed beyond the trees. But I heard the river. Even with the ice closing in on both sides, I heard the river. It still ran in the middle, just like what Barnum said."

Henry stopped to listen to the church. The furnace had started up, and heat hummed inside the walls.

"When I came back in, I saw the stillness of Rommel at the bottom of the steps. I went down and touched his eyelids with my fingers, because that was what Barnum said they did on TV. Barnum told me that in the coatroom. He even made me sit once and keep my eyes open, pretending I'd been shot by old Rex. He said, 'It should look like you're watching a dark forest far off, a forest that isn't as scary as you first thought.'"

Barnum had touched Henry's eyelids, closing them, and Henry had counted to zero once, and then to zero again, until he was dead long enough, and Barnum leaned back and Henry couldn't smell the boy's honeysuckle skin anymore.

Leaning over Rommel's body, Henry had thought of Barnum's words, of that forest. *Because that was what I saw in Rommel's eyes. Rommel was looking into that dark forest—and I knew he was there—that he'd made it in among the branches that swept over him with their shadows.*

Henry stopped under the third Station of the Cross. He looked up to Jesus in the white robes. "I knew he made it in then, Jesus. Just like You wanted him to. He was covered by dark branches and willow. Though when I touched his eyelids, a great coldness rose through me, a coldness I felt all the way in my teeth."

A fierce shudder passed through him when he remembered touching Rommel's eyelids—so that his lips moved up like he was smiling. "And I thought I smiled then too, Jesus. I thought I smiled touching his cold eyelids, bringing them down, to know that he was in that dark forest, that he was in his own zero and not with me and Mabel anymore—that we were free."

Shadows from the candles along the wall rose under the third Station of the Cross. Henry stared at the flickering light until the flames slowed into pictures again. The pictures rose and fell across the wall. "And now it's slower here. Rommel can't limp up from the basement to tell me to start the next chore no more, to scrub the pews or change the candles. There's only me now, Jesus...there's only me. And just look—I can walk straight all by myself." Unlacing his boots, Henry shook his feet out and stood very still. "I can stand straight because of Mabel and all the grace You gave her. I even found a new pair of boots under Rommel's cot. So when I stir the soup at night and make the sandwiches, I don't have to lean over on one leg when I get tired. It's easier to scrape the ice from the steps too, and the priest and churchgoers all agree I should take over for Rommel. I even heard someone whisper about the *grace* of my being here. As if I was supposed to be here all along. That the good Lord gave the grace to Rommel to see that I should stay after walking all the way from Baltimore. Can you believe it? They all say I have grace now." Henry took a smooth step on his bare feet, on the balance of his straight legs, and stared up through the picture of the slow falling light—and smiled.

THE NEXT AFTERNOON, as Henry worked in the coatroom after the service, he heard the same whispering about the grace of him being here to replace Rommel. As the crowd stood near the coatroom, he caught snatches of what they said.

"No...he walked from Cumberland all the way without his shoes and fed off green onions and fern..."

"Well, I heard he come down from Antietam, where they have the home for people like him. Though when the priest called they said they hadn't lost any men in a while, so the priest just ended it at that."

"Or from Washington...I heard he walked from DC. He was supposed to be here all along with some family or something but the family was gone, and so he spent some weeks by the river, living near the canal."

When Henry heard them whispering about the canal, he felt all those days from before in his body. Each muscle returned to the hauling and digging up of stone and junk. His feet remembered wading in the marshy grass, the river water on his fingers. Stepping from the coatroom, he tasted cooked turtle and mint and had to breathe in—once, twice—to stop his body from shaking.

"Henry...*Henry?*" Barnum's voice sounded somewhere in the aisle, and when Henry looked, Barnum was at his side. "Do you want to go sledding again? In the hills?" As Barnum touched Henry's side, Henry sipped another deep breath and saw Barnum in the lockhouse naked by the fire. "Geez, I see all the veins in your neck," Barnum said. "The blood beneath your skin is blue." Barnum's voice brought more people to the coatroom. They touched Henry on the arm and shoulder. One lady even put her hand on Henry's neck and said he was warm, until they all repeated it now:

"He's warm; he's warm; Henry's warm."

They took their coats from the hangers on their own after that and said Henry should lie on his cot for the rest of the day. But instead of lying down, Henry sat in the pew beneath the white robes of Jesus in the third Station of the Cross. "This is where I need to rest," he told them when they asked. And after he stared for minutes on end at the white robes in the glass, with the light falling and the mountains darkening behind, he moaned, putting his hand against his stomach. His stomach was clenched tighter than ever before so that even the priest put on his coat and said Henry needed to be alone.

When Henry heard the last shuffling noise dissolve, he knew it was late and that Barnum might be waiting for him to go sledding, but he didn't want to move. *Not till I see Mabel*, he thought. *Not till she comes to loosen this feeling in my stomach. But she hasn't showed yet, anywhere*, and he wondered if maybe her mother had died, if Mabel's mother and Rommel were in that dark forest together?

"Because there's a dark forest by the canal too," he said, and he saw the canal again and how he pretended it to be before he left. The surface was blue: mules stood on the towpath. They pulled barges behind them. He could hear their creaking steps, and when he blinked his eyes, he saw the mules wearing red saddles in the center of the church. They came right down the center aisle. He arched his head up and sniffed their hot mealy hooves and rich hairy skin, but focused mostly on the red leather saddles and how they glowed in the sun. He thought that maybe in that dark forest there was a blue canal? Maybe you rode that blue canal all the way up? If you were lucky, you got to sit in the red saddles because the saddles fit every part of you. Both your feet fit in the stirrups, and both your legs were the same size riding into heaven—and then he remembered what he wanted to ask the priest—about the size of his legs. Standing up, as if to catch the priest on his walk home to tell him, he stopped beneath the shadowy robes of Jesus in the third Station of the Cross.

"Why shouldn't I?" he said, looking up.

The candlelight fell across the pews and drew a zero around his feet. He followed the zero from point to point until he came back to the first point beneath Jesus way up. But Jesus wasn't as way up as he first thought. When he looked again, it felt like the pews and church had dissolved. Until he saw the canal stretch out from wall to wall, and he knew that where he stood was really down in the marshy grass. Down where he toiled to set it right, and that Jesus—when Henry looked back up to Him—Jesus was really on the towpath above the canal. Jesus was pulling up with his white robes to Henry's body beneath a depth of blue water.

"Why shouldn't I know about my leg?" he asked louder, and his stomach clenched tighter; he'd never raised his voice to Jesus, even on those days scrubbing the pews. *Because scrubbing the pews was its own kind of talking with Jesus. When I scrub the pews, I only see my hands going out and in, and there's nothing else for me to know.* "The scrubbing always makes the pews like a sheet of paper. And maybe I could write my question in letters to Jesus, if ever I had the letters to write like how they wanted me to have in the rectory. But I only have the numbers. The numbers from one to zero." And he counted standing beneath Jesus. "One two three four five six seven eight nine ten zero…one two three four five six seven eight nine ten zero." When he came to zero again, he thought he saw the zero of the candlelight turn a darker shade with the sun gone behind the mountains, and he wondered if his numbers were enough. "Are they enough to ask the question about my leg?" Passing his hand along his right thigh, it felt smooth and steady, even when he leaned on it with all his weight.

"Henry?" A small voice from behind frightened him.

Henry thought it might be the Lord answering him, though he'd never heard the Lord before. So he whispered, *"The Lord wouldn't speak to me. The Lord only looks for very long when I stare into the slow center of the candle. Because with the world slower, and the pictures of everything slower around me, I've often felt the Lord's eye inside me, looking into the very center of me. That's what the clenching and un-clenching of my stomach is.*

It's an answer." His belly grumbled beneath his voice, and he had to pinch his belly hard with his hands. "Though the Lord's eyes have not shown me all the way to the center of that answer yet—not yet."

He looked up at Jesus, pressing his hands against his belly.

"The Lord leaves me on the edge of something very large and fuzzy. It's like when I step out from the church to watch the people drive off after service. I have to stare very long because of the glaring snow. And I know that the Lord's answer about my legs is like that too: it's white and fuzzy and will only come into focus from far off..."

"Who are you talking to?"

Startled, Henry shifted on his leg, and the steadiness in his right leg tingled. The tingling went all the way through his waist to his shoulders before shuddering across his cheeks so that he felt his cheeks move again on their own. He thought he might smile, so he brought his hands up to feel the smile, but it never came like he thought it might.

"It's me, Henry." Mabel was at the front door. She smiled in her yellow slicker and galoshes, and when she tugged at her yellow slicker, Henry saw her smooth brown belly. "I saw Barnum waiting outside, but he said you weren't coming out. He asked me to sled with him, but I told him I haven't had a chance to pray, not since I missed the service, so I wondered if I could, and if you'd get me the candle?"

"The tallow?"

"Yes, the tallow. I know how you like to say that." She smiled and watched from her seat as Henry walked to the basement stairs.

Henry came back from the basement with an armful of candles. He looked at Mabel's bowed head and saw the zero from the candlelight beneath the third Station of the Cross. It expanded across the floor and almost touched her as he worked. He started at the altar. Replacing the melted candles with clean candles, he bowed, just as he'd seen Rommel bow so often before. While he replaced the melted candles, he watched Mabel and listened to her streaming prayers move across the church. Putting the candles in the sack, he felt his legs move as light as cotton sheets across the wood. He'd never noticed how smooth and straight he'd become. Since he'd gotten a bit of grace from Mabel, he felt his own grace rise that much more so that he didn't even think why he walked so much smoother from pedestal to pedestal. Though he had an idea: he could tell he was walking smoother because Mabel was watching him work.

Mabel is always watching me, he thought. *Even when she prays she looks from up in the air where she rests, praying and watching me so I do right by her, so I get her the tallow that helps her pray for her mother. She can see me even when I'm behind her like this, and I'll stand behind her like this for as long it takes before I know she wants me to come closer, before she wants me to reach up like in the lockhouse to her red-blossom bumps. She'll want me to do that because she is un-bodied now, and when she's un-bodied she's up in the air wandering from the earth, and it's only the touch of my fingers that can bring her back to her body.*

"It is." Henry let his words rise louder so that they merged with Mabel's smooth flowing stream. "She does not want to leave her body yet. Not with all the prayers she still has to ask the Lord about her mother. And maybe that was what Jesus wanted to tell me but couldn't when I looked into His light beneath the third station? Maybe Jesus wants me to bring her back to her body? Maybe Jesus wants me to *always* bring her back to her body, so she can pray for her mother again and again? Maybe that's what Jesus wants to tell me with the voice I never hear?"

"I can feel him there, Lord," she said, as his words faded away. "Because it's You behind me, isn't it?" Her voice grew louder as Henry edged closer. "And I have come all the way from my thoughts and prayers to be with You. I have climbed up to You in heaven, and You have come all the way down to be beside me. And I never once doubted You. I never once thought You wouldn't come to me—especially in the church 'The way we must pass is through the church, through these prayers, through Your touch.' My mother always said. And I will reach out to You now like I was afraid to reach out before, though I knew it was what You wanted me to do, but I held back in the lockhouse. But in Your church there can be no fear of giving over to the heat inside me, the heat that burns to be closer to Your touch, to the touch You'll give to me through Henry."

As she finished, she turned to Henry, rising from her prayers. She stepped right out of her stream like Henry thought she would, because he stood there watching her. But now that she turned, he knew it was the sign he was watching for, so he slid into the pew beside her and put his hands to the edge of her sweater. Though as he began to reach under her sweater, she touched his hands with her fingers.

"Lord, these are the hands I've wanted to touch for so long, because I know these are Your strong hands too..." And as her fingers fluttered across his, Henry felt a deeper heat burst from beneath her waist. She took his hands and pushed them down to the seam beneath her. "Because this is how the Lord is settling me," she said. "The Lord has His hand on me now, and raises me up. I can feel it."

When Henry looked at her face, he saw her chin rising like she said. It looked as if the Lord was placing her chin on a ledge in the air.

"That's because the Lord feeds us," he said. "The Lord feeds us with the light."

"Yes, the light." She leaned back against the pew so that her legs and skirt spread out so that Henry could move his finger in and out of the seam beneath her where the heat was rising to warm his whole arm. "*Ohhhhh,*" she moaned. And Henry was not sure if it was her voice or the Lord's moving through her because he had his eyes on her face. The flush came to her cheeks and made her skin brown with the cinnamon he liked. "*Mmmmm,*" she said and turned her head as Henry moved his finger and felt the heat rising off her limbs in waves. And down below, his dangling thing stood straight up against his belt. "Yes," she said as her hands fell against Henry's waist. Pulling his zipper down, she had her hand along the inside of his waist to touch his dangling thing.

"*Ohhhhh,*" Henry said, and when he turned to face her, she kept moving her hand up and down and he kept moving his finger so that they both said, "*Mmmmm,*" together, and "*Ohhhhh.*" *And it's much different than the lockhouse,* Henry thought. *It's much different because the church is different and the church is watching and letting this heat pass through us, because I'm rising up now to where Mabel is.*

His eyes were closed, but he could still see her flushed face. He was above the room with her and felt her hand working on the center of his being, and yet he was floating above it all. His body was lighter and straighter, and he couldn't feel how his right leg was once cramped and shorter than the left. And he thought he must have reached back far enough to be near the beginning—when his legs were the same. This was *before the beginning*; and this was the rising above; and this was the light of Jesus staring into the center of his being with the answer Jesus could not speak, because there was no speaking at this level. There were no letters. Or numbers either. *And maybe we're beyond the zero now*, he thought. *Maybe we've passed beyond the zero and might only be outlining everything between, so that the world inside our circle is this heat, this quiet heat, this quiet rising and falling away, and this bright hovering.*

18

$\mathfrak{T}$HE NEXT WEEKS SNOWED OFF AND ON, and the people said it was the hardest winter yet—as Henry took their coats, he watched for Mabel. When he changed the candles and shoveled the steps, he also watched for Mabel—but she never came to pray like she had the night they sat so close together. That was when the heat passed between them, and he felt himself rising into the rafters to where she must have been. Because when she did fall back to her body and open her eyes, neither of them could move their lips to say a word. They only stared at each other before walking to the front door.

Henry wanted to call to her then, as she walked off, heading up the side road that led away from town, but he didn't feel the words rising in him then. He didn't know what the words would be for what they'd shared between them. So he let the urge pass to speak to anyone after Mabel left. Even when the priest talked to him now as they prepared for a special evening mass, he only nodded and made the sound, "Mmmmm-hmmmm," as if to say "Yes" to the priest's instructions.

"We want the pews scrubbed extra-clean," Father Whitney said. "The cardinal from Baltimore is visiting tonight."

"Mmmmm-hmmmm," Henry said.

"And I'm not sure if this means I'm to be reassigned or not, but we'll have to wait and see." The priest straightened his collar as his voice trailed off. He looked above the basement stairway to the seventh Station of the Cross. The station was dark with purple glass, and in it, Jesus stumbled to the ground. It was the second time Jesus fell, marching up Calvary, and Henry counted—*one two*—on his fingers as he looked up with him. "Every decision is watched, Henry," the priest said, turning to stare into Henry's eyes, "and everyone—all under the Lord's perfect eye."

Henry watched the priest mutter about his sermon before shuffling to his office, and as Henry watched him go, he thought about the Lord's perfect eye. *Because I know the Lord has watched the center of my own nature for years now. The Lord has watched me my whole life. Even before Mabel sat with me, I felt the Lord watching from the center of the candlelight, from when I burnt the matchsticks down.* He rubbed his fingers, remembering the oily heat. *And now the cardinal might sit in the same pew that me and Mabel sat in, when we had the floating feeling.*

The idea of the cardinal sitting in the same pew had Henry staring at the grainy wood. He dipped his hand in the water and drew the suds back and forth in a slow circle.

"So maybe the pews weren't the right place for me and Mabel to pass the heat between us? Maybe it was wrong to sit here? Because it happened here. The floating feeling happened here. That was when I felt what it was like to have both legs from before the beginning, when they were straight. And maybe I could ask the cardinal about it too? Like what I always wanted to ask the priest." Henry looked at the priest's office door. It was hidden in shadow behind the altar. "The priest said he had a special sermon to write about *forgiveness*." And when he remembered the priest mumbling about: "Forgiveness for even the worst sinners and traitors to their kind," he wondered what his own kind would be—and what the priest meant by it?

Leaning over, he saw the reflection of his face in the soapy water. His lips were pressed together, his eyes wide apart. Jostling the bucket, he watched his face dissolve into ripples. Turning to Jesus' white robes, he wondered about his kind and breathed in and felt his stomach rise and fall beneath him. The picture of Jesus' eye was all he could see. The edge of everything else was black and dissolving, until he only saw those eyes—those burning eyes—and he thought he heard a questioning voice drift down to him, "*Why?*" the eyes seemed to ask.

Henry heard a faint voice like Mabel's. The voice came in a small, curious way. It was like what the real Mabel might ask if ever she were confused about the heat passing between them that night. "*Why'd we do it?*" The eyes seemed to repeat the question, and he dipped his scrubber into the bucket.

"But I don't want to speak about her." Though as soon as he said the words, he realized he *was* speaking about her, and his stomach un-tightened from its fist. "I can only speak about her with You then, Jesus, because You asked me to, and nobody else can. Because I know it was You who let my leg grow longer. I know it was You who took me up into the rafters and released my leg from its cramping. That was when I felt what it was like before the beginning, with how we floated above everything. And I knew it was right for me to touch her then, since You let me."

Henry kneeled beneath the third Station of the Cross. He scrubbed the pew until the wood glistened like a piece of paper, until he could imagine his words spilling across the surrounding page. "I touched her even though I knew Hiram would call her a whore and say she took me away from my redeeming. That the tugging and rubbing were not a redeeming at all. But I say, 'No,' to Hiram now, Lord. I say, 'No,' to him and I mean it."

Dipping his scrubber in the bucket, he felt the water swallowing his wrist.

"And maybe You always wanted me to say 'No' to him like that? Because I never knew 'No' was so strong. That it could stop others from what they wanted. Not until I met Mabel. Not until I knew You had given her that grace so I could walk straighter, so I could say 'No' to Hiram forever."

Light was rising in the window. As Henry watched, Jesus in the white robes loomed larger until the colors in the glass buzzed into focus. The colors moved across the pews flashing clear and then dull when the clouds drifted by. And as the windows rattled now with each stronger gust, he knew the flashing light was from the changing sky.

"I'm changing too, Lord," he said and reached out with his rag and brought it back across the pew. "Mabel changed me so that even now I can bring my right leg up as fast and swift as my left, and I know You've seen it. You've seen everything just as the priest says, because I know You've set everything as only You wanted it."

Henry was quiet then. He had said all the words inside him. There were only the pews to scrub now, because that was what Jesus had set out for him to do. And as soon as he started scrubbing again, he felt this body submit. This was a special scrubbing. *I've never been up so early to scrub like this,* he thought, *and it's all because of the special visit of the cardinal of Baltimore.* So Henry scrubbed harder. Once he worked his way over the pews, he started over from the beginning, sliding on his knees. "And I don't mind," he said as he worked. "I don't mind at all."

Moving toward the front door, he looked out the window to the white patches of snow on the lawn. The road beyond the lawn was a black runny sludge. Henry remembered walking beside the road when he was out scraping ice. He even put his foot inside the iced-over gutter and felt his leg slide along. The iced-over gutter reminded him of the canal. *Though I haven't seen the canal for so long, not since I took Mabel to the lockhouse.*

"*Or the mattress,*" he whispered and scrubbed the pew by the door and looked across his hands. "When I held my hands to the stove."

Scrubbing harder, he felt his arms push up and out before returning in a smooth arc. He thought of the stove as he worked and of the heat glittering below the rafters. So that when he looked at the rafters in the church, he imagined the silver glittering raining over him until he was scrubbing across the pews in the outline of a zero. He was marking glittering zeroes as he scrubbed.

"Maybe I've always scrubbed like this? Maybe I've always marked zeroes here and here and here. I've marked every inch." Scouring the church, he saw that everything was drawn within a zero. Everything was set apart for him—the whole church glowed inside his glittering zeroes.

"It's all mine. Even the altar, when I put the red tablecloth on, because that's what the priest wanted—to have the special tablecloth."

He looked at the shiny velvet cloth with its soft carpet feel.

"First I set the tablecloth and then I fringed the holy water, just like he said, just like before the Christmas pageant."

He looked at the holy water's silver basin.

"I remember the rehearsals, when Barnum spoke about Baby Jesus. Then the three wise men brought their presents to the manger. But that was all before Rommel fell, before the manger scene was cancelled."

When Henry remembered the rehearsals, he saw the white styrofoam bits they used as snow. The manger was light and creaked when he hauled it back and forth to the shed. Though when it was inside the church, it filled up the whole space beneath the third Station of the Cross.

"When I put the manger in, Jesus looked down on Himself as a baby. Jesus watched Himself from the windows when Barnum spoke about the crowded inn and the presents with the three wise men. Then the three wise men spoke about the one shining star they followed, and it always made me think of the stars I watched in the lockhouse above the mattress. I wonder if they helped guide me here too?"

He couldn't see the sky. The shingles above him weren't broken like in the lockhouse, and he knew the ceiling would never show him anything higher here. Not the unfolding hills or the sparkling night, so he thought of Mabel instead. He thought of how he'd watched her all during rehearsals.

"Because she was Mary and not herself then. She was Mary and beautiful and not herself at the rehearsals. She was wrapped in white robes like Jesus, and seemed not like herself at all. And I could un-wrap her if she came. I could un-wrap her all the way."

Looking out the window, he rubbed his thigh thinking of Mabel. With his eyes, he followed the black road all the way to the left. That was the way Mabel had walked whenever she wasn't picked up after praying. On those nights, he watched her walk up the road that followed a hill and turned at a bend. Opening the door, a gust of wind rushed in, ruffling his shirt. Peach-colored light was lifting the darkness from the mountains so that it looked like daylight's brighter skin was being revealed bit by bit. Just like when Mabel lifted her skirt that night, when he saw down to her pearly white underwear—and to her seam beneath.

Standing in the doorway, he traced the rising color above the trees. *And what if I walk to the left too? What if I walk all the way around the bend to where Mabel is?*

He edged out on the first step. His hand trailed the railing.

"Then I could be at her window. Then I could watch her in her white robes and un-wrap her from being someone else. I could un-wrap her all the way."

The peach sunrise warmed him. Farther down the valley, Henry watched glittering bits of snow high up in the trees. The bare limbs were patched with ice, and when the wind got the trees swaying, Henry saw through their tips to the river.

"The river is made of ice now. The glittering bits are like stars." Watching the river, he felt like he was back on his mattress in the lockhouse. He watched the glittering river far off. "I could show Mabel the bits too, if she were here. We could watch the night in-between the rafters like how we watched it with the heat. And she could sing while we watched. She could sing."

Henry saw Mabel in the lockhouse then. He kneeled beside her on the mattress as she sang to him. He held her waist as they both watched the stars pulse one by one in the night. "But that's only after I bring her back. We'll go to the lockhouse only after the church, only after she sees the cardinal. Because if the cardinal stays long enough, she could ask him to pray for her mother?"

He imagined Mabel kneeling before the cardinal. Her head was bowed, showing her black hair parted. "The cardinal must be as big as the altar, with a red velvet robe to be so close to the Lord." Henry rubbed his hands thinking of the velvet robe. It was as bright as any fire, and he watched Mabel in his mind warm her prayers against the cardinal's flame. "The cardinal will bless anyone who comes before him, so I must make Mabel the first one."

In a moment, he was back inside scrubbing the pews much faster on the other side. As he scrubbed, his strong hands drew zeroes across the glistening wood until the conversation of his arms against the shining pews spun around him with a steady hum.

"She'll be the first. I'll make sure of it."

The pews shook with such a vibration that a hurried trembling rose to his cheeks—until he felt like his lips moved on their own a moment. Lifting his hands to his teeth, he felt the skin rise in a broad arch. Scrubbing even harder, pushing up and out, he heard his teeth hum as he brought his arms back in, drawing out each countless arc.

"Mmmmmm," he said and felt his cheeks quiver against his jaw. "Hmmmmm," he said and drew the zeroes up and out. "Mmmmmm-hm-mmmm," he said, and leaning forward, he pushed until he knew every part of the pews. Until every zero on every plank rose through his arms to his face so that his cheeks hummed with a light chattering laughter. He thought he heard himself laughing, and he realized he was done much faster with the pews than before. In the basement, he dumped the bucket in the sink, so he could get his coat and hat and gloves. Rommel had found him clothes in the boxes months ago, and when Henry saw Rommel's empty cot—with the wax steeples and angels still on the blanket—he remembered the words the priest had muttered about his sermon earlier.

The priest spoke something about, "Traitors to their kind." Then he'd mentioned the death penalty and the sins of the fallen, and Henry had never heard what the death penalty was, but he didn't ask. He thought the priest would tell him in his sermon. Henry hadn't missed a sermon since he'd arrived, so he could wait. It was still early. Even the cars that usually passed outside hadn't appeared. The tall silver Amtrak that came through each morning hadn't passed with its shuffling clacking sound. So that when he stepped to the sidewalk, drifting down the—*one two three four*—steps, he felt as light and free as he'd ever been. He didn't limp and looked to the mountains to see all the peach loveliness lift into the air. The darkness was gone. The trees were white and glittering, though he still found the icy gutters as hard as in the morning when he shoveled the sidewalk all the way to the road.

"It won't get much warmer than this though." He pressed his right boot against the black ice, and his foot didn't tingle. It hadn't tingled for a while, and he wasn't used to that absent feeling. Each day of his life had always been filled with a thousand racing needles. They shot up through his toes and knees, scattering like buckshot through his hip, but now it was gone. And it was this absence that made him skip once by himself. Henry skipped and landed beyond the black ice, and the tingling didn't race up his right leg, so he skipped again. He skipped once and then twice, skipping up the road that led away from church because there wasn't anyone to see.

"This is a different way than to Barnum's." The words passed from his lips into a white steamy mist in front of him. "I'm going up farther into the valleys and dells. And I've only ever seen up here before when I sledded that night on the hill. Now here I am, up farther than I've ever been."

With each step, he felt the river falling away. He stepped up and down, smashing the harder tufts of ice beneath him, and it was this crunching sound that had him walking faster along the side of the road where the snow was swept by the trucks and plows. He usually watched the trucks from the church those snowy nights. He liked how the plows swept the snow into waves over the edge of the road, and when he remembered the trucks riding by with their bright lights, they seemed like stars to him. Like bright yellow stars shining through the storm, and he thought Barnum, more than anyone else, would like to stand here with him, thinking of the yellow stars moving on the edge of the road.

"He'd see all the snowy waves and it would be just like standing in the rapids then—in Carter's Coffin—with the river rushing over."

Henry looked back to the church. It was farther away than he'd ever seen it. In town, the houses were clustered near the church. He'd never realized there were so many. He couldn't possibly count them on his hands. But from up here, the houses sagged fewer between. Snow clung to rooftops and gutters as fences drew jagged lines back from the road. So that he had to stop now to look with his hands brought up to his eyes to shield the sun. The light streaked in rays off the unbroken lawns and left silver traces when he squinted. When he closed his eyes to stop the glare, he still saw silver traces. He even saw the black sludgy road when he closed his eyes. It was a deep line between things, dividing the world. Though he realized that if he kept his head down, the glare wasn't so bad. When he saw a driveway, he followed it with his eyes, to see if Mabel might live there because he didn't know where her house might be.

"Her window will be white though. It'll be white and glittering." Saying the words comforted him. Because with the town far off and quiet and the wind dying down—now that he was sheltered by the high and wide drifts—the soft river sound had left him alone, and he didn't know where to go.

"Her window will be white and I'll see inside and she'll be on her knees praying that I come." He stopped as another driveway stretched off to his left. Snow dripped in white sleeves from the roof. In the front lawn, a boy stood in a blue snowsuit. Henry hadn't seen anyone up this early except the priest, so he watched the boy sled down a small crest. The boy raced down again and again until Henry counted to six. "But he ain't Mabel. Mabel will be in her room waiting for me, praying. And I'll know it'll be her because I'll feel her un-bodied eyes in the air. She'll be watching me."

Farther up around the bend, he saw another driveway a hundred yards to the right. It sloped down to a stone house behind a hedge, and he liked the look of the stone walls and corners so much, he crossed the black sludgy road to look closer. As he reached the middle line, skipping over it, his right leg suddenly throbbed. Pressing his hand to his hip, he squeezed the muscle until the throbbing went away. "It's nothing," he said and touched his lips. When he made it across, his leg tingled again, and he had to remember the small grace he'd gotten from Mabel walking in the aisle. *Just remember the grace she gave you. Then think of all the grace you'll get with her waiting by her window, praying, because this might be her house.*

He stood at the driveway's edge.

"Just look at the stone," he said, surveying the house. "Mabel liked my lockhouse. She knew the stones could protect her like I could protect her." Henry saw the side of the house from the road. The front porch wrapped around into shadow, and with the window glittering and throwing handfuls of light into the yard, he thought there must be a candle inside. "Maybe it's the tallow I gave her? And it's low." He reached into his pockets to take out another candle, but there was nothing. His hands were empty, and he held them to his face to warm his cheeks.

The house was etched against a towering pine, and with the hill rising behind it and the sludgy road stretched out front, he thought it looked like the lockhouse for a moment—and he knew that Mabel had been comfortable in his lockhouse; she'd been happy. *I'd passed my hands along her bumps till she was un-bodied and floating above me. So her own house must be like my lockhouse; it must be comfortable and strong.*

"It should make her float too. Her house will let the glitter come in like in-between the shingles. So this is it. This has to be it." He looked at the smooth stone walls and stepped off the road and then walked along the yard to where handfuls of light fell in the shadow of the hill, below the window. "So I'll just sit here till she wakes, till she comes to find me watching for her."

The handfuls of light fell to the yard at his feet. He was below the window as the wind rushed down the hill, racing through every part of him. The picnic table he sat on was covered in snow, and he shivered as he rocked back and forth to ward away the cold. It was only the light that he could see in the top of the room that kept him going. He saw the white ceiling and oak rafters and knew that this was it—where he should wait.

"I can see the light that Mabel must be wearing," he said, shivering as he spoke. "And maybe she's un-bodied in the rafters even now. Maybe even this early she sees me." He put his hands in his pockets and repeated, "She sees me, she sees me, she sees me." As he whispered, he felt the wind rise again as the light flickered at his feet. "*She sees me*. I know it. *She sees me, she sees me, she sees me*. Because I'm here; I'm with her, waiting, to protect her."

19

ENRY SAT IN THE SNOW outside the window for much longer than he expected. He sat there as the sun rose over the mountains, as the snow dripped from the rooftop. Once, he thought he heard voices inside the house, and he rose to look. But with the window closed and the wind whipping against the hill, he wasn't sure if he really heard anything, or if anyone was inside. Only the white ceiling showed beyond the window. Vague shadows seemed thrown against it. The shadows reminded him of the church with the candles along the walls, and he realized after sitting there for as long as he could that he had to get back to the church and attend the service. So when he left after not seeing Mabel, after she didn't come to the window as he thought she might, he limped once stumbling over the middle line on the sludgy road. When he looked down at his right leg and tried to raise it as high as his left, he limped again, and thought she must not have been un-bodied in the air after all. That she must not have been praying to see him at the window, and he limped whenever he thought of her not as he pretended.

"But she'll still be first," he said, feeling his mouth. His lips were cracked and dabs of blood showed on his hand. Rounding the bend, he saw a sea of cars crowding the road near the church. The parking lot was packed, and he thought he must have missed the cardinal. That all the people must have already come, and the priest must have had to take their coats and hats and scarves himself.

Henry's stomach fell away from him then when he thought of all the coats and hats and scarves piled in the priest's arms, especially after the priest had to work so hard on his sermon. But when Henry got closer, he heard a great many voices. He saw a great many churchgoers too. They were gathered in a swarming choir on the porch. Their boots trampled the icy drifts into a hovering white powder as they sang, and as he got closer, weaving through the crowded sidewalk, their words rose in a clear chorus.

> *Amazing Grace, how sweet the sound,*
> *that saved a wretch like me*
> *I once was lost, but now am found,*
> *was blind, but now, I see*

It was the song he liked more than any other, the song Hiram sang those nights when the radio played nothing but static. The song with the word *grace* in it, for when he heard the word, he thought of his own grace and of the fleeting bit Mabel had given him when he passed her that day in the aisle—and his limp fell away from him. Arching his back out, he stretched his arms and moved through the crowd, striding toward the door.

"*Henry!* I've been looking everywhere for you." Henry looked down and saw Barnum's cheeks glazed with sweat. "I been here the last hour and nobody seen you so I run down to the lockhouse." Barnum panted for a moment. "But the lockhouse was empty, so I run back up, and the priest says he seen you walking up the Coulter Road?"

"He saw me?"

"Sure did. Said you were walking faster than he'd ever seen."

"I was skipping." Henry arched his eyebrows when he said it, like he'd seen Barnum do before.

"Well, he ain't seen nobody walk that fast in the snow—especially you."

"Was he mad?"

"No, he just wondered where you were going. And he said you was just gliding along, like you weren't even touching the ground."

> *Twas Grace that taught my heart to fear,*
> *and Grace, my fears relieved.*
> *How precious did that Grace appear,*
> *the hour I first believed*

The choir called above Barnum's voice, and Henry looked at all the singers. Some of them smiled when they spotted him, and some stretched their hands out to touch his shoulders. The touching was what they wanted to do most—the touching above the singing and smiling. Though after some of them had touched him, their voices grew higher and more forceful as if they had the answer now to their question, as if his presence had solved some greater mystery.

"And I wondered why you walked up the Coulter Road. But then I thought you was probably sledding down Coulter Hill. Is that what you done?"

"Coulter Hill?"

"Didn't you ride down it like when we road Clarke's Hill and almost Jimson's Hill before? You remember—when me and you and Mabel seen that crazy train—that red-painted train that ain't nothing like the Amtrak."

"*Mabel*," Henry whispered her name as the singing swelled over them. "Where is she? She don't pray no more like she used to."

> *When we've been here ten thousand years,*
> *bright shining as the sun*
> *We've no less days to sing God's praise,*
> *than when we first begun*

"She ain't been in school neither. I think she got pulled out when her Momma got better. At least that's what they say."

"Pulled out?" Henry took a step up into all the swaying people. "But I sat for her and waited in the handfuls of light?"

Henry took another step up and another until he was on the front porch among the loudest singers. Their hands were outstretched, and as he stood in the middle, he felt his right leg tingle to his foot. He could tell he was leaning on it again and that his right leg was coiling beneath him like before.

"I sat there for her. And I thought she'd know it because she'd be floating above me—that she would feel me."

"*Feel you?*" Barnum had followed Henry up the steps.

"And I was gonna sit there for as long as it took." Henry held up all ten fingers, showing Barnum. "I was gonna come back even the next day and maybe the night and sit there for days and days until she showed, so she knew I was waiting. *But I knew I had to work here. I knew I had to come back for this,*" he said, shaking his arms out at his sides. "When I could have just sat there in the light, waiting for her."

"Sit where, Henry?"

Amazing Grace, how sweet the sound,
that saved a wretch like me

The chorus had started again, and the churchgoers packed in tighter around Henry until he could only feel his leg. Only the tingling in his right leg rose up from his boot. He hadn't felt the tingling since Mabel gave him that first bit of grace when his leg straightened out. *But now I'm standing in the middle of them again, in the middle of the rising heat from all them bodies, and not one part of that heat is hers—not one.*

He turned to the street to look away from the church but couldn't get away from the sound. The song had merged with every noise surrounding him—and he could only think of Mabel. He only saw her walking away that night when he stood at the door. *Because that was it,* he knew, *the last night I saw her. When we touched, and the heat passed between us on the pew.*

"On *our* pew, and now all these people are gonna go in *my* church and sit where *I* touched the pews, where *I* drew a zero over everything." His eyes were closing in. Black smudges appeared in the corners of what he saw. "And it's *mine* inside. Everything is mine and set apart for me. It's not fair." Henry pressed his hand to his head to try and stop the darkness. Shaking his head from side to side made him feel better. He saw clear again and felt his leg tingling with the arms and hands pressed around him.

"What isn't fair?" Barnum said.

"She's not gonna be the first to see him anymore. And they're gonna ruin everything. They're gonna cross over everything we already touched."

Barnum looked up at Henry and mouthed some words, but the sound of the singers repeating the song had risen above his voice.

"And they're gonna know the special spot then," Henry said, "where we passed the heat between us—me and Mabel."

"*The heat?*" Barnum shouted as the crowd quieted down a bit.

Henry pressed his hand against his hip. He felt the tingling rise in needles across his thigh. "Then their voices are gonna rise up to where we both floated in the rafters, when we were free. And the un-bodied feeling is gonna fall away from everything."

Henry saw Barnum watch him as he brought his hand to his lips. Henry's lips were cracked and flaking and smeared in blood. An iron taste like pennies coated his tongue when he licked his lips, when he thought of the church falling away from him.

"Jesus in the white robes is gonna look down on me then, into the very center of me—and He's gonna see that Mabel's gone even though He already knows it. Even though He already let it come to pass."

"She sure is gone. Her Momma just pulled her out. Just like that."

Henry shook his head because the blackness was threatening to crowd his eyes again. "So then Jesus is gonna talk with *her* voice again. He's gonna talk with her voice all about, '*Why?*' About, '*Why I let her go?*' About, '*Why I didn't follow her that night around the bend forever?*' I know it. But *He* let it come to pass, didn't He?" Henry stared at Barnum and then reached out and shook Barnum's shoulders.

"Who's gonna say that?" Barnum said, quivering beneath Henry's strong hands.

"Jesus." As Henry let go, he wiped the blood from his lips. "When He talks to me."

> *I once was lost, but now am found,*
> *was blind, but now I see*

Barnum shuffled back from Henry. Looking up, he bit his lip.

"He's gonna talk to me, can't you see? It's just gonna be me."

Barnum smiled and rubbed his hand against his brow. He was pressed against Henry by the throng of bodies and had to raise his hands along Henry's chest; otherwise, the people would have crushed him. "But it ain't just you, Henry. You got all of us now. Just like I got you. I got you and I got the river. Because I think it's more like the rocks in the rapids here than anything else." Barnum giggled at all the bodies pressing in. "I even fell once and it was like this. All the air came out of me—so that I had to raise my hands up to let the air come in—just to breathe."

As Barnum shouted, more people surged up from the lawn. More arms and hands swayed around Henry, and as the street filled with cars stopping in the middle of the road and honking for spots, Henry felt his right leg tingle so that when he turned to look at all the people, it looked like they were circling around him in a row of zeroes. Their arms stretched out into lines, and the lines ran into larger zeroes until the zeroes covered the whole length of the lawn and porch—until everyone was inside a zero.

"But they can't be in here with me. Them's my zeroes and Mabel's zeroes and Jesus' zeroes. And that's it. That's it."

The final singing note wavered above the whole swirling mass. The lingering sound, echoed up and up, and some of the voices went even higher at the end and held the last note much longer so that a brighter, louder hum spread among them. Though when this final hum had finished, someone said: *"There's Henry! He'll let us in!"*

And another voice said: *"There's Henry! There's Henry!"* Until they all started shouting and smiling so that the last of the song vibrated through them again.

Henry heard the voices, and as he turned his head, he saw the whole lot of them swirling around him like when he was in the river fishing and the fish jumped and drew a zero around his body. *I was alone then, I was separate, and it's like that now, being among them. I'm with them, but I'm not. Because there's only my leg now. Only my leg coiling and tingling beneath me. Only my leg comforts me. Only my leg tells me that I'm different, that I'm set apart. Cause even Barnum's against me now, even Barnum will cry out with the rest of them, saying, "There's Henry! There's Henry!" just to be like them, just to be gathered in.*

And sure enough, when Henry looked down, even Barnum's high piercing voice chanted along, *"There's Henry! There's Henry!"* so that Henry looked at Barnum's head where the boy had fallen that day in the lockhouse and didn't feel as bad about the cut that drizzled blood when they pulled back and forth over the mannequin.

"The mannequin," he whispered, and when he said the word, he felt the soft canvas bumps against his waist; he smelled the river water deep in the body. But then Barnum started calling, *"There's Henry! There's Henry!"* and it chased the image away. Barnum had his hands on Henry's ribs, holding himself up so that Henry had to step away from him into the swirling mass toward the front door.

Henry knew the door wasn't locked and wondered why they were all standing here without going in. But it was a ceremony now, and he remembered how the priest had talked about the ceremony earlier. Because when the priest said the word, "cer-e-mon-y," and drew out the long thin syllables, purring between his lips, Henry thought it sounded like how Hiram said: *Flor-i-da* and *Kor-e-a*. So he thought *cer-e-mon-y* was a place you could visit until the priest said, "The cer-e-mon-y this Sunday will start with you."

Then Henry knew the *cer-e-mon-y* wasn't a place at all, but a moment, and that the moment would start with him.

"The churchgoers know this is a special day. When we have a special day, we try to mark it with a special color or banner or with a special gesture. Gladys—you know Gladys—she prays afternoons near the front; well, Gladys will start the choir in a rendition of 'Amazing Grace.' When they've gone through it once, they'll want you to open the doors."

Henry had said, "Mmmmm-hmmmm," and continued scrubbing as the priest walked away, humming the tune to himself. And now, as Henry stood at the door, he heard that same humming behind him. The cries from the choir had died down so that it seemed as if the whole world had died into one long ashy hum.

He stood with his hand on the handle and heard the river again. He heard the water in the rapids rushing against the rocks on the edge of the ice. He hadn't heard the river in so long. When he'd sat in the handfuls of light at the picnic table, there had only been the sound of the wind rushing down the hill. Even on the walk back, he'd only heard his feet slushing through the ice. He hadn't heard anything until the singing started. But now that the singing had died down, he heard the river rushing beyond the trees, and he felt it in his leg. It moved up through his foot and thigh to his stomach. The river felt like it was flowing through every part of him, that it gave him the strength to watch these people crowd into his church—into the church he had set aside for him and Mabel.

Because all these people are gonna sit on the same pews and look at the same Jesus and maybe hear the same voice inside them that I did. And I'm gonna have to stand there and watch it. I'll have to take their coats and hats and scarves, and I'll have to feel the tingling rise up through me like the river—and I'll take in the strength of it too. I have a strength that is not like these people at all. A strength not even like this church or priest or cardinal, my strength is like the river. My strength comes from inside me, just like the river, from inside my shorter leg.

"*Henry's got it!*" Someone cheered when Henry lifted the handle, and as Henry stepped in, opening the doors, the crowd came in humming and buzzing with words and praise, and when each person gave him their coats and hats and scarves, they touched him on the shoulder saying: "Bless you, Henry." Or: "Thank you, Henry." Or: "By the grace of God, Henry," and he hurried to the coatroom with Barnum helping. The boy hung the coats on the hangers and watched Henry work. Henry moved smoothly again. He felt the river rise through him and brought his right leg up as fast and swift as his left. The tingling in his hip had died away as the church filled, and when he had a chance to look, he couldn't see where Mabel had ever sat. He couldn't see the pew where they'd passed the heat between them. He stood in the back as the church filled up and shut the door to keep the wind from rushing in. The wind made the candles flicker, and Henry thought about the wind edging in at the cracks all while the priest began his sermon—because the wind felt like the river rushing in, surrounding him.

It feels like fingers, and he felt the wind like the river rising up, covering his back and shoulders and neck, like when he sat in Carter's Coffin in the rapids. He shivered with his back to the door to feel the fingers of the river rushing in with the wind. The fingers moved over his knees and ankles and cheeks, and the current even worked over his lips so that he felt a smile rising on his face. It was a smile brought out by the river—by the hands of the river—and not his own hands floating at his sides.

So he didn't even look at Jesus in the third Station of the Cross during the whole service. He didn't even look at the cardinal when the cardinal was announced, when all the churchgoers swooned in the pews and Henry had to pick up a lady in front of him from fainting. He didn't even look at the cardinal when the cardinal said some somber things just like what Father Whitney had said, about, "SINNERS," and, "KILLERS," and, "TRAITORS TO THEIR KIND," because it sounded like the cardinal said all these words in capital letters, shouting into the center of Henry's soul. Though as the cardinal said each word, pointing to the crowd, Henry felt the letters dissolve inside him into nothing. There were no letters now. The letters were swept aside from his body by his fast river leg, by the tingling river moving through him. Even when the priest offered the body and blood of Christ to the people who stood and swayed, spinning out from him on both sides, he didn't look. He was beyond looking now.

He was beyond watching the ceremony of things.

So that when Barnum helped take the coats down after the service was done, Henry didn't even look at him either. He didn't look at the churchgoers even after everyone said it was the best service they'd ever heard and the greatest warmth they'd ever felt. They said all of this smiling to Henry as they touched him. But Henry did not look at them and did not speak and did not kneel as everyone else kneeled when the cardinal was led by his handlers out to the white Cadillac waiting in the middle of the road. Henry did not do any of this. But he did stand there for longer than anyone else. He did stand there leaning on his right leg after everyone left, and as he swept up the scraps and bits of slush with the mop, he listened all night to the river of his leg.

Part Three

Part Third

20

HENRY FOUND THE LOCKHOUSE like he left it. He hadn't been back since that night with Mabel when he first passed his hands along her bumps, and he wondered what it'd be like without her. *She'd been un-bodied then*, he remembered, *and I'd crouched behind her, pressing my waist against her back.* Yet he couldn't remember if he'd seen it that night or not—the mannequin—and if it was in the lockhouse. He hadn't seen it by the window where he left it. He couldn't find it in the canvas tarp either. In fact, the room had been changed without the mannequin, and there was only Mabel to touch then. Everything else was the same.

The radio was as he left it. The sink and kitchen were the same. The windows still looked out on the canal on one end and on the railroad and mountains on the other. The kitchen glass was still blacked out. Withered bits of cardboard hung in the panes.

"And the water?" He wondered about the cistern in the basement. "Is the water like I left it?" He wasn't sure. But when he went down that first night, he saw the junk still piled around the cistern's edge. He'd arranged it that way to keep the rats away. A rusted box spring and bicycle frame, an old metal locker and broken dresser drawer all looked in their arrangement like a miniature city. As he traced their jagged outline, the pieces reminded him of Baltimore's harbor.

"It's *just* like Baltimore," and he saw the city again and the errands he ran for Hiram. Often he went for groceries. Or to the shoeshine with Hiram's boots. And always on Sunday mornings, he walked the docks to where the men with ice-cooled trucks sat by their bushels of crabs. All the crabs were heaped in baskets. Hiram gave Henry enough money for a half bushel—which was a lot of crabs—and when Henry leaned over the baskets, all the blue crabs were pinched together until the sun made bay foam ooze from their bellies. Henry carried the basket to Hiram with the boiling pot to steam them up, to turn their blue shiny shells to red rusted shells right there in front of him.

"And then the picking." Henry remembered picking the red shells from their bodies. He saw crab guts and belly roe and claws heaped in mounds on the table. He liked pulling the cartilage inside the claws to make the big pinchers work. And often, he'd play like that until Hiram told him to stop, until Hiram had him concentrating on the picking instead because Hiram picked much faster than Henry.

"I like the knuckle meat most." Hiram said, his hands wiry as they pried open the minute stores of muscle and tendon, and then when he took a long drink from his colored water, he said, "*Ahhhhh*," when the cold liquor went down. With the way he said, "*Ahhhhh*," Henry though it sounded like bay water oozing from him, just like from the crab bodies he picked hour after hour.

The picking was for the crab cakes Hiram made, and when Henry was back upstairs in the lockhouse, he caught a whiff of spicy bay water coming off the stove. It mixed with an oily lingering that made him lick his lips and shake his hands. He still felt the crab picking in his fingers, just like the pew scrubbing. He saw all the zeroes on the grainy planks like the pages in his mind because he knew the pages held the heat that passed between him and Mabel. *It was the same heat those churchgoers tried to sit on and pray into. But they can't take the heat away like they wanted. And if only they knew about me and Mabel, if only they knew.* So he decided he would not go back to church; he would never go back. Shaking out both legs, he clenched his fists.

"I don't even want to sit beneath Jesus in His white robes anymore. Especially after the crowd sat in all my zeroes. Especially after the priest and cardinal talked about forgiveness that's not even here, that's up in the air somewhere, up where we can't even see it. I don't even think Jesus would say such things, that forgiveness is up in the air. That it's not set aside down here, in-between the lines of our lives."

His right leg quivered when he remembered looking into the cardinal's creased face. He hadn't been able to shake the image of the cardinal this whole week. *The cardinal looked like Rommel with his pinched-up eyes, with how Rommel had to throw his hips out and bring his feet under him when he walked.* "Rommel even tried to break into my zero." That was something he couldn't forget, when Rommel tried to break into the zero that held him and Mabel, and that was why Rommel had fallen away.

"But the priest will want to know why I fell away too." He grabbed a handful of leaves and tossed them on the glowing coals. "And when Barnum sees I'm not at the service today—at the service right now—he might tell them where I been. So I'll have to watch for Barnum. Because even if they do find me, I'm not going back. Not without Mabel praying there. Not without Mabel sitting so I can see her from every pew."

When he spoke about Mabel, he stood mesmerized as a blue flame spread along the stove's leaves, curling the crinkling ends into black flaky fists. He threw another handful on and watched as the leaves curled up, curling into black fists that shook apart, scattering atop the coals. After the last handful, he kneeled to look closer and heard a speeding car along the road: it was a late churchgoer rushing to pray.

With this last rushing sound, he knew he could build the fire up higher in a few hours once darkness fell, once this easy warmth—so unusual this early in March—was pushed away. It had been so warm, the ice along the riverbanks had broken. All week the river had flowed louder. All week the rapids had roared with a hum that Henry let come back to him after he'd released the image of Mabel praying in her pew. He let go of Mabel and let the river return. *Because the river sound goes on and on. The river sound is not up in the air and away in a place where I have to search to find it.* "The river sound is here," and he touched his right leg, thinking of the river. Then touching his belly, he said, "The river sound is in here too. And maybe the river sound has always been in here?"

Closing his eyes, he heard the river rushing over the land. As he listened, the wind crept in the door, so the river smell washed over his curly hair and cheeks, his crinkled ears and lips, until it felt like he was kneeling on a hill overlooking the river and that the river was high up with him. *The river runs all the way up to the sky too. And if it runs all the way down to the earth, it's not anywhere but here.* He touched his chest because the rushing sound was like the blood he often heard when he'd slept on the cot in church.

"When I couldn't sleep, I'd listen to the furnace and its whispering flame. Then I'd tug my dangling thing thinking of Mabel. I'd tug until the release fell over me." Henry saw, when he held his ear to his pillow after the tugging was over, the blood rushing in his skull. The blood rushed harder then softer, and he wondered if Rommel heard the blood rushing then too? But Rommel was always asleep. The air came from Rommel's lips until Henry rolled back to listen to the furnace's quiet song. He loved to hear the blue flames twist and touch together. The flames pushed a brilliant light between the furnace cracks, a light covering his arms and legs, his cot and blanket, until he only heard the whispering flames. They were like the sounds the river made rushing by now—rising through the door—whispering to him. "It's always whispering to me."

With his eyes closed, the river was speaking to him like the small voice of Jesus had that day in the church, when Jesus spoke like Mabel inside him. *But the river isn't Mabel—and she isn't even here anymore.* Though when he heard the river rushing through the valley, he knew the river was here instead. "It's inside. *With me.*" He felt his body floating in the watery sound and knew that he was un-bodied now too: that he was separate. *I'm un-bodied and floating. I'm following the current down to where the current hugs the rocks, and the rocks hold the water, so that the river doesn't uproot the earth. I'm floating down to hold the rocks and river together.*

He heard the wind rising from the canal. A minty smell blew through every part of him. "I'm holding myself down with the rocks. Down where the rocks hold the earth and river apart. This is the zero I've found." In his mind, water spun in circles around the rocks before flowing off and away. "This is the zero of the earth holding the river up. And this is the river letting the water fall away."

We're separate now, he knew, *me and Mabel. She's not here anymore. But I still have her; I do.* He saw Mabel floating in his mind. Mabel was blue like the feeling that flowed around him because he was whiter and all limbs now. His legs were the same length, and his arms stretched out so that he was a collection of white limbs that a vast blue vapor held together. The vapor flowed around him until he knew that Mabel was this vapor. "Mabel is the air. But not just air. She's much more than just air."

Raising his hands in the lockhouse, he trailed his fingers along the blue vapor in his mind. The blue vapor absorbed him and held him, and he felt all his limbs were even and steady in his mind with how they tingled. "And it's not just my right leg now. It's not just the same tingling. This is a different tingling than before. A tingling like the river passing through me, passing through the world."

With this last word, his eyes opened, and he lost Mabel's blue vapor. Though he wasn't sure if he was still un-bodied and floating in his mind or just kneeling in the lockhouse, and when he brought his hands to his eyes, pressing the lids open, he heard a small voice inside say, '*When?*' The small voice was like the call of Jesus, when Jesus had spoken as Mabel, asking, '*Why? Why didn't you follow her? Why didn't you go?*'

That was the last day he heard the voice of Jesus, after the heat passed between them. He had thought there would be many days like that to come, many days when they would meet and touch, so they could feel they were floating and free. And on all those future days, he'd already imagined how his legs would feel: *They'd feel like how Mabel made them feel—before the beginning—with each touch and rubbing.*

But then she'd left. She'd walked up the road and hadn't come back, and now the voice inside him was smaller and sounded like Mabel. It was rising from the river, and it was the river's voice, and it was Jesus' voice too, and it was Mabel's voice all in one. They all spoke to him now, saying, '*When, Henry?*' He closed his eyes to feel Mabel's blue vapory voice. But he couldn't feel or know anything except that he was un-bodied and bodied all at once. That Mabel was always with him and not always with him. That the river was whispering and flowing away but also rising and returning to him. And he didn't know how things could both be separate and so close.

"Because of the zero of the rocks," he said, "that's why." As if naming the sermon he'd spoken, the tingling of his whole body rose up with the river. "*The zero of the rocks is both life and death.*" His teeth were uncovered now, and his lips trembled to feel the muscles rising across his face, and he knew the service was over. He heard the bells far off. Though he wondered who would get the people their coats and hats and scarves? Who would sweep out the nave? And change the candles for the next day and the next? Swaying on his knees, he felt the wet bristles on his fingers. He smelled the waxy soap bubbles surround him, and his leg tingled...before dissolving. It had dissolved, just as quickly as the coiling had begun, skipping along the road.

It's gone. The muscle just eased out, after saying the sermon of the rocks. He felt both legs strong and straight, and when he looked around the lockhouse, he knew Mabel must have helped him. *She must have watched from the air with her grace. She must have given me another small bit of it,* and he knew he couldn't disappoint her now. Not with her touch. Not when he had to straighten out the canal like before.

"But I'll be more careful. So the man with the walkie-talkie don't chain the door like before." At once, he knew he had to sweep out the dust and straighten the tarp, so it wasn't creased like Rommel's face. At the door, he looked across the canal, and his stomach fell away to see how the weeds had crept back and how countless leaves had filled up all his earlier work. Looking to the forest, he heard the river hum beyond the trees. A new growth of fern and ivy spun out in circles as far as he could see. And above everything, an afternoon mist smelled like rain falling later. So closing his eyes, he forgot about all the work he'd have to do. He forgot about all the hauling and digging and threshing still deep in his body, and he listened to the world instead. He listened as the world unfolded for him, pressing into his skin and bones, his eyelids and jawline, until he heard that small voice of Jesus inside him like the small voice of Mabel rise again, saying, '*When, Henry?*' And he knew his work was much more urgent than before.

21

"**THE PRIEST HAD TO STAY MUCH LONGER** than he wanted because all them gray-haired ladies were worried about you." Barnum had come from town after church, just as Henry thought, though Henry didn't see him arrive. He only heard Barnum's high-pitched voice when the boy appeared by the lockhouse. "And you shoulda seen the tears in their eyes. Them old ladies were walking around blind, coats hanging from their arms, bumping into pews, till the priest asked me when I seen you last."

"He asked you?"

"He knew I worked with you in the coatroom and that we went sledding."

"He knew we went sledding?"

"I guess Rommel told him—or Mabel maybe. But he weren't worried."

"Who weren't?"

"Father Whitney; he said you'd come back. Said it was only a week gone by so far, and he knew your kind—that you'd come back."

"*My kind?*" Henry whispered.

The sky was turning from its brighter open-blue to a later falling-blue, and Henry looked to see if Barnum had talked to the others about the canal. Scrunching up his eyes, Henry locked his attention on Barnum to see if he told the truth, but as soon as he saw the boy teetering on the canal—in his white Sunday school shirt and brown jacket—he heard Jesus' small voice inside him and had to look away. The voice said, '*When, Henry?*'

In hearing it, what Henry really thought the voice meant was, '*When are you going to fix the canal?*' Or, '*When are you going to do some work?*' So he bent to his task much harder as Barnum stood on the crumbly lip.

"The priest even grabbed my arm after all them gray-haired ladies shuffled off. Said, 'I seen you running with him, if you know where he is, you should tell me.' But I didn't. Not like what most people think—because even Momma says I talk too much."

Henry didn't say anything about how Barnum talked. He only remembered how the boy chanted with the rest of them before the cardinal's special mass, when they wanted Henry to open the door. That was when Henry didn't mind so much the cut Barnum had gotten on his head after they pulled on the mannequin. He tried to forget the boy's chanting and focused on the log beneath him and rolled it to the edge of the canal.

"You don't think I talk too much, do you?"

Henry looked down and rubbed the lines in the wood with his fingers.

"If I did talk too much you could tell me. That'd be something I wouldn't mind, so I could learn. Because we're still partners, ain't we?"

Henry saw the buttons on Barnum's jacket were mismatched, and his nails were bitten to the ends, and as Henry breathed in once and then twice, he counted the—*one two three*—clouds drifting in the sky above Barnum's face. *Linen in the sky.* "We're still partners," Henry said, before hoisting the log up in one shuddering heave.

"Boy, you sure like fixing things." Barnum smiled as the log landed beside him. "That's why I brought you this shovel." Barnum had hidden a long-handled shovel at his feet when he arrived but held it out for Henry. "I wasn't sure if we were still partners." Barnum shook the long handle and it looked awkward in his hands. "I bet it's better than just working with your hands."

Henry held the handle a second to feel its weight, and when he sunk the blade into the mud, the shovel made a *whummp* sound going in. When it did, Henry felt the shattered earth rise along the handle to his arms, shuddering through his shoulders. Lifting the shovel, he brought away a heap of mud with some roots cut off, smelling of sassafras and fern, and it was like the earth was pouring out of its cold slumber. A stew of mint and cinnamon mixed above him; the grass stems were like the green onions Hiram used to chop and put in the crab cakes. "To give it that little kick," Hiram always said. When Henry thought of Hiram, he dug the shovel in with another *whummp*, edging the blade around a stump he'd been having a hard go of. Working with the shovel brought a loose feeling to his arms, and digging in again and again, before he knew it, he hauled the stump up like pulling a tooth from the ground.

"Jesus, you work with that thing like you been doing it all your life."

"It's easy." When Henry held the shovel, testing its weight, the scar above his lip flushed a deep red, and a smile crept over his face. Though before he could enjoy it, he brought the shovel down with another bright *whummp* and wedged the blade in the mud.

"Just wait till you try the hoe." Barnum held up the other tool he'd hidden at his feet and made a motion with his hands like pulling in string or fishing line. Henry set the shovel aside and felt the hoe. When he placed it in the leaves, he pulled back like what Barnum did, and at once, he felt the earth pulled under the same even lines the hoe made.

"That's not bad." Looking into Barnum's eyes, Henry felt another smile crease his lips. *Yet I wonder if he notices how easy the smiling was? Because if only I'd known how easy it was, and that all I needed was a bit of grace like what Mabel gave me those weeks ago, all these years might have been different. I might have been different.* Henry stopped working with the hoe when he thought of the rectory. He felt along his leg. It was straight and steady from his hip to his toes, and he took in a deep breath as he glanced at Barnum.

I wonder if Barnum sees it and if he knows how grace can change a man? Even now—even after I haven't seen Mabel in days and days—I still walk like a man with both legs smooth and steady. I still walk smooth above the earth.

To show Barnum how smooth and steady he could walk, Henry stepped out from where he dug up the stump. He walked down the length of the canal, away from the lockhouse, so he could come up the easier, more gradual sloping side to the towpath.

"What you way over there for?" Barnum said.

Henry walked back along the towpath toward the lockhouse, the stump trailing from his hand. Stopping before the narrow footbridge, he straightened his pants, and there was no limping in him, no lagging leg, no tingling in his right boot. *I'm moving smooth and the tingling has gone away. And I'll always move smooth now, just like what Mabel would have wanted, if she'd wanted such things.*

"Oh, I know, you're gonna throw that stump in the fire."

The long dangling roots skittered against the footbridge as Henry stepped onto the uneven planks. Looking to a patch of weeds, all he could think of was filling up the lock, filling it all the way. *Because that's what Hiram said about the canal, that the water would fill it up when we brought back the barges and raised them from the lower portion to the higher. That was what Hiram said all that long life ago, that it would fill up if we let it.*

"And it feels like another life," he mumbled. "A life that only comes in pictures whenever I work in the canal like this." As he swayed on the footbridge, the pictures were all he could see. So that as he came across, he watched Barnum sit in a sun-splashed spotlight on the ground. Henry remembered the picture of Hiram: he saw Hiram's stomach dangling over his belt, smelled his egg-smelling lips, but he couldn't see Hiram's hands, not like the boy's hands now. Hiram's hands had fallen away, ever since Mabel had let the heat pass between them. Though when he looked at the picture of Hiram in his mind, he saw Hiram's mouth moving again. Hiram said: *The water is raised up in the lock, Henry, don't you know that? Just look at that boy—he knows it. He knows all kinds of things.*

"Like what?"

Like about the canal, Hiram said. *That it moves from Washington all the way to Cumberland. That the barges rise from the lower portion to the higher, all with the water. Shoot, you get raised up with the water too, Henry. Everyone knows that. You get raised up when you touch other things. Like when you touch the boy.*

"No," Henry said and shook his head, standing behind the boy. "I thought I said 'No' to you forever, and even the Lord knows I said it."

But the Lord ain't here—you left Him back in the church.

Henry shook Hiram's voice from his mind. "The Lord is here with me. The Lord is everywhere with me."

As Henry stepped closer to Barnum, he shook his head and saw the river in his mind. Because even with Barnum in his Sunday best, the boy still had the river smell on his hair and lips. And as Henry watched the boy run his fingers along the stump, he remembered Barnum leading him to where the two glowing birch trees were toppled over when they'd fished for trout and bass. When he'd dipped the net, the water had gone over his waist, and he'd seen all the zeroes spinning off the logs—and he remembered feeling raised up in the water, just like what Hiram said. The water had risen up Henry's legs so that when he walked on the rocks, it was like walking on the hands of people. They raised their silky fingers along his skin like feathers tracing his legs. And as he watched Barnum now, the boy's thin marble fingers fluttered on a knotted groove, and Henry thought the stump must be warm to feel Barnum's heat passing into it.

"*The heat*," Henry whispered, but Barnum didn't hear. The damp wood held his attention.

And there's something about his hands, Henry thought. *There's something about his hands that are like Mabel's.* As he watched Barnum, Henry saw Mabel's hands working along his dangling thing. He saw Mabel's hands all over him in the pew. Her fingers had squeezed and pulled him how he liked it, yet he had to forget her hands to keep working. He had to forget her hands, so he stepped back and looked away.

"I bet you worried about the smoke?" Barnum looked up from the stump. "If there's smoke from the fire, they'll know you're down here and the priest might come ask you back. Maybe all them old ladies too? Can you imagine? They'd just stand on the other side of the railroad yelling, '*Come back, Henry! Come Back!*' Then you'd have to stop working on the canal like I know you want to. *So I was just wondering*," leaning closer, he whispered. "*If they do come call you back, can I work on the canal for you?*"

"You want to work too?"

"Well, sure, I brought them tools, didn't I? After we work, we could fish. Then I could cook the fish right here on your stove, and we could sleep on the mattress and wake up and do it all over again. Until it's done. Day after day, and I'd never have to go anywhere else."

When Barnum spoke, Henry remembered the boy's naked body.

"You know I seen a picture of a canal in Momma's almanac. I seen how to get the wooden doors to work to raise the water. It's even got diagrams and numbers…"

"It's got numbers?"

"All kinds—and I could bring down the almanac if you want? I could bring a few hammers too, so we can chip all them stones till they fit."

As he talked, Barnum's eyes opened wider, and it was like he was pretending right in front of Henry, because a peculiar thing happened to the boy as he talked. The more he talked and stared vacantly at the crumbled lock, the more it seemed he was in the same imaginary place with Henry. Until it felt to Henry like they were the same person—that they were set apart—and together with what they felt. *He's pretending right here*, Henry knew. *He's pretending right in front of me. And it's like he's back in an older world, along the canal, and I like his pretending. I've always liked it.*

Henry rubbed his hand along his thigh as he watched Barnum speak about a day they were going to make real again. As his hands fluttered in the air, as he talked about fixing things and sawing boards, Henry knew Barnum was just the kind to see all the way back with him. All the way to the older things that had gone rotten since, falling to waste.

"And neglect," he said, as Barnum's talking died down, and his eyes snapped back to the present.

"*Neglect?*"

"Sure, but I won't never neglect you if you can see all the way back to what I see too, now that we're the same kind." Henry started drawing a zero with his boot in the dirt.

"We're the same kind all right." Barnum nodded to Henry and patted the stump with his hand. "And we won't never have to hide behind each other's backs no more—like with each other's women."

Henry stopped drawing in the dirt. His stomach clenched into a fist wondering what Barnum meant.

"You know, with how you took Mabel from me in the snow."

"*What snow?*" Henry shook his head, staring at Barnum.

The boy smiled as the black smudges crowded Henry's eyes. *Because if he seen us, if he seen me and Mabel in the lockhouse, that would be it.*

He'd be like Rommel stepping into our zero. He'd be like Rommel at the bottom of the stairs.

"Aw, you know. With how I wanted to walk off with Mabel that night, but she went with you instead."

"Went with me where?" Henry saw the shovel in the corner of his eyes. The shovel was shiny and not in the blackness at all.

"When she went with you into town. I wanted to tell you I had your mannequin then, under my bed. I wanted to tell you I took it when I saw the door unchained. I thought it would be a surprise for you, because you hadn't seen her in weeks and months. Ever since you started working in the church."

"*You* had the mannequin?"

"I wanted to give her back to you. But you had Mabel instead. You just walked off and I couldn't even speak to her…So I threw your mannequin in the river. In the ice. I threw her in to get back at you, Henry—to get even."

Barnum's face had receded into nothingness, and he looked like the new children in the rectory. Whenever a new child showed up, Henry watched to see how blank their faces were, scowling at the sheets the nuns handed them, or spitting on the cots and bunks. And he wondered if the new children would ever laugh at his short leg when he tried to do something, his right leg tingling against the laughter of being left out.

But Barnum never laughed at me like that. He never even spoke about my short right leg. Of all the words Barnum said, he never once mentioned my leg, and that was one of the things I like most about him. So I can't neglect him now, especially if he wants to be my kind. Especially if he can see the finished lock. Only my kind can see the blue water along the surface. Only my kind can see the mules in red saddles. Henry knew he had been lifted from the blackness, that he'd been lifted by the power of some hidden grace to see the clouds above the boy. He'd been lifted up to see the linen.

"Okay." Henry looked at Barnum and the white puffs in the sky had taken the black smudges from his eyes. "It's okay. But we're gonna fish her up as soon as we can. And you're gonna make it up to me. We're gonna work at night, so no one sees. And we ain't gonna tell nobody about it because I don't want to go back to church. That ain't my kind no more.

Even after I drew all them zeroes out and brought them back in. Even after I touched all them pews."

"And we won't never neglect each other no more, because we don't have to." Barnum glanced to the roofs and antennas in town. The antennas were cold metal fingers far off. "We're closer now, Henry, we are."

When they shook hands, Henry held onto Barnum's fingers like he did when they first met. As he did, a train whistle rippled downriver, and Henry snorted at the boy to feel how soft the boy's grip was and to know how much like Mabel's glowing fingers they were, squeezing his skin—squeezing and tugging his skin.

22

THAT NIGHT, WHEN HENRY RESTED on the mattress after Barnum went home, after they listened to the evening train rumble past, after Barnum apologized again about the mannequin and said he couldn't work tonight anyway in his Sunday best, Henry watched the stars appear in-between the holes in the roof. The stars came out one by one, and he counted the lights across the ceiling: *One two three four five six seven eight nine ten. Zero.* With his finger, he drew from point to point until he saw the circle of one large zero cross the sky.

Listening to the wind slither between the walls, he knew everything he heard and felt now was his. "It's mine. I drew it out with my fingers and brought it back in, and I'm beneath the zero too. The zero takes up the whole sky. It takes up everything below the sky as well—because even the canal and river are mine." He heard the murmuring river through the woods. "And even the trees are mine to work with. Because when I work on the canal it'll be like before the beginning before I know it, because the hauling and digging will go much faster with Barnum helping, and with Barnum fishing up the mannequin, I'll have her back soon with me forever."

When Henry thought of the mannequin he passed his hand along his right leg then up across his lips. He felt along his scar and remembered the scar Mabel had above her lip. He saw how her face had flushed a faint red when she'd bowed in prayer that last night. That was before they touched, before she was un-bodied and floating in the rafters. She had taken him up into the air with her hands, and he wanted that floating feeling to return and wondered where she was and if she knew he needed her.

"And what does she pray for now that her prayers for her mother have been answered? Maybe she prays for me? Maybe she prays I'll finish my work, so she can come back and see it? She'll want to ride one of the first barges, when she sees the mules in their red saddles. When she sees it all spread out for her."

He sat up as he spoke the vision of his world into being.

"She knows all about them red saddles. She knows about them because she's my kind like Barnum's my kind, and like the mannequin's my kind. She can see them red saddles because she's probably un-bodied right now, right here in the rafters."

Peering at the rafters, he raised his hands to the glittering stars.

"She hears me even if her body isn't here. Even if her body is still in the house where her mother is—because that place is only for her body... *and it's strange*," he whispered. "It's strange to think she can be in that room and this room at once."

Staring at the worn grooves in the dusty boards, he clapped his hands. As the sound vibrated above him, he heard an echo against the walls.

"It's strange to have two bodies like the echo—with my clapping hands and the sound. Because I know where she lives is only for her eating and sitting and praying; it's for being with her mother. But this place—this lockhouse—is her other place. This is where she's always un-bodied. Where she wanders when she wants to feel the floating again, and the heat." Looking at the light-dappled corners, he clapped again, and as the echo rippled around him, he watched leaves swirl in circles with the wind. "She's always here." He felt the wind brush harder against his cheek. "And when I have the mannequin back it'll be like having Mabel back as well, so I can touch her—so I can know."

He watched some leaves settle on top of the radio. "She's in the sounds of the leaves and the sounds of the wind and in the sounds of the river too. She's in the sounds of the radio—if the radio would work—because the radio would sing with her voice; it would sing." Throwing in another log and some crumbled newspaper, he settled back and watched the shadow of the brightening flame dance across the dusty radio—before edging into the rafters. The light and darkness were interchangeable, flitting back and forth, until what he really watched were the colors in his mind dancing above him, touching and dissolving into different shapes and forms. As the shapes grew brighter and darker, twisting together and pulling apart, he thought of Mabel twisting beside him on the pew. "Because I thought she would be here with me, that she would come."

In the shadows, he saw Mabel's waist. Her moist brown skin felt like clay to him, and he thought of the seam below her waist on the pew that night and her sugary river smell. *The smell was like Barnum's hair—though not entirely.* He knew Mabel's was a different smell, a female smell, and hovered like a dark honey on his fingers. When he thought of her heat, he felt a wave from the stove throw handfuls of light across his face.

"She was warm below. Warm like what I was warm when we first started, when she unrolled my pants at the waist."

As he spoke, he felt his lips for the dryness he thought might be there—but there wasn't any. His face was moist, and so he moved his hand to his pocket.

"And I thought she was watching me even then, even as her eyelids fluttered up when she led my fingers beneath her dress." He felt his hard dangling thing standing against his waist. "Then she put my fingers all the way in at her seam."

Concentrating on the shadows, he saw the church pew. Rubbing his dangling thing, squeezing from top to bottom, just as Mabel had done, he saw the people in the church, when the cardinal had spoken about forgiveness.

"If they really wanted forgiveness, they wouldn't ask Jesus for nothing. They'd know Jesus is inside them even when they're not in the church, even when the cardinal isn't there, or the priest, or those old ladies with their prayers and '*Mmmm-hmmms*'." He said, "*Mmmmm-hmmmm*," as he rubbed harder, as his dangling thing tingled at the top. "They'd see Jesus' white robes wherever they looked, just like I do. Just like now. I see Jesus in the third Station of the Cross."

Squeezing with all his might—he saw Jesus in the night. He leaned back and saw Jesus in the third station, in a zero of stars spread along the rafters.

"He's here, and I know he'll speak to me about the things I have to change." Rolling to his side, he pulled the canvas tarp back. Sweat glazed his thighs as he pulled his pants to his knees. "Because these are the things I have to change: I have to change the canal." He kicked off his boots as he shook his legs out, squeezing harder.

"And the lockhouse, I have to change the lockhouse." As he spoke, he licked his lips to keep them moist. "And the church, I have to change the church, but only if I can."

He shook his legs again, twisting with his hand grasped firmly to his center.

"Though the people may not want it. They still want someone to forgive them." He pursed his lips as a dull spark flared in his groin. "Even You said we should only look inside for forgiveness. That only *we* can set apart what we want."

He felt the tingling rise in his dangling thing. It surged through his arms and neck, molting in spidery shivers, until his whole body vibrated with the ecstasy. Until squinting into the shadows, he saw the zero of the stars hovering around him. The zero came down from the night to touch the mattress and radio, crossing his shoulders and eyes, until he felt a last rising wave course through him, and he said: "*Ohhhh,*" shivering on his side. He said: "*Mmmmm-hmmmm,*" as a quivering jolt coursed through each inch of his flesh.

He was inside the zero of the night. The zero came all the way down to touch him as the heat surged out, as his body shuddered—once, twice—before he rolled to his back. He snorted in once, coughing, and let the air rush out. Reaching over, his hands came away from his dangling thing, and the crumpled newspaper was sticky and warm. But he knew he was calm now, he was set apart, and he thought of all the other things he still had to set apart, all the other things he wanted to keep and touch.

"*One:* I want to set apart Mabel—and the mannequin." He sat up and pointed a finger in the air. "She is first, because how I feel about her will be set apart, so her heat is my heat—*always* my heat. And *two:* I want to set apart Barnum. Because Barnum talks to me and never spoke about my leg and will help me with the lockhouse even though I think he'll tell the others what we're doing. The others will come down and I might have to tell them about the church and why I won't go back, because I won't, Lord, I won't go back." He nodded to the black window facing the railroad.

"And *three*." He held up a third finger. "I want to set apart Hiram—even Hiram—because I don't feel Hiram's tugging hands anymore, and I don't feel his lips." Henry pulled up his pants and wrapped the tarp around his neck. "All of that has faded from me, Lord—though Hiram's words are still with me. Hiram's words about being free in the lockhouse are what I'll set apart from him. Because I'm free here, Lord; I am."

Rolling onto his side, he heard the river beyond the trees. "I wouldn't have met Mabel without Hiram. And *four*," he said louder, his voice brightening as he held up a fourth finger. "I want to set apart the red saddles on the mules, when the barges return. That'll be when we make the lockhouse gates, when the blue water trembles in the wind. And: *Five*." All five fingers were held out as he pointed to the darkness of the world. "I'll set apart the river, so I can wade out and find the mannequin and hold her again. So I can watch the zeroes spin off from the logs and rocks forever."

When he finished, he drew the zero of the starlight across his chest. It came through the roof to touch him, and as he took in a deep sipping breath, he listened to the beating rhythm of his life. His life spread out across the river and mountains, across the sky and sleeping town—until the sound of another train far off crossed into his expanding zero. It was the late train, the midnight train, and as the sound grew louder, as it pounded across the land, it pounded in time with his heart's steady voice.

"*The train*," he whispered, thinking of the sound, because when he heard the train rumble closer, when he watched the lockhouse shake as the shadows from the rafters melted with the starlight on the radio, he pretended all the sounds were from the radio. He pretended the world was playing its sweet smoky song for him, and he didn't have to feel anything else in this moment—not the mannequin or Mabel, not even Barnum's marble hands. There was only the sound of the world resting inside the zero of his life.

23

ALL DURING THE NEXT WEEK, Henry and Barnum waded in the river. Each morning, Henry went out in the water searching for the mannequin, and Barnum would hurry after school to help. And whenever Barnum appeared, he was always sorry for the searching they had to do and for all the bruises and split shins and stubbed fingers they got from all the lengths and rapids and crevices they searched.

"I'm just glad it's the warmest March ever." Barnum had brought his fishing rod and whistled as he tied off the lure. "This is the one," he said, motioning to Henry. "This is the one that's gonna catch her—I'm sure of it."

Wading to a rock behind where Henry stood, he cast out once and then twice with the line ticking near Henry's ear. After letting the line drift down with the current, Barnum reeled in and pulled off some green weeds from his hook before casting out again. He made a slow rising up and snapping off motion with his wrist, and when Henry watched the pole bend and the line sing out on the fourth cast, he knew Barnum had a fish for them to keep, but not the mannequin.

"Did you see that?" Barnum pointed to a rock jutting out in the middle. "The line drifted behind that rock."

Henry watched the dark current swirl around the rock Barnum pointed to.

"If you can just get down there with the net." Barnum handed Henry the net, unclipping it from his belt. "Then we can at least have something to eat when we start in on the canal. Because I told you I'd give you all the fish I catch until we find her."

The sun was setting as Henry watched the water reflect the fading orange and purple light. Stepping out, he wobbled a bit and felt his right knee buckle. Looking to the dark surface, he balanced himself, holding out the net and feeling the cold water rise along his waist—then over his waist.

"I thought I'd be used to it by now, and that we'd already have her." As the water got deeper, he breathed in quick short bursts. The coldness was part of him now. He saw zeroes swirling away with each wobbly step. Zeroes were swirling off his waist and away in the current. "Look," he said and turned to Barnum, forgetting for a moment the anger he held toward the boy for throwing the mannequin in the ice those months ago. But when he turned, Barnum was already farther off than Henry thought. The small rock Barnum sat on had shrunk into a gray dot on the edge of the water.

It's like the edge has been erased. Even the banks from here look like they're gone. When he leaned closer to the surface, the wind blew ripples across everything he saw. Ripples stretched across the whole river—until even the zeroes that spun off from his waist dissolved into myriad cascading lines. Looking around his legs, he realized he was in the middle of the river and that even the zeroes had left him stranded so that he teetered standing there. He teetered on his tingling right leg and felt his head grow heavy until he felt like falling under to hold the rocks close to his chest, to hold the zero that he knew was underneath—the zero of the rocks he'd spoken about before. Though almost as suddenly as it had arisen, that windy breath eased off and the zeroes came back, reforming on the surface, and he put his hands inside them again.

I'm okay. He swayed a bit, so he could stand up straight and tall again. Moving slower, he followed a diagonal course toward the rock Barnum had snagged his line on where that large trout hovered behind, re-gathering its strength. "And look." He knew Barnum couldn't hear or see the zeroes he trailed his fingers through, but he said it anyway. "Look at how the zeroes pull right through the edge of where I put my hands. They pass right through. I'm passing from one zero to the next—until all the sides are together—until all the zeroes are linked across the whole span."

He looked along the fast-moving water. The river was a chattering conversation of white rapids and choppy calls and swirling laughs, until he had to stop and listen to where he was. He had not been in the middle during this whole week. He had stayed close to the banks, near the rocks Barnum said would be the most likely place for the mannequin. But out here it sounded different. In the middle, Henry heard the river speaking louder to him. It rumbled around him, pulling the other ends of the current into its middle strength, into its faster, thicker weave.

"*That's what it says*," he whispered, scouring the surface. Crouching, he bent his knees as his right leg tingled. It was sore from passing over the uneven rocks these last seven days. "I can hear it all around. The river wants to pull the other ends into its center. The water of the bank is slow and shallow and does not have the thirst for the darker life out here. It does not speak."

He looked at the darker water ahead, swirling near the rock. Taking another step, he sunk into a hole all the way up to his shoulders so that he was floating toward the rock, holding the net above the chattering surface.

"Whoa," Barnum yelled from far off. "You all right?" Barnum's words echoed higher up and didn't seem to hold onto anything Henry could know: not the river or the bulrushes that stood up here and there, not even the rocks. Barnum's words didn't seem to hold onto anything at all.

Henry couldn't swim and floated to the rock gulping breaths of air. He saw where the line was caught and flailed his boots in the murky deep until his left leg held fast to the bottom. As he shifted his weight, easing his right leg down, a host of bubbles scattered up along his thighs when his trousers billowed out, so it felt like fingers were rising up his waist. The water clambered all over him, before stopping in the middle of his chest where he thought his heart must be.

"My heart is along the line of the river. And the river must have wanted to touch it just to know it, just to know me and what I want. But I want nothing, River—nothing but the girl." Henry spun around, broadening his voice. "I want nothing but the girl, and to be beside You like this, to be with You and to hear Your chattering and to know why You would want to pull the other ends into Your center? *Why?*"

Swaying in the current, he watched the zeroes spin off as the river chattered among his legs. The river babbled near the rock too, now that he could put his hand there, steadying himself. Barnum's yellow line glowed above the surface and was caught in-between a slit in a groove. The line was as taut as the guitar strings Henry imagined in the radio's smoky music, the music he hummed along to with Hiram those nights in the apartment. *I always imagined those guitar strings like this. That they'd quiver with the music dripping from them.* Reaching out to touch the line, he felt the life of the trout on the other end. The trout quivered in the dark where the river eddied into a host of zeroes unlike any before. The zeroes swirled and broke off into one another, merging and touching and setting everything apart.

"*Yes.*" Henry felt the living trout beneath the zeroes of the river. He knew it was deep because as he followed the line around, trailing his fingers along the glowing edge, he saw it slant into the darker water, slanting—*one two three*—feet down until he couldn't see the line any more. "It's the darkest water yet. Only the purple light reflects on the water here, now that the orange and red have fallen away."

Looking up, he saw that even the purple had faded into a blue bordering on the blackness of night. Sinking the net into the water, he saw where the glowing line dissolved under the darker zeroes spinning out. He was amazed at the endless number of zeroes falling into one another. With both hands, he swung the net around, plunging it with his arms to where he felt the glowing line ended. The water was up to his chin, and he could feel the life of the fish sag in the broad mesh. Pulling in then, he pulled harder like on the pews in the church when he pulled in the zeroes he'd drawn out, scrubbing across the blank surface.

Because the river is a page of words, he knew. A page that holds all these words together, and all these voices—everything.

Though in listening to the chattering rapids, he realized the water called much louder now that darkness had fallen, now that the river's voices could be much brasher without being seen for the noises they made or the thoughts they carried. "The river is a page of zeroes," he said and pulled back on the dripping net, which came up much easier with each tug. "The river is a zero."

The looser glowing line curled in the water at his waist as he pulled in harder. He saw the white fleshy side of the trout even when the net was still a foot below the surface.

"My," he said as he brought the net all the way up, as he saw the whole white bulk rising through the zeroes and dark water. "This is the biggest fish Barnum has ever caught. It's bigger than any other. And he'll talk about this fish forever, always talking about the fish as large as any stump."

Though when the net was in the air—with the water dripping down, drizzling from the sides like squirming lines—he could not say another word. He saw that the fish was not a trout at all. Barnum had not caught the largest fish ever: he had caught a body. It was the same body Henry had been searching for, the same body he imagined holding and rubbing so that he could know the girl again and have her always.

"It's the mannequin!" Henry raised the net, so Barnum might see the white flesh of the torso. "It's the mannequin, the mannequin!" As Henry shouted, he lisped like he hadn't done in so long that he had to stop and suck in his lips because the dry cracked edges were starting again. "It's the mannequin!" he called again, licking his lips. Bringing the familiar body close, he touched the worn canvas with his hands. He smelled the river smell of the curving body with the bumps like Mabel's bumps beneath her shirt. "It's the mannequin," he said, cradling the body to his heart. "She's come back to me."

24

"**W**ELL, WHAT YOU THINK OF THAT?" Barnum stood on the banks as Henry waded through the shallows, the mannequin in his arms. "I told you we'd get her back."

As Henry came up dripping from the river, Barnum's fingers fluttered in the air as he helped Henry up the slick, tangled roots. Henry only offered one hand to Barnum to help pull him up with. The other he kept clasped to the mannequin, and now that they were on the bank, he wrapped both arms around the torso.

"I bet you didn't even think we'd find her after looking so long." As Barnum edged closer to the mannequin, Henry turned from him and started up the trail. It had gotten colder since they began looking, and Henry walked faster, limping as his knee buckled with each step.

"Well, how's she look? Is she all right?"

Henry started the fire, and they both shivered in their dripping clothes as they waited for the flames to catch. The mannequin smelled of river water and river stones, and Henry didn't want to let go of her as Barnum started talking about how he knew they were going to find her. He'd stayed up each night all week with a map, scratching off sections they'd searched, retracing each rapid in his mind. "I swore I wouldn't stop until we found her."

Henry rubbed a leg with his free hand. He was sore from all the hunting and searching, dragging his hands through the cold water, bumping into rocks.

"Each night I just shivered going up the hill and promised myself I'd fish her up for you. So I could make it right. So we could be like before."

"And you think it's like before now?"

"Ain't it just like before all the way around?"

Henry cradled the mannequin in his arms. His fingers rubbed against the slick bumps as Barnum watched.

"I'm back here with you and we got the mannequin and we can start on the canal straight away, as soon as we eat."

Henry re-asserted his grip on the mannequin as Barnum peeled his shirt and trousers off. He watched the boy hang them from the wall behind the stove. Flashing a broad row of teeth, Barnum leaned back from the stove and ran his hands across his hard-blossom nipples. Henry remembered those same rosy nipples that night long ago, when he watched the boy undress all the way, and he saw the seam between the boy's buttocks. And as Henry watched Barnum rub his hands against his chest now, he thought of stepping closer to touch him, and he grabbed tighter to the mannequin.

"*Because I thought this was over with you here,*" he whispered to the torso. "*I thought this was over after Mabel passed the heat to me in the pew. But Mabel is gone now—and I can only look at you. So I don't have those thoughts like Hiram would have about the boy. So maybe you'll help me push those thoughts away?*" Shifting from his left leg to his right, he leaned on his tingling foot. He felt how strong his short leg was, how it raced with needles all over.

"After I dry up, I can fetch some biscuits Momma bought last night and some chicken," Barnum's voice echoed off the walls and brought Henry back to the room. Barnum still had his dripping underwear on. "With no one on the towpath, we can start clearing with our shovel and hoe." Barnum threw in more twigs and leaves until the fire spread, casting a higher light across the walls. "And ain't it just like it was before winter?" Barnum shivered near the fire and rubbed his hands along his legs.

"But your legs look longer." As soon as he said it, Henry shut his mouth, tightening his grip on the torso.

"Teacher says I've grown an inch." Hanging his hands at his sides, he rubbed along his legs, rubbing back and forth. "I wanted to show Momma but she had to work last night when I told her my jeans don't fit—but heck," Barnum giggled, twisting out of his wet underwear. "I bet I could wear your overalls one day. You'd let me. I know it."

The heat from the open grate splashed across the room—and when the boy turned, shifting his weight—Henry breathed in to see the boy's dangling thing flop back and forth against the top of his thighs. He saw that Barnum had smaller wisps of hair around his dangling thing like what Henry had below his waist: a brown nest of twisting curls. And Barnum had his hands down now too, around his dangling thing. He was smoothing out the thin wisps with his fingers. Once he smoothed them all the way down, he'd let go and then giggled as the threads coiled back into brown wispy waves.

"Look." Barnum thrust his waist out in the heat. "I done this in the locker room once because all the other boys said I couldn't have hair down there yet, not since they didn't have any." Barnum rubbed his fingers along the hair, twisting it between his fingers. "You want to smooth it out? Everybody wanted to try, but I wouldn't let them."

When he asked, he thrust his waist out, so that only the width of the mannequin separated them. Henry saw the boy's dangling thing rising up the more he swayed back and forth. The boy had both his hands around it too, so that they looked like Hiram's hands—raw and wiry—and Henry brought the mannequin to cover his own dangling thing. Raising a hand to touch his lips, a dab of blood came off on his fingers. Grasping the torso tighter, he saw a small red smear on the front bump, and Henry breathed in to see the torso marked like that.

Well? What are you waiting for?

It was Hiram. A shifting breeze had hissed under the cracks in the window, rustling the newspapers.

You just gonna stand there stuttering when this boy's ready for you to touch him?

"*No*," Henry whispered and watched Barnum pull a log from the floor for the fire. "I thought you were gone. I thought Mabel's heat pushed you down forever, that she burned your words to ash." Henry pulled the mannequin closer to his waist.

Aw, she can't hide you anymore.

"Who can't?"

Your friend there, the one you just fished up.

Henry felt the damp torso in his hands. The canvas had grown warmer in the heat.

I might not have even come back if it wasn't for her. You've been hiding behind her so long now, Henry, why don't you just set her down?

Henry leaned on his right leg and felt it tingle with the wind rising across his skin.

That's right, just set her down. You don't need her with the boy here. Hell, he's like your own son now; he's practically family.

As Hiram coaxed Henry, whispering across his skin, Henry felt all the hair on his arms standing like needles. It was like he was in Hiram's apartment again, at the window, with moonlight falling across his face, and he let Hiram's pink breath work across him, soothing out his arms and legs, easing his fingers from the torso.

That's right, just ease her down so the boy can see your legs for once. You haven't showed anyone your legs in so long, and you don't have to carry that burden anymore, not with the boy here, not with the boy.

"You might be right," Henry whispered as his fingers relaxed. "I am rising up." As he wiped his lips clean, he felt his skin rising as he spoke, rising as he watched the boy. *Because I can see the boy standing there, his legs all warm in the firelight. And with the voice of the river far off, calling to pull everything in from the banks—everything to the center—I want to pull him in too, to pull him in and feel below his seam and along his dangling thing.*

That's right, Hiram said.

But Henry shivered when he thought of Hiram being right. He shivered from his higher wandering thoughts and put the mannequin in front of him. Unbuckling his belt, Henry slid his trousers to the floor. When he did, he sucked in his stomach because the heat of the room and the wind from the door crossed his bare buttocks with their trailing fingers. Turning from the stove, Barnum giggled to see Henry's dangling thing swing from side to side as he stood out of his trousers, shaking off his boots.

"I'll get them," Barnum said. As he bent over to pick up Henry's trousers, Henry looked below his dangling thing and saw the boy's knobby spine curve in an arch to the floor. When Barnum stood up, his hair brushed like a feather against Henry's thigh, and Henry's dangling thing shot straight up like a fishing pole to feel Barnum's touch.

"And your shirt." Barnum smiled, leaning up to Henry.

Sliding off his shirt, Henry felt his red-blossom nipples stand up hard and pert when Barnum stepped closer.

"Geez, you got all kinds of hair down there. And it's standing straight up—your jimmy. Mine does that when I wiggle." He pointed to Henry's dangling thing, which was hotter than Henry could remember it being for so long. Not since Mabel moved her hands up and down on it in the church.

There had been the floating feeling then, he knew, *when I was un-bodied with Mabel, when we floated above everything: Above all the silver haired ladies saying, "Mmmm-hmmm"; above the priest talking of, "Sinners and traitors to their kind"; above even Rommel's pinched-up eyes, with Rommel's refusal of our love.*

Henry still saw the creaky way Rommel fell down the basement steps. He saw a picture of Rommel crumpled in his mind. But Henry didn't look at it long. Not with Barnum here. *That was Rommel's fault for passing into our zero, for passing into what was set apart for me and Mabel. And I ain't gonna let Rommel ruin the floating feeling. Not with the zero edging around me, and with the boy so close.*

"Because I'm starting to feel that way again," he said as he watched Barnum hang his shirt beside his trousers. "I'm starting to float over all these things, even over the feeling of my legs—my uneven legs."

"What's floating? In the river?" Barnum turned and stared at Henry.

Henry stood behind the mannequin, which sat on the floor. The mannequin, slick and glowing white with the river smell, was between them and held the same pale color as Henry's legs. And as he nudged the mannequin, inching it out with his toes, he watched Barnum look along his body to his legs.

"Oh."

Henry had taken his trousers off before in front of Barnum, but that was when the boy fell back after wrestling over the mannequin, when he hit his head on the radio, and he hadn't seen. But now, after finding the mannequin in the river, and after feeling his knee buckle walking up the path,

Henry knew his muscle was coiled again and shorter, and he wasn't afraid to show Barnum what he'd always kept hidden from the others—what had always set him apart—not with the floating feeling returning.

"Well, I'll be." Barnum looked as Henry pulled his toes back from nudging the mannequin. Henry's left leg was bent at the knee and compensated for the shorter right leg—the right foot of which rested with the tips of the toes on the wooden floor. His left foot rested flat. Barnum had never seen Henry's legs before, and when he bent down, he reached out to touch Henry's right foot.

"*Fffffftp.*" Henry made a sipping noise when Barnum touched his foot, but he didn't shake the boy's hand away—not with the smooth fingers on him or the floating feeling returning, with his skin rising in the wind. He didn't mind at all and felt a warmer pulse in his foot. The more Barnum kept his fingers on the wedged toes, the more Henry felt a lighter fire spreading through his body.

That's right, Henry, bring him in bit by bit. Let him touch what he always wanted to touch—and then bring his hands higher, to where he can squeeze and maybe put his lips on as well. Just like what I done for you, like what I needed.

"*Hiram.*" Henry shook his head as Hiram's voice brought him down from the floating feeling. Henry wasn't in the air anymore, though when he looked again at the boy, he felt the boy's fingers melt like warm drops of sand along the inside of his arch. If Barnum heard him whispering, Henry wasn't sure, because the boy didn't stop touching with his melting fingers. He seemed so focused on Henry's shorter leg, that when he bent over, Henry saw in-between the boy's buttocks to the line where the two halves met. The flesh was cleaner there. Henry saw a pure snowy whiteness where the sun had never touched the flaky skin.

"Has it always been like this?" The right foot had flat edges to it and hard corners. The toes stuck out and couldn't move or fidget like what the toes on Henry's left foot were doing, with Barnum's hand running across the ankle and all the way up to the knee.

"Always."

Henry felt the touching was warm like river stones in the sun, and the more Barnum felt along the lifeless toes and ankle, the more the boy's touch swallowed Henry's mind. *Because the skin is thicker than I'm sure even he thought. It's thicker and there's a chord of muscle running down the center, along the back of my leg, the same chord he's touching now. The chord with a thickness unlike any root he could pull.*

"There aren't even any bristles like on Charles' face, your legs are so smooth." Barnum moved his hands along Henry's shins, up to the bottom of his thighs, crossing his jagged boney knees. "It's like a lily pad, the skin." Barnum brought his hands back down until both of them rested on Henry's right foot—a foot trembling to feel the sand-melting sunshine of Barnum's fingers. "Jesus, it's just an inch shorter." He cupped the ball of Henry's right heel, and with both hands underneath, Henry stood much straighter. "See." Barnum giggled as Henry shifted over and stood straight up. "That's all the difference it's ever been—just two thin hands worth."

The door swung open with the wind rising, and Barnum and Henry smelled the muddy river grass and heard bullfrogs in the night, waking from their slumber.

"Everything's warmer than it should be," Barnum said, and as he moved his hands back and forth under Henry's heel, Henry swayed a bit.

Henry reached to touch Barnum's shoulder, and when he leaned over, his dangling thing brushed Barnum's head, and a darker flare sparked in his groin. Henry stepped off Barnum's hands and reached down to pick up the mannequin, holding her over his hardening waist.

Now that wasn't so bad, was it? Hiram said. *It wasn't so bad to feel yourself touched by the boy's soft hair?*

"What is it?" Barnum looked to see Henry in the light of the stove, staring at the rafters. "It's like you're listening to something else, like the church choir or something. Is something up there?"

Listen to him, Henry. He's waiting just for you. He's naked and waiting to touch anything you want him to touch.

The odor of Hiram's egg-smelling lips wafted with the canal grass. The egg-smelling lips slithered against one another like the sound of a bull-frog's bumpy legs brushing its glazed body.

Just listen to him, Henry. The boy wants to make up for making you wobble, when he put his hands beneath your heel. Henry? Henry!

Hiram screamed and Henry rocked to the side to stop the screaming. He shook his head because he did not want to look at the boy. Not with him so close. Even when he knew Hiram was right. That maybe Barnum did want to help, that Barnum wanted to hold him up and make up for throwing the mannequin in the river.

He just wants you to be even. He just wants you to feel what it's like to be even.

And way off, a rattling metal jolt echoed across the land. A train was moving; the sound brought Barnum from his knees to stand beside Henry. "That's the night commuter. We can start working on the canal as soon as it passes. Nobody's gonna be out now." When Barnum leaned over to where he'd hung his trousers and shirt, Henry turned his eyes to watch the boy's thin buttocks quiver in the light.

That's right, Hiram said. *Just get a taste. Just draw him in slow and steady and wait.*

"Here you are." Barnum held out Henry's trousers, which were still moist from not having dried as long, and as he brought his hands back, he trailed his fingers along the edge of the mannequin.

"I guess you've got to put her down if you want to start working," he said, smiling as Henry put the mannequin on the sink.

Henry remembered leaving the mannequin all those months before on the sink, and as he turned again and pulled on his trousers, leaning on his short right leg—he wondered what the boy meant by trailing his fingers along the torso. *What did he mean?*

He just wants to be like you. Hiram's breath cooled Henry's face as they stepped out to watch the train rumble past. All the tin-can cars raced past in the dark, and Henry could see some of the commuters in the lighted windows. Some of the faces yawned, while others looked across the canal. Henry even saw some of the faces winking on and off as the lighted windows passed speeding along to Harpers Ferry. *And you can let him if you want to. You can let him be what you and I always wanted.*

25

THE NEXT DAY, Barnum brought a hammer with him. He said it was a rock hammer his Momma's boyfriend Charles bought a while ago when Charles was supposed to be interested in collecting fossils from the rocks that slid down the mountain. Quartzite and limestone and shale: Barnum looked up all the rocks in the almanac his mother gave him and in the encyclopedias at school during lunch.

"This hammer has a pointed tip," Barnum said and rubbed his thumb over the blade. "We can chip away at all them rocks lying around at the bottom." Barnum pointed at the rubble near the lock, and Henry looked up from where he was working the shovel.

It was dusk. Henry stood on the towpath and had been working for half an hour trimming the lip. He had watched Barnum appear after the last commuter train with its silver tin-cans and sleeping faces rumbled past. As Barnum waved the hammer, Henry looked to the railroad tracks and still saw the train. The windows went by light and then dark and then light again, and he tried to count them from one to zero, and then to zero again, but the numbers swarmed over all that he could ever add up in his life. That only made him stare at the faces that much harder. He saw the faces even when they weren't there. It was like being in church all over again when he used to watch Mabel's face when she prayed in the pew.

Mabel had bowed her head those nights beneath the Stations of the Cross. Henry stood in the back corner as the light crossed the stained glass and brought out the brown pools of her eyes. And often, as she rose after he lit the candle for her, he watched her face's reflection on the shiny floor from wherever he stood. When she stepped from the shadows to the lighted altar so that the light shot across her eyes and lips and skin, bringing the whole circle of her face into focus, he knew it was like he held her close to his heart, that they were together, and he stood for many moments like that, watching her reflection in the glistening wood.

So when he slid into the canal with the shovel trailing from his hand, he still saw her face over all the other faces he'd ever seen. The faces were spread like zeroes in his mind. They went on and on, and he knew if they were zeroes to him, then they were his; they were set apart and different. Though he still wondered about Mabel's face and her zero? Was she still set apart for him? He hadn't seen her in so long and wanted to be with her again, to be close. He wanted to see her on the train and wanted the train to stop right here at his lockhouse. She could look across the water and fixed-up canal. Mules in red saddles would shuffle on the towpath, and a band would play on the first barge. Then he knew she would sing to him as dusk fell across the valley, the stars pulled one by one from the night. *She would sing.* When he thought of Mabel singing, he felt along his lips and watched Barnum move along the top of the canal, shaking his arms at his sides.

"We just got to break that pipe is all. That pipe brings down the stream from town." Barnum pointed with the rock hammer to the thick ceramic pipe running down the mountain. "It brings all the rainwater too."

The pipe went under a drainage ditch beneath the railroad into a gully before running south along the lip of the canal. Farther down, the pipe went beneath a worn-down section of the canal, right below the part Henry had cleared away before emptying out on the other side of the towpath.

"We just bust that pipe right here," Barnum said and pointed to Henry's part of the canal. "And block up the lower portion where it slopes, so the water stays in the part you cleared out. Then you've got your canal all fine and dandy and we can even sail a boat if we want. Shoot, we can ride whatever we want after we clear out the higher part."

"*The higher part?*" Henry looked back along the seventy or eighty feet he'd cleared, to where the canal rose up slightly above the lockhouse. The higher section was as overgrown and cluttered with junk as this lower section had been when he started. He'd cleared out so much and never once considered raising the barge up, about actually using the lock. "I just wanted to close it is all, so the water stays in this lower portion." He searched in his mind for any plan he held for the higher portion but couldn't find one.

"We got to raise it up; we just got to." Barnum walked along the top lip and looked to where Henry had cleared away the junk and brush from the last fifty years. "We'll start on the other side after we bring the water in. It'll be easier to start on the higher portion once this lower portion is all swamped through." He pointed to the muddy grass at Henry's boots. "What we've got to do is make a dam below where we bring the water in." Barnum pointed to a worm-eaten stump Henry had wanted to dig up for weeks. "Leave that stump. We'll start filling in all the other stones and logs so the water stays with us forever, so it's even."

"We can make the water even?" Henry stood very still thinking of how even the water would be, how blue and shiny and calm. He stood so still he didn't even hear Barnum come back with a log as big as the boy's leg. Barnum tossed the log down, and as Henry placed it beside the stump, he realized how deep the canal really was.

It's as high as me and more, and maybe only if I leaned on top of myself would I be able to see above it all the way. And with the dusk falling, and the river louder, Mabel would be proud to see what we done, to see the bit of grace we've given back to the canal, because it's all because of her—this work. It's all because she still holds the grace of her prayers in her hands for me in her room. She still prays for me.

Barnum came back with a stone the size of a watermelon. The boy was huffing and sweating, and Henry had never seen the boy sweating like this before, especially doing work. He watched Barnum plunk the stone down near the stump before walking back for another load.

"I chipped that one off," Barnum said and came back grinning, his arms half as full with a freshly chipped rock. "Did you hear me when I did it?"

"No."

"Well, I was up there and found a rock too big to haul myself, so I decided to use the hammer." Barnum wiggled his hips, so the hammer waved from his belt loop. "And sure enough, the hammer chipped it in two. You swear you didn't hear me hammering?"

Barnum plunked the chipped rock down and Henry held it in his hands to feel the edge. It was a smooth cut. Henry saw all the layers packed together in the rock so that the rock looked like it had its own world of years and lives and lines packed around some middle-bunching-knot. He traced the middle-bunching-knot with his fingers and saw the packed lines more clearly once the moon pulsed from behind some clouds.

Instantly, the canal flashed a smoky gray. Crickets and frogs all started at once or came back to Henry with the moon pulsing brighter. He hadn't heard any of it with the train rumbling past, and then with Barnum's voice. He only saw the faces in the tin-cans and pews; because when he saw the faces in the tin-cans and pews, he felt his arms drawing out the zeroes again. He saw himself scrubbing with the brush and bringing the zeroes back in, and his arms had that ragged worked-out feeling to them. It was like he was letting out rope, letting out rope. It seemed like his arms were constantly letting out rope so that he couldn't feel his arms even as he held up the chipped stone. Barnum stood above him with another chipped half. He plunked it down beside the stump near Henry's feet. "My arms are gone," Henry said.

"No they ain't," Barnum giggled. "I see them right there."

Henry glared up as the boy skipped back along the canal.

He don't understand I can only feel my arms when I'm not holding nothing, when I'm not hauling or hoeing or shoveling. I can only feel them when I'm not touching things. And I wonder where my touch goes when I do hold something like this rock? My touch is gone then. It's inside the rock, so that the rock holds my touch closer to its middle-bunching-knot—till my touch is a part of it forever. And I wonder if that's like Barnum's hands when he touches my foot? Does he still feel his hands? Or do they become part of my foot then, when he makes my legs even?

"Here's another one." Barnum plunked another stone beside the log Henry hadn't touched yet. "There's enough junk in that higher portion to fill another basement. When we haul it up, we can burn it," Barnum said. "We'll burn it at night so no one sees."

"Sees what?"

"The smoke...Momma thinks I'm at the church for the recital. She thinks I'm gonna be in the Easter pageant—and I am—though I only got a shepherd part. I didn't get to be Jesus and go through the resurrection like

I wanted. You know who they gave that part to: Josh Frye, as if he'd make a better Jesus than me?" As Barnum spoke, he waved the small rock hammer in his hands. "And I told Miss Abigail the same thing. I said, 'You just wait, Josh'll mess up the resurrection for sure. He probably thinks it has something to do with the thing below his waist—with his jimmy.' And she slapped me on the wrist and made me say ten Hail Marys. Said I needed to talk to the priest for what I implied. And I said, 'Well, I didn't imply nothing, you can't leave the resurrection up to Josh and Mabry. Though Mabry plays Pilate, so I guess that's about right."

Henry watched Barnum's hands as he spoke. As they trailed in the air, drawing a frame around the picture of his words, Henry imagined them resting under his foot. *Because those are the hands that made me even as easy as putting his palms beneath my heel. He put his palms beneath my heel and I was even, and I wonder if it was the palms that made Hiram even too?* From across the canal, Henry felt a pink breath brushing his face. *Did I make Hiram even just by letting him tug me with his hands?*

On the river, a motorboat buzzed like a bumblebee. Henry heard voices echo before dying away. Then only the night flowed through. The rapids far off were a soft chattering. Looking up, he felt the sky flow like its own darker current. And the *tink tink tink* of Barnum's hammer came to him like a slow ticking, like a clock. Barnum's hammer sounded like a clock that Henry could hold in his hand, like a perfect ticking body. The steady *tink tink tink* filled the whole canal, spreading over the weeds and stumps, the fern and oak, until Henry felt his body tingle with each sharp falling sound.

IT RAINED OFF AND ON the next three weeks, and whenever Barnum didn't have to practice for the recital, he helped Henry in the lockhouse. As the clouds dripped large cold drops, he sat in the doorway and chipped the stones Henry brought up for him to shape for the lock. While he chipped stones, re-shaping them into smaller bricks, he kept the fire going. He heaped in leaves and twigs so that when Henry finished heaping up stones and stumps to make the dam bigger, the lockhouse would be warm enough to dry his clothes. When Henry came in for breaks, shivering in those moments, he looked with Barnum over their work as the dam held better and better with each new addition.

"The rain's backed up in puddles already. Just shows you how well it's gonna hold once we bust that pipe. That's when the stream really trickles down, when we can hold it on our own."

"We'll make it even then." Henry's teeth chattered beneath his blue-tinted lips. Standing by the stove, he took off his shirt and trousers like he was used to doing now. The two of them had a routine. Henry would stand by the stove, raising his hands to the flames, while Barnum would rub Henry's legs up and down to help stop them from shivering. After Barnum rubbed Henry's legs, he cupped his hands beneath Henry's right heel, like he'd done before to make Henry stand even and flat. "Oh," Henry would say, whenever he felt Barnum's hands beneath his heel. He was always surprised with how warm they were. The boy's thin marble hands felt like they were melting into his foot.

The boy's soft brown head bobbed right below Henry's dangling thing, and whenever Henry looked over to feel the boy helping him like this, Hiram's pink breath circled louder to see the boy so close and ready to touch. *You can touch him now if you want. You've brought him in and brought him in and now you can use the mattress behind you.* Henry looked at the mattress. *The mattress is where you want to lie after drying yourself, Henry, because the heat gives off the sleepy feel.*

Henry had often thought about lying on the mattress with the boy. But he knew the mattress was where Mabel had sat before, kneeling in the heat. She'd prayed for Henry to pass his hands over her, and he had done it. And now, when Hiram's breath awoke in him the memory of the mattress and Mabel's small kneeling body, he turned to the sink and saw the mannequin with the bumps glowing red in the heat thrown off the fire. He stared for a long moment—remembering the bumps against his hands—and as he did, he felt Barnum's hands melting beneath his heel. "Oh," Henry said.

Barnum rocked to the side by accident, adjusting his hands.

"Sorry."

"It's okay." Henry's thick lips chattered above his teeth. The blue misty sound of rain swarmed across his mind. Henry felt the blue water rushing in, with the sound of the river rising higher, and didn't mind the blue coming in so much. He didn't mind the blue as long as it wasn't the pink—Hiram's pink breath rising up to make the mattress seem brighter and warmer and the place for him to lie with the boy. Henry knew that place was only for Mabel now. *That's her place, and it can't be anyone else's.*

Barnum coughed, and when he did, he brushed Henry's dangling thing with his soft curling hair.

Okay, Hiram's pink breath whispered again. *The boy has his hand beneath your heel and can't you feel the skin again, the gold-dripping skin?*

"*Yes.*" Henry felt the boy's marble fingers dripping into the golden sand of the heat. The boy's hands were heat now, melting into his heel.

His fingers are turning from marble to clay even as I stand here, even as he re-shapes me like the stones he chips with the hammer. Because he's re-shaping me with his fingers, re-shaping me so I'm like the stones. I'm like the stones on the tomb of Jesus in the last Station of the Cross, the stones of life and death. I work with the stones and haul away the stones and have felt the stones underneath me and everything else: beneath the river and canal, the lockhouse and cistern, where the water flows between the rocks. The water flows over everything, and the boy's fingers have flowed over my hard short heel to make me even again. I feel even with the golden sand of his heat.

"*And Mabel*," Henry whispered. "*Mabel should see how even I am.*" Whispering her name, he thought he saw Barnum look up, but the boy's head didn't move. Barnum kept his hands beneath Henry's heel. *And he'll keep his hands there until I touch him on the shoulder. Until I brush him with my hand and say*, "Okay, Barnum, I've rested enough."

They'd repeated this ritual the last three weeks, and Henry couldn't feel where the boy's hands began or ended anymore. He couldn't feel where anything ended anymore. He only felt himself growing in these moments— growing even—and he never wanted these moments to end. *Because he's just like Mabel now*, he thought. *His hands melt into my heel like Mabel's hands melted into my waist, melting over my dangling thing. Because I was un-bodied then too. I was un-bodied and perfect, just like her.* Arching his head up to the rafters, he felt himself being lifted as if he were floating higher. He felt his body arching up—straight and even with the help of the boy's hands—until he was floating. *I can see the golden rafters again, with the purple Stations of the Cross. I floated with Mabel in the church like this. I heard the scrubbing then too, with the pews and my hands pushing out and always out—until I couldn't feel them going out anymore. Until I only saw the zeroes, all the many zeroes.*

From the door, Henry felt the wind. The flames in the stove fluttered as Hiram's breath circled around them.

I can hear him breathing again. I can hear Hiram's pink breath falling beneath the blue sky of the boy. The boy is as blue as the sky. The boy is young and raw and blue, and he's brushing my dangling thing with his hair. He brushes me without knowing. His hands are gold and dripping with the wetness of sand, dripping like fire in the darkness. Because the fire is dripping up to touch me in the darkness, to touch my floating body. Yes, my floating body is perfect and even and ticking like the clock of his hammer. Because his hands are part of my leg now—though he is so far away from me. The ground is far away and the tingling I've known forever is gone. There's only the ticking now. There's only the perfect ticking, the even ticking, the perfect even ticking.

"Henry?" Barnum looked and saw Henry's head arched back, so only the egg-whites of Henry's eyes flashed in the firelight. "Henry, I have to go. My Aunt Remmie is coming over. I was supposed to be there tonight, so she sees how good we are together—my Momma and me." Barnum watched another long moment, leaning back. "I want to stay with you; I do. I want to stay with you forever, and I don't know if you know that or not because you probably can't hear me now." Sliding his hands out from Henry's heel, Barnum watched Henry stand against the firelight. "You're up in the air, aren't you? Up there wandering in your mind, and I know you don't know nothing about what I want."

Henry's right leg leaned down as Barnum let go.

"I'm sorry." As Barnum shuffled to the doorway, he left Henry standing there alone, naked, his gaze fluttering in the glittering heat—his egg-white eyes rolled-up in his head—with the dark mist falling over the canal.

26

HENRY DIDN'T SEE BARNUM for a week after the boy left him standing there alone. Henry didn't even know the boy was gone until the late freight train rolled past, and the veils of dust he was so used to sifted down across his skin. The falling dust made the firelight waver when he blinked to see the boy's hands gone and that his right leg was coiled again and tingled. He worked in the canal without Barnum that whole week, and with each new stone he shaped, with each space he filled, he repeated to himself how he'd stood for so long without the boy's help, repeating it over as he dried himself. Leaning back from the stove, he wiped the water from his cheeks and drop after drop hissed on the iron grate. "I bet I stood for another hour without him, all by myself."

It had rained hard all day, and Henry pulled his wet trousers and shirt off. After hanging them by the stove, he stepped to the radio and spun the knobs. As he did, he hummed a half-formed rhythm he may have heard before but couldn't place the words to.

> I once was hmmm,
> but now hmmm hmmm,
> was blind, but hmmm,
> hmmm hmmm

There weren't any words in him now. There was only the smoky feeling of the radio coming from inside, the radio rising up to fill his life. He listened as his voice mixed with the chattering rapids far off. This last week he'd slept with the mannequin close to his waist. After being lodged in the river, the torso had dried to a flakiness that rubbed off in his hands, and each night as he held the bumps with his hands, he saw Mabel's bumps instead.

He saw how her hard-blossom nipples had stood straight up between his fingers as he rubbed them again and again.

"This is Mabel, my girl." Cradling the mannequin, he fell back to the mattress and watched a fine sheet of moisture drip from the rafters. A wave of heat was pushing up from the stove to meet the leaky raindrops. Where the two edges dissolved, he counted to zero once in his mind, and then to zero again. "This is Mabel, and I can rub her and be with her."

But this is also Barnum, Hiram said.

A pink breath hovered under the tarp, hovering close to Henry's waist. *And Barnum's hand is melting into your heel, because you've brought the boy in, Henry. You've brought him in but still you don't lie with him like you should. You don't move his hands along your waist, and I think it's over now, Henry. I think the waiting's over.*

Henry sat up on the mattress, his hand on his lips. "But Mabel is everywhere here. I still feel her here instead of the boy."

Mabel is gone. The pink breath rattled against the blackened windows, shaking the glass. *There's only the boy to make you even. There's only the boy like there was only you to make me even before.*

DURING THE DAY, HENRY KEPT HIMSELF AWAY from the lockhouse. The swishy-colored people had returned with more frequency. They jogged and rode bicycles and some even rode horses along the towpath. But mostly, they walked past the lockhouse and looked. Occasionally, they stopped to take pictures of the dam Henry had constructed, the dam he'd finished.

During the day, Henry wandered along the river. He brought the mannequin with him so that they might never be parted. When he reached the riverbanks, he placed the mannequin against an oak and watched the current spin out in ever-widening zeroes. The zeroes spun off from the ends of logs and stones, from the occasional leaf or branch drifting by, and he spoke to the mannequin as if he were talking to Mabel or Hiram or Barnum. He spoke even without Mabel or Hiram or Barnum there.

He said, "The days are much lighter now without the cold."

Or, "I don't think lying on the mattress with the boy is the best thing.

Especially with Mabel in the rafters the way she is. Even if the boy touches my heel with his hand, even if he does, I still see Mabel above me. I still see Mabel."

Or, "We'll break them pipes soon, Barnum," and he pointed to the mannequin. "But only after we finish putting them bricks you shaped in. Then we cut those boards I found by the tracks—to make the lock's gates—and we can break them pipes sure enough."

And then again to Mabel, "You'll come back because I know you have to see the end of what I done—the end of the work—when we make the canal new again. You'll come down from your rafters and you'll be on the banks on a mule in a red saddle for sure. Then I'll see you smile, because I know I can smile if you were to show up riding in the red saddle, because only you can ride in the red saddle."

He touched his lips and tried to raise a smile like he'd done when Mabel had given him the grace of her touch, but couldn't. So he watched the zeroes on the river instead. He leaned over and watched his face inside the zeroes. The air was warmer. April had arrived, and he wondered if he would go see Barnum in the Easter pageant. Barnum as a shepherd.

"I'd have to go inside the church and see the pews that the other people sit in and don't know the feel of like I do. They don't know the pews have the paper feel with the words spilled on them. How the zeroes touched every inch of the pews in the light from the Stations of the Cross." He turned to the mannequin. "They don't know about all that. Not about the purple light and the blue light and the pink light in the glass. They haven't seen how the light draws shapes on the floor. And they don't know the strength of my leg either. They only think they can tell me how to hang the coats and hats and scarves."

The mannequin leaned against an oak. As he edged closer, he took the mannequin in his arms so that the reflection of the torso was in the river with him.

"They'll just want me to hang their coats up for them again."

Leaning closer, he touched his lips to the mannequin's smooth neck, and the taste of river water spread across his tongue.

"Mmmm," he said, when he tasted the river rise up from the canvas.

It was a sugary nectar, and he leaned back as Barnum's smell returned to him. *Because the boy had the same taste, that honeysuckle feel.* Though he shook it away when he thought of the church again and what they'd want from him. "They'll want to touch me with their hands and fingers. They'll ask me where I been since their coats have been hung up by Barnum instead. That's what they'll say. Because what they *really* care about is Barnum talking too much. They'll say he talks too much and that he never brings them the right coats. That's what they'll say. Then they'll ask me if I seen the priest yet, because the priest was very sad when you left, Henry. He was very sad."

He looked at the reflection of the mannequin in the water. A single zero on the surface encompassed both the torso and his face.

"The priest didn't even come out of his home for several days after you left. He only sat in his room with his arms folded and said he'd lost one of his own, that he'd lost a member of his flock. He knows now that he wasn't close enough to you, that he hadn't consoled you enough after Rommel's accident."

Henry looked at the mannequin when he said Rommel's name. He knew the mannequin was not Rommel.

"You'll never be Rommel, so I don't have to talk to you like that. You'd never try to pass into the zero with me and Mabel, to pass into the zero that was not yours. Because even I know there are zeroes that can't be crossed into. Even I know that."

AT DUSK, DURING THE WEEK BEFORE EASTER, Henry worked on the lock with the stone bricks Barnum had chipped during all those days of rain. It was dull, heavy work. He looked at the places where the older stones had crumbled and held up a brick to see if it fit. If it didn't, he held up another brick to see if it fit. He moved the bricks left and right, up and down, rearranging how he held them, turning them over, backward, forward, in every possible arrangement, and in this way, the bricks approached and receded from the holes they were meant to fill, and the work progressed. When he did find a brick that fit, he scraped his hand in the shovel for the gray clay he dug up. With a handful of clay, he smeared the brick and placed it in the space it would fill from then on. In this way, he worked each night, now that the rains held off.

"They have to hold off, if I'm ever to finish." The rain was a gray line in the sky that week, and he watched the gray line tremble above him almost as much as he watched the trail coming down from town. But Barnum never showed, so Henry looked from the gray clay in the shovel, to the gray trailing sky, to the gray footpath descending from town, and he built up the stone locks on each side so that the canal narrowed between the locks. It edged closer so that the barges and boats could flow flanked by the two great stone sides, and he wondered what Barnum would say when he saw all the work he'd missed. "Because Barnum is the Good Shepherd now," he knew. "He's been rehearsing all this while. That's why he hasn't come this whole week."

Henry finished placing the stones in their rightful places Saturday night and let out a long breath when he was done. He had found new shapes for all the holes, and when he looked over the new gray bulk of the two stone locks, he thought he had passed into the years before the lock was ever broken to begin with.

"I've passed over," and he thought of Barnum as a shepherd in a land long ago—guiding a flock along a mountain path. "I've passed over, just as Barnum has passed over into that older way." When he said it, the moon appeared, rising above the mountains. It sent down a silver glare illuminating everything Henry had worked on: the canal and dam, the lockhouse and towpath, even the two stone locks.

Everything was silver and looked like it had come from some silver past, rising like from the old black-and-white photo books Hiram made him look at those nights after the tugging was done. Because on those nights, Hiram would often listen to the smoky music before calling to Henry for his colored water. After Hiram drank the colored water and dozed in his chair, he woke with a snort and turned the pages of his picture book. Henry still remembered the pictures Hiram liked most: the jet fighters and soldiers and remote hills with hidden caves. In the caves, there was always a man camped with a rifle and some sand bags. He might have been lost or positioned there by his platoon. Or, he might have been the lone survivor from a plane crash, but the man was always alone. Supply boxes surrounded him. His eyes were painted black, and as he drew the numbers of the days on the wall so that he would remember the world he'd left behind, he always stared into the camera as if this was all he'd ever been trained or fated to do.

"I don't know why he made me look. But he showed me pictures even when I tried to leave."

Henry sat on the large stone in front of the lockhouse and rubbed his hands along his thighs. He'd worked hard this last week, from dusk to sunup to get the two locks done by Easter so that Mabel could see, and yet all he could see now was his own hunched body as he stood beside Hiram's chair after the tugging was done. He felt how his legs and back had ached as the silver photos passed beneath Hiram's shaky hands, the same hands that tugged and pulled below his waist

"Even when I tried to leave, Hiram would say, 'But I have to show you the ones with the dead *Kor-e-ans* in it, the ones from the ambush, and what I did.'"

Henry saw the dead bodies in a ditch as Hiram and another soldier posed in front of them. A tank and some burnt huts were clouded in smoke. Hiram's face was thinner in the picture, his belly wasn't as big, and as he knelt smiling, he held his hand to a dead boy's face, touching his shattered cheek. And on those nights, when Hiram made Henry look at the pictures, at the silver bodies, whenever Henry did finally make it down to his cot to sleep, he often saw the dead bodies in his mind. The silver faces in the ditch, their arms grasping for air: grass huts and treetops scattered in the wind—with Hiram leaning over—holding the dead boy's cheek.

"He always made me look so that I always see the pictures now, whenever it's silver like this. I always see the faces." Henry looked across the stones at his feet and they were silver. The moonlight on the dust from the chipped stones made the grass and leaves and even the rock hammer at his feet all silver. Everything was silver. He placed his hand on the rocks, wiping the silver dust away, but it only got on his overalls when he rubbed along his leg.

"*Everything's goddamn silver.*" When he looked at the stones, he saw the silver bodies on them. The silver bodies reached out to him. Their eyes burnt, their tongues torn. Their mouths gaped like black zeroes screaming about Hiram's egg-smelling lips. *"No!"* Henry yelled. *"They ain't like the zeroes on the river; they ain't!"*

Picking up the hammer, he felt its compact weight. He hadn't worked with the hammer at all, he'd let Barnum do the shaping and chipping, but now he liked its smooth feel in his fingers. He also liked thinking about hitting the stones beneath him, with the silver bodies on them. He liked thinking of smashing the stones with the hammer to send Hiram away—to send all the things that Hiram had ever done away.

"Forever," he said, and raising the hammer, he brought it down with a loud smack, cracking a stone in two chalky parts. "There," he said. "There you are Hiram."

He brought the hammer down again, feeling his strength spread across the stones. *"There!* These stones ain't death no more. They ain't!" He brought the hammer down and the stones flew apart as the silver dust spread over his outstretched arm. "There's another body gone, and another body that ain't broke no more. Because I sent them all to heaven, to where Jesus can make them even for Himself, where Jesus can take them in and let the bodies rest."

Henry raised the hammer and slumped to his knees in the silver dust, shattering the stones of the bodies beneath him.

"There!" he screamed. *"There!* I done it. I sent them all up to heaven, up to where you can't touch them anymore!"

Panting from the effort, he leaned against the larger stone and wiped the sweat from his brow. Swinging the hammer again, he brought it down, shattering another picture, and swayed a bit doing it. When he swayed, he had to put his hand out to steady himself, and the hammer fell with a bright rattling sound. It lay slanted on a clump of silver-dusted leaves. Rubbing his lip, Henry sat on the stone, nudged his sluggish right foot out, and kicked the hammer. It sounded with a bright *tink* and a clump of silver leaves scattered, revealing the shovel Barnum had brought. Pushing his foot out farther, the shovel teetered against the hammer, and he heard a bright ticking like the wings of birds rise to him, and he reached to touch the bright ticking away.

When he felt the smooth hammer, he tapped it against the uncovered shovel. The tapping sounded like the ticking he remembered Barnum making when he chipped the stones into bricks. He remembered how that ticking made him feel when he worked in the hospital burning linens. On those days, he knew his body with its shorter right leg would never be as perfect as the ticking clock he punched with his card in the morning, or in the evening when he left. Not with its smooth perfect circle—and its perfect ticking legs.

"But only Barnum made the ticking before. I never touched it to make it perfect like this, with the sound." He looked to the sky. Stars had brightened the night. And raising the hammer (only a hands-width now), he brought it down against the blade. *Tink.* The sound echoed across his hands. He brought it down again—*tink tink tink*—with a small tapping until the ticking started again and spread across the whole canal.

"*It's perfect.* The sound makes a zero in my mind." As he tapped a constant rhythm with the hammer, he felt a tingling rise in his right leg. "I can see the zero of the legs now too. I can see the legs spinning round and round—in the circle—in the zero. A short leg and a long leg. Together. Just like me."

He shook his leg, and the tingling rose from his foot to his thigh, and as he hummed along with the wings of the perfect zero ticking around him, he knew he was much closer to the perfect sound now, to the zero. He looked at the window in the lockhouse and saw the mannequin watching him through the darkened glass. The mannequin was in her special spot to watch him work.

"See," he said to the darkened glass. "I'm that much closer to the zero, with the sound." He tapped again, so that he felt a steady rhythm absorb his body, absorbing the canal and lockhouse, the window and mannequin, the walls and trees—until the rhythm merged with the sound of the chattering river far off. "See," he said, looking at the glass. "I'm much closer inside the zero, inside the perfect ticking clock—with the legs—I'm that much closer to being even."

27

THE NEXT MORNING, when the church bells rang, Henry woke near the river. He was on the banks of the Potomac, lying in a sandy patch of grass beneath a canopy of fern. The mannequin was beside him, and the river was full of zeroes from rain falling across the surface. He watched the circles spin across the chattering current, mesmerized by their motion until the tolling bells dissolved in the surface.

"Easter," he mumbled, and reaching beside him, he brought the mannequin to his chest. Trailing his fingers along his thick, rubbery lips, he felt how swollen they were from the early dew. "I wonder if you're there, Mabel? I wonder if you've come back with your mother. Maybe you're sitting in the same pew where you prayed to Jesus before, when you prayed for her to wake up?"

Imagining Mabel, he saw the zeroes of the river pulling down more raindrops. The drops moved out, rippling across the surface until the mist scrawled a prism in the air, and he saw the colors of the world pulled into the descending zeroes.

"The colors are everywhere." Dragging his hand through the water, he touched each fading color. "But they're leaving me." He watched the zeroes swirl away from him. Leaning back, he kept his wrist in the water, and the coldness chilled him, rising from his arm through his chest and down his leg.

"Don't worry," he said, looking to the mannequin. "Your mother will sit with you in the pew soon enough. And at the end of service you'll say, 'The tallow?' to her, just like I said it to you, when there was only you and me and the Stations of the Cross. Even then you talked about how raising her up from her dreams wouldn't be so bad, and I see it wouldn't be so bad to be raised up like that, un-bodied and free. It wouldn't be bad at all."

Standing with the mannequin, his right leg was a wet bag of sand. It was heavier than he'd ever felt it, and as he limped to shake the tingling away, he couldn't get the feeling back. Inching closer to the lockhouse, he looked to the towpath and along the tracks, considering he wasn't used to being at the lockhouse during the day. But he figured with most everyone at church, and the priest keeping them for as long as he could, he might not have to worry about anyone seeing the smoke rising from the chimney after he got the fire started. In the red light of the room, he saw how wrinkled his fingers were from the mist he slept beneath that morning. Shaking out of his clothes, he hung them above the stove and stood by the open grate. The wind picked up then and shook the windows and door, scattering newspaper around him, and as he listened to the whirring sound, he heard faint footsteps on the path, running down from town.

"I knew you'd be here." Barnum came running into the lockhouse. Henry shivered to see the boy so close. He shook his leg out to stop the tingling, but his heavy right leg barely moved. "You shoulda seen all them folks in church. They're praying and waiting for the play, which I know Momma's gonna find out I'm not in."

"The pageant?"

"I got kicked out on account of Miss Abigail thinking Josh made a better Jesus than me. She said I was a shepherd and that was all I would be, but I told her Josh didn't even know how to die the right way. Don't you remember how I died in the basement with you?" Barnum looked at Henry, and Henry saw the cluttered walls in Barnum's basement again; he saw the radios, smelled the fish-gut bucket, and remembered when they went there with the TV. That was when Barnum slumped on the floor near a cardboard box, when he pretended he was an outlaw shot by a sheriff.

"I remember."

"Of course you do, because it was real. And I told her so. I said he wasn't dying right, and nobody would even know he was dead if they didn't already know the story."

"Of Jesus?"

"Of course. And you shoulda seen her as soon as I said it—she got rid of me right there in the church basement with everybody milling about upstairs." Barnum rubbed his hands together like he was washing them clean. "And I told her, just ask Henry, Henry would know. I died the way a person on TV is supposed to die—so everybody knows."

Barnum raised his hands to the grate, and when he realized Henry was naked and shivering, he stooped in front of Henry's right leg as if there had never been anything he was as comfortable doing. Cupping his hands, he put them under Henry's right heel without Henry even realizing how quickly the boy had done it. Both Henry's knees were aligned, and he stood straighter and breathed a sipping breath as Barnum talked. "I crept upstairs after rehearsal was over and watched all the people milling about because I wanted to see if everyone was hanging up their own coats or not."

"Did they hang up their own coats?"

"I seen Josh and Mabry up there working the coatroom, and I even had a mind to tell Miss Abigail how bad they were hanging up the coats, but then I saw Momma wander to a pew near the front by herself. When she did, I thought of you, and snuck outta there."

"Me?"

"I thought of you down here by yourself—on Easter—with how you never came back to church after you left, and I wanted to know, why?"

Henry looked at the boy hovering below his dangling thing. Breathing in with a slow sigh, he released the air in a low moan. "I guess I just didn't want it no more."

"You even had a bed there and everything." Barnum peered up at Henry, leaning to his left, and when he did, Henry teetered to his left as well. "I figured if it was good enough for you to leave the church, with everybody asking about you and me not even telling that I seen you—not even once— then maybe it was good enough for me to leave too. Especially after Miss Abigail wouldn't listen to me. And all I wanted was to make the resurrection better, so everyone would know."

"Was everybody there?" Henry felt a hot tightening in his stomach. It went straight to his toes, and he knew he was going to ask about Mabel. As soon as he looked to where the mannequin sat by the sink, he thought he could still see where the head of Mabel should have been, atop those slender shoulders, perched in the window. *That's because she's deep inside on*

the riverbank, leaning over the water. We're both inside the falling zeroes.
"Was she there with her mother?"

Barnum's two hands melted into Henry's heel so that Henry couldn't feel anything but the warm golden fingers beneath him.

"Is who there with what mother?" Barnum turned his face up and smiled to see Henry looking down on him.

"Mabel," Henry said and counted to one on his finger. She was a number to him now. A number he wanted to repeat until the number burned into every part of him and never let go. "Mabel," he said again.

"I haven't heard about her since her mother come back. That's what her friends say. They say she moved to where her real Daddy lives so they can be a family again."

"*A family?* But everything's ready for her with the mules and the red saddles?"

"Red saddles? Where'd you get red saddles?" As Barnum's voice echoed with the excitement of the red saddles, he rocked again to the left. When he did, Henry had to hold onto Barnum's shoulder with both hands. Bending low, his dangling thing brushed Barnum's hair, and Henry felt a red hardening in his stomach. Barnum turned to look, and Henry's dangling thing brushed against the boy's cheek making a slapping sound so that the boy laughed to hear the noise and to feel the fleshy rod bouncing up from Henry's waist like a fishing pole. "Well," he giggled and lifted his hands from Henry's heel to Henry's dangling thing. Henry thought the boy might have wanted to make his dangling thing sway against his cheek again and rocked to the side and almost fell over. Looking over, he saw the mannequin by the sink and thought of Mabel un-bodied in the rafters, watching at how he'd leaned over on his short right leg, leaning away from the boy.

See, Henry thought, *I stopped him*. He looked up to where he knew Mabel was watching. *I stopped him from touching me*. Henry leaned back up from the wall, naked and red, and felt Hiram's voice rustling in the heat:

He just touched it and giggled and even reached up for it again. And I know you don't want to hear me now, but the waiting is over, Henry. Just push the boy over on the mattress. He'll think you're wrestling, and you can get on top of him.

Henry eyed Barnum as Hiram spoke.

Then you can make the slapping sound against his cheek. Like when I slapped you against my lips and felt the warmth rushing out so I didn't see the bodies no more. I didn't want to see the bodies no more, and you helped me push all that away.

Hiram's voice hesitated as Henry saw the silver bodies and all the stones he'd smashed along the canal. Henry thought he heard a ticking noise, and he remembered the smooth hammer tapping against the shovel's blade.

Just push him over, Henry. He'll make you even again. Because he feels like Mabel now—he's young and warm and trembling.

When Henry righted himself, he heard the ticking grow louder. Barnum was hunched beneath him and seemed mesmerized by the tapping rhythm he made with the hammer he'd found. He was tapping against the stove until the ticking was the only noise inside Henry's mind, and he thought of Mabel's heart. *Her heart beat just like that when I brought my hands along her bumps. It even fluttered against my fingers when I rubbed her nipples, and maybe I could feel Barnum's ticking chest too? Maybe I could feel how close he is to Mabel, how warm and small and ticking?*

Barnum stopped tapping with the hammer once he saw Henry leaning over him. Trailing his fingers against his cheek, he touched where Henry

had slapped him with his dangling thing and looked up from his knees. "It felt like a rubber hose."

Barnum smiled and started as if to say something, wetting his lips, but Henry nudged him with his leg. When he did, Barnum giggled to feel his side being nudged like that and fell tumbling to the mattress.

"Well, I didn't know you were going to be like that." But before he could stand, Henry fell on top of him, so their bellies touched. Henry had his hands on Barnum's shirt, like he was going to rip it over the boy's head if he didn't help.

"You're like Mabel now," Henry said, his voice slow, heavy. "Mabel is here with us. But she can't make me even like you can—not since she moved away."

Barnum rolled with his back to the wall.

"She's up in the rafters watching." Henry felt Barnum's chest ticking beneath his fingers. The boy's chest ticked like the clock in his mind, and when he brought his hands along Barnum's chest, it was like passing his hands along a smooth, quivering leaf. Their stomachs were pressed so close together, they were glazed with sweat.

His skin is a leaf, Henry thought, *a leaf brought up from the current. And I can touch it now. I can draw my hands across it and bring it back in—because he's mine now—and he can make me even.*

"*You're a leaf.*" Henry whispered, and his lips brushed Barnum's ear as he brought his fingers to the boy's nipples. They weren't hard and pointed like Mabel's, and Henry had to stop rubbing to look at the nipples, to see if he was rubbing the right way.

Don't stop, Hiram hissed. *Even if his nipples aren't like Mabel's, isn't it nice to feel someone smaller underneath? Isn't it nice to feel him squirming and laughing at your touch, like you were the only touch he ever knew, like you were his father?*

"*No,*" Henry whispered. He pressed harder against the boy's chest, and Barnum's giggling rose higher.

I don't want to be his father. I want him to feel like Mabel and be un-bodied, but he's not. He's still down here with me, and I'm still down here watching him. We aren't in the rafters like I thought. We aren't un-bodied at all.

Barnum squirmed against Henry's waist. When he did, Henry felt another rush in his groin as Barnum's waist brushed against his dangling thing as he struggled.

"Wait, Henry," Barnum said, gasping for air. "Let me take my pants off. Then we can *wrastle* all you want and I'll show you what I done to Josh when he tried to grab me in the locker room when I was changing. I rubbed my hard thing like your hard thing all over him when I got him down."

Barnum pulled his trousers to his feet, and Henry heard Hiram breathe in with a loud *Ffffffffipp.* It was like when Hiram used to breathe after drinking from the colored water Henry brought him after the tugging was done.

Hiram said, *Ffffffffipp*, and Henry said, "*Shhhhh*," breathing in. Their chests ticked against each other, and Henry felt the ticking was like one of the songs on Hiram's radio when the drums and cymbals reached up for one last great sound. He knew then that Barnum's ticking wasn't like Mabel's at all. Mabel's ticking was smooth and centered, and Henry had only felt a ticking in her bumps when he put his hands on her chest. Barnum's ticking came from all over; Henry even felt a ticking in Barnum's dangling thing. It was pressed against his own dangling thing, and it made Hiram hiss to feel the boy's hot center, though Henry couldn't hear Hiram as much. Not with the church bells tolling far off. The bells echoed across the canal and in the lockhouse and brought Henry up from the heat rising all around.

It was Easter. The church bells rang for some special moment in the service. Henry looked to see if the boy heard, but Barnum still wiggled to free his hands, so he could try a wrestling attack of his own. When Henry saw Barnum pressed beneath him, he rolled his belly away to let the boy loose.

No! Hiram hissed. *Use your weight, or he'll leave. Then you won't be able to bring him back where he's wedged in for good. Because this is my boy now too. You've brought him here for me, for my fingers and my mouth and my lips. And I've been waiting long enough to get a young one like the one I killed.*

Henry arched his head up to the rafters and felt the heat from the stove. *Don't you know you've brought him here for me, that I'm inside you now? Don't you know I brought you to this house to be free?*

"He's not my boy and he's not your boy and I won't, Hiram. I won't!"

Henry felt the boy's fingers holding onto his dangling thing. Barnum squeezed and Hiram hissed to feel the small fingers melt below Henry's waist, melting like how the boy's hands had melted into Henry's heel. But this wasn't Henry's leg. This wasn't the same feeling of Mabel's hands moving up and down when they sat in the pew—and the hissing was too much for him. Hiram was too much.

"*Stop!*" Henry rolled off the mattress toward the stove. There was a terrible echoing in the lockhouse. A broader thunder had started, and as he stood to shake Hiram's hissing away, Barnum laughed to see Henry almost fall over, stretching his hands out to steady himself as his dangling thing jumped up and down.

"What you do that for?" Barnum said, and Henry saw in Barnum's eyes that he was really asking why his touch wasn't what Henry wanted.

"I didn't mean to squeeze you against the wall. I thought we was just playing." The boy tried to bend over in front of Henry then and put his hands beneath Henry's heel, but Henry backed away. He backed away and heard the ticking of the smooth body in his mind as he lifted the mannequin from the sink. Pulling the mannequin close, he heard the beating grow louder inside until he heard the beating like the ticking of Mabel's heart. "This is Mabel," he said, and he held the mannequin out. "And I can hear her ticking in the rafters. She's ticking above everything, and only she can make me even. Only she can see and feel the things inside. I know that now."

"*That's Mabel?*" Barnum raised his hands to the mannequin's bumps, and Henry had a mind to pull back on the mannequin like before when Barnum fell against the radio, but he let the boy touch the mannequin.

That's right, Hiram whispered. *Let him touch every part of the bumps, and then you can set the mannequin down and the boy will be touching you instead. Then you can move his hands up and down like how he squeezed you before.*

From far off, Henry heard a sharpening metal cross the land. A train moved on the edge of hearing. It moaned over the land, echoing on the river, and he looked to the blackened window toward the tracks.

Don't turn, Hiram said. *Don't you turn from this boy or bring your eyes off his hands; that'll raise him from his mind. That'll raise him from the feeling forever.*

The river chattered beyond the walls. Henry heard it rising like a bright chorus of coins. And closer—in-between the space of his own breathing— he heard the chattering rain drip down to the puddles in the canal, before rising up to where the stream flowed down from the mountain, in the pipe along the canal.

Don't turn from him, Henry! Hiram shouted, circling the room. *Not with everything so close!*

Henry kept the mannequin and stepped past the boy who turned, following him.

He's right there for you. He's everything you want—young and new and even! Just look at how even he is!

Henry stood in the doorway and looked at Barnum's legs.

Just think of him rubbing your foot every night, making you even. You could even kneel over him right now and put your dangling thing near his mouth. Then you could move the boy's lips over your dangling thing and he'd like it, I know it; he'd like it.

"No!" Henry shook his head to shake Hiram away. Cradling the mannequin, his eyes were clouded with darkness, and the shouting helped bring back the light. He saw the stove when he blinked his eyes. He saw the boy. Hiram was shouting at him for more, but Henry didn't want any more. He didn't want the rising in his dangling thing to shoot up with Barnum's sun-dripped hands. Not when he could see how excited and eager the boy was, with how he reached out to touch the bumps as Henry pulled back on the body. The train rumbled closer. Henry heard the river and chattering puddles. The canal was waiting to be born again, to be brought back to the beginning—*before the beginning*—when everything was even and new and shimmered in the sun. *Because it isn't Mabel, it isn't Mabel that can keep me here. None of it is Mabel.*

"He isn't Mabel!" he shouted. "He isn't Mabel! He doesn't know," and he limped through the door, cradling the mannequin.

28

THE RAINDROPS WERE COLD on Henry's lips as he hurried along the top of the canal. He could see into the puddle forming by the edge of the dam. The reflected mountains and gray sky looked back at him when he leaned over. In the puddle, he saw his naked body trembling. "Barnum doesn't know not to touch me like that because he's young and just starting with how he thinks. And just look at my face." Henry traced in the air with one finger his thick lips quivering in the reflected pool. His orange curls wilted as he leaned over.

"Henry?" Henry turned and saw the boy standing behind him.

"You must've hurried." Henry pointed to Barnum's pants. The zipper was down.

As Barnum zipped up, he leaned into the rain and cupped his hand around his ear. A train was just below town. "Do you hear it?"

Henry's fingers fluttered across the torso cradled at his waist.

"I didn't know that was Mabel." Barnum pointed at the mannequin. "I wouldn't have done nothing she wouldn't have liked if I'd known." He stepped closer. "Shoot, you've seen me. When I'm pretending, it's like nothing else is there. So I know what you mean by saying it's Mabel—that she's with you."

"*Pretend?*" As Henry stepped back, the muddy earth oozed between his toes. The boy reached out to touch the mannequin, raising his hands along her bumps.

"See, I'm sorry. I'm touching her, ain't I? And I know she'll come back as soon as the canal's ready, as soon as she can ride in them red saddles like you said. With the mules—because I can see them too." Barnum pointed across the canal to the towpath. "I can see them mules over there all alone. It's just like looking at the TV with you; them mules are all bright and shiny in the sun. Towlines trail from their harnesses to the barges in the blue water."

"You can see the blue water?" Henry pointed to the towpath where the—*one two three*—mules were lined up waiting for the lock to open. The mules would tow the barges from the lower portion to the higher portion. That was when the water rushed in, when it did its job, raising everything up. "The water will raise us up too," Henry said.

"I know it." Barnum moved his hands back to the canvas bumps, cradling them.

"The sun will shine too." Henry had turned from the canal to look at the rain falling from a gray oneness. The gray oneness spread over everything and didn't allow even the darkest hint of light. "The sun will shine like it shines now—over everything." Limping up from the canal, he looked at the railroad. The wet lines hummed with the train just below the bend. Henry saw a plume of steam edging along the ridge. The steam drew a white current through the grayness.

"Well, it sure ain't no commuter train if it's got steam." Barnum looked at the edge of the canal, but Henry was already wandering up to the tracks to be closer.

"*They're ticking*," Henry whispered. Limping into the middle of the tracks, he felt the vibrations race through every inch of his body. Bending over, he held one hand to the humming metal. "It's ticking like the clock is ticking, like Mabel's heart is ticking."

With the train's weight compressing the steel around the bend, the line beneath Henry ticked in intervals, arching against its rivets.

"This is the metal that has to stop," he said and passed his hand along the wet, ticking steel. When he did, he felt Mabel ticking beside him. The mannequin was ticking in his hands. "I've lived beside it and slept beside it and dreamed beside it for so long, but I never seen the zeroes become part of the train like with the river and pews." Raising his fingers in the air, he traced a zero on the line. "But now they can if I just draw them out. If I just draw them out here and here." He pointed along the steel. "It'll be mine then, because I'll know it and it'll be slow. I'll slow it down with the pictures I see."

Henry looked at all the zeroes swirling from his fingers. He tried to count them in his mind: *one two three four five six seven eight nine ten. Zero.*

He counted to zero again.

"The canal is older," he said, rising from his zeroes. "The canal is older and cleaner, and the people will come to see the canal instead of the train. They'll even ride the canal instead of the loud, rusty train. Because the canal ain't the ghost around here no more—the canal ain't the ghost no more at all. The train is the ghost."

Henry watched the white steam rising from the train as it rounded the bend. He knew it wasn't the silver tin-cans of the commuter train he was used to. It wasn't a train hauling cattle or pigs. The cattle and pig train had thin slots on the sides, so he could see the animals and hear their sad lowing long after they passed. This was the other train. The red train with the wooden panels and thin smokestack. The train with the engineer he'd seen twice before. He remembered and counted—*one two*—on his fingers. And as he watched the train race toward him, as he heard its whistle blare out a warning, he could see the engineer's wide green eyes and lips stretched out into a screaming mouth as he saw Henry, naked, standing on the tracks.

"Henry!" Barnum yelled from the gravel slope.

Henry heard the boy, and when he turned, the boy reached out with both hands. He was trying to bring Henry in from the tracks that were not real to Henry anymore, the tracks that were ticking and rusty and not as clean as the canal, or as slow and pure.

"Move, Henry!"

"But I haven't drawn out all my zeroes yet..."

His voice was swallowed beneath the train's screeching brakes. Henry raised his hand to draw out more zeroes, and Barnum screamed above the chattering river. The world had slowed down. The river was shouting to Henry above everything. He heard each sound. The chattering river was pulling everything into its center—even the bells—because even the bells were ringing again. Henry heard the bells ringing over everything.

He let go of the mannequin when he heard the church bells. The tolling vibrated through his body like the ticking rail. The bells rose from his toes, through his legs and waist, quivering through his arms until his hands shook—and he let go of the mannequin. He watched Mabel fall to the tracks as Barnum pulled him clear. Both their dripping bodies tumbled to the sandy weeds as the engine rumbled past, as the train careened around the bend, and the last white steamy veil lifted into darkness.

HENRY'S RIGHT LEG TINGLED WHEN HE SAT UP. The red train with the wooden panels and steaming smokestack went right past, even after slowing as much as it could, even after Henry saw the engineer's shouting face as if it was held right before him. The engineer had watched Henry and the boy slump in a heap to the side of the track. But he hadn't stopped. Only the hot metal smell of burnt steel lingered now. In the space where Henry had watched the train exist, he smelled tar, burnt timber, and ash. The train passed by in a moment—passing across the zero he tried to draw out. And he'd lost Mabel because of it, because of Barnum's tugging hand. As he limped up the gravel slope, he saw her on the track, in smoldering pieces. His right leg tingled as he trailed his hands along her ripped seam, along each crumpled bump. Gathering the shards, he carried them smoldering at his side and put them in a pile by the edge of the canal.

"You okay?" Barnum limped beside him, rubbing his hip.

Henry disappeared into the lockhouse and returned wearing his overalls. He had the hoe in his hands. As he moved along the top of the canal, he could feel Hiram's pink breath hovering above him like a wing.

"No," Henry said and shook the hoe as he limped along the canal. The ceramic pipe echoed with water beside him. "She's gone, Hiram, and I don't want to hear from you no more." Henry shook the hoe at the sky. "The boy is not Mabel and will never be, even he said so. So that's it for you. When I break this pipe, that'll be it for you forever."

"Henry?" Barnum pressed a torn opening in the side of his shirt, and his hand came away smeared with blood. "Did you say something?"

Carrang was Henry's reply. The sound of the hoe crashed against the ceramic pipe. *Carrang carrang carrang.* Henry swung the hoe down with all his weight, with all his fear. He was alone now and knew it, and he never thought he would be alone without Mabel—not since they'd fished the mannequin up from the river. But now Mabel was piled near the canal in smoldering shards. *But even those shards are not her*, he knew, and he felt lighter because of it. Setting the hoe at his feet, he remembered her and drew a zero in the sky above him, then a zero beneath him on the pipe. Then picking up the hoe, clenching his whole body, he brought it down with such a terrible swing, it seemed as if he were thrusting a dagger into Hiram's pink heart.

Carrang, and the hissing voice of Hiram lifted into the air. *Carrang carrang.*

The voices of the priest and the cardinal fell away from him. He couldn't hear them preaching anymore above the pews. All the people who'd ever stared at him and his leg and didn't know it had always been perfect like the clock was perfect all flew away from him too.

Carrang carrang.

He brought the hoe down and the hospital fell away. The linens he'd burned rose above him. The linens were the people's souls that had passed into the sky. They were redeemed.

Carrang carrang.

The Stations of the Cross disappeared with Jesus' smooth legs, and even the lockhouse dissolved. Barnum's squeezing fingers did not hold his dangling thing anymore. Henry couldn't feel where the boy had touched him—and didn't care. He didn't want the boy like Hiram would, not with Hiram dissolving above him along that great pink wing.

Carrang carrang.

His arms ached as he raised the hoe again. His leg hurt from falling into the weeds by the railroad. His right leg was just a heavy stone, but it sung to him now with each crashing blow. It sung with a bright rustling of rapids and wings and he knew it was perfect no matter what. Like the clock legs. It didn't have to be even. It could be short and long. It didn't have to be smooth to push Hiram's pink breath into bits and puffs of chaff. He would do it on his own, and brought the hoe down more fiercely to rid himself of Hiram forever.

Carrang carrang carrang.

The pipe finally cracked. The first mountain water spurted at his feet.

"You did it!" Barnum shouted and staggered to the lip where Henry stood.

"I've done it. He's gone. Hiram's gone." Henry's toes were soaked, and he laughed to feel the cold mountain water against his skin. It was blue. He could see it. With another *carrang*, the pipe cracked all the way, and the water flowed faster, filling the canal. Breathing twice, he listened to the river and mountain stream. The echoes of both watery voices met in the air above him. Their merging sound pushed Hiram's weak wing away like bits of fluff downstream, and Henry smiled to hear it. He smiled and felt along his upraised lips with his fingers.

"She'll come now," Henry said and breathed heavier. Gulps of air came from his wheezing lungs. "She'll come and see it—she has to. I can wait for her and count."

"Sure she'll come," Barnum said, and he rested his hand on his sore hip.

Breathing in again, Henry sat on the lip of the canal. His right leg wouldn't move. He rubbed his hand along his leg before bringing his fingers to cover his heart. His heart ticked louder in a rasping, chugging rhythm until he felt the ticking spread across the whole canal. Until he felt the whole canal vibrating with the sound, and when he leaned over to look into the water, to see the reflection of his smiling face, the moist earth crumbled beneath him, and he slid down the steep bank all the way to the bottom.

"Whoa," he said. A bright clump of brown mud sat on his shoulders. He felt his heavy right leg wedged into the earth.

"It's getting deep," Barnum said. "You okay?"

Henry could feel the water already over his ankles. Then after a moment, it pooled over his knees. He sat there staring at the canal walls until Barnum hurried off. Henry heard the boy say something about getting help, but then all he heard was the water chattering around him. The mountain water rushing down chattered like the river.

"She'll see me now," he said. "She'll see everything I done for her," and he raised his hand to his lips, smiling. He could see the mules above him on the towpath. The mules were waiting. Towlines hung from their harnesses to the barges. The mules were waiting for the blue water to rise over his tingling leg. He could see that now, and the water. It rose above his waist and up to his arms as he slumped down farther. His arms were weak; his right leg didn't move anymore, and he felt like he was floating with the linens in the sky. The rain had stopped. Maybe it stopped a while ago? He wasn't sure. White clouds raced above him, and sunlight poured through.

Linens were in the sky. They drifted above the mules in red saddles.

But them mules are waiting for me, he knew, *because they'll watch me until the water rises up to my eyes—and then over my eyes—until the bubbling feeling in my chest goes away. Then they'll watch until I float in the sky like I'm floating in the water, rising up like in the rafters until I see the tops of trees and antennas and hills far away. Until I count everything on my hands, because everything will be far away then—when I'm un-bodied and free—because I can see them mules on the side now too. I can see their towlines dragging on the blue surface. I can hear their sad shuffling snorts and grunts, and I can see their saddles, with how fine they'll fit me. I can see their red saddles glistening in the sun.*

Acknowledgments

As always, I'd like to thank my family for their steadfast love and support in all my artistic endeavors. Without them, none of this would mean much, and I hope they know that.

I'd also like to thank all the talented writers, editors, artists and thinkers at April Gloaming Publishing. Their unwavering support brought this story to its finished form. April Gloaming supports the voice of the South (in all its strange shades and inflections). And I feel a cacophony of different voices is what we need to listen to most these days. And to recognize. With my work, they are supporting the soulful voice of the Blue Ridge Mountains and the meandering pulse of the Potomac River. Ancient sources of growth and movement.

I'd also like to thank the peculiar heritage of the Chesapeake & Ohio Canal. First envisioned as a passage from the East to the West for goods, services, and people, I believe it became much more than that over its near 100 years of operation—it became a conduit—a way of tracing the wild interior and mysterious development of this American experiment. A mystery my book celebrates unflinchingly.

About the Author

Christopher Kritwise Doyle grew up in Brunswick, Maryland, a small town nestled on the banks of the Potomac River and Blue Ridge Mountains. After receiving his MFA at the University of Baltimore, he has written about the origin of country music, an embattled elementary school teacher in urban America, and the C&O Canal. He lives in Baltimore with his wife, daughter, and Rhodesian ridgeback, all in a cramped rowhouse.

Also by Christopher K. Doyle